HEARTS AND STONES

STORIES OF CELTA

ROBIN D. OWENS

FOLLOW YOUR HEART

ISBN-10: 978-1-951612-03-0 ebook

ISBN-978-1-951612-04-7 print book

Created with Vellum

HEARTS AND STONES
COVER COPY

Before Celta ... *Passage Through Stone*: In the UStates Colorado Area, Levona Martinez is determined to find a berth on the starship, Lugh's Spear, and escape the psi mutant ghetto for a new life on a new planet. But she's missed her chance and the ship is full. The leaders might not consider her worth taking, but what about Pizi, her prodigy cat?

Celta, a place of magic, telepathic animal companions, and adventure! Five stories highlighting some fan favorite characters:

Homing Stone: As his magic emerges through fever fugues, nobleman Holm Holly fights death duels in the Downwind slums ... and catches the attention of blacksmith Rand Ash, who needs a noble to help him with his revenge on an equally noble family ...

Fractured Stone: Struggling with his disinheritance and the loss of his identity, Holm Apple strives to make a new life in a new city with his HeartMate and their Fams.

Hidden Stone: Garrett Primross didn't expect to be hired by a Cat, let alone two of them, and their idea of payment doesn't match his. When a GreatLord appeals for Garrett's help, he's reluctant to take the case, but finds that solving the mystery unexpectedly leads him to inner answers.

HeartStones: Losing his sight and psychic power, treasure hunter Zane Aster wants to make one more score. He discovers a House on the cusp of sentience, but missteps might trigger their deaths.

Stone in Zanth's Paw: It's time for the best FamCat on the world of Celta to return the irritating sea turtles to their mother in the ocean. Perhaps time to learn a big lesson, too.

DEDICATION

Like most books written during the Covid 19 Corona Virus pandemic, these words are dedicated to the front line people, especially our courageous health care workers, but also those who staffed the grocery stores and other businesses. Blessed be.

ACKNOWLEDGMENTS

Thanks for all my readers who hang on Facebook with me and can answer the odd question when I'm hurredly writing, and my critique buddies who see portions of almost everything...

Passage Through Stone: Thanks to my dear friend and long-term critique buddy Alice Kober for doing a full edit under a quick deadline.

Homing Stone: Many thanks to the readers who helped out with Holm's death duel details as related in Heart Duel: Kelly Self, Kendal Ogles, Melanie Luther, Shawna Lanne and for my excellent and new beta reader and fellow writer: Karina Steffens.

Fractured Stone: I'm grateful for everyone who read the Staying At Home story and enjoyed it daily and helped me keep on working. I must also mention Rebecca Ho for her suggestion in the scene with the young cats and rules in the fighting salon, and Shara Forrister who reminded me where the rules were originally laid out. (***Heart Search*).**

PASSAGE THROUGH STONE

Colorado Area, UStates Middle Region, Earth, WorldStates Year 236, Spring

A massive shadow in the sky angled over Levona, and noise enveloped her in a thunderstorm. She cowered in a mud-slush coated gully, frozen like choice prey of a predator.

Booms sounded, and terror flashed through her. Then she glanced up and saw the white, angle-winged aircraft. *Spaceship.* Stunning sight, no starships around for more than a decade.

The ship passed. Not a military plane, a government threat. No, a vehicle to escape the UStates and the Earth and sail to another planet.

Months ago, word had spread through the underground mutant network that folks in the psi ghettos had pooled their money and bought three starships. They planned to escape Earth and establish a colony on another planet. She hadn't believed it.

Now she'd seen a starship just overhead and her terror transmuted into hope.

Hope. Her whole body shuddered with the vigor of her breath.

Since the Earth's space colonization era had ended about

fifteen years back, Levona thought this sighting indicated the rumors were true.

She popped above the lip of the gulch and watched as the huge ship headed for the city of CentralConglom. She'd scrambled her way out of her hometown, home slum, a little over two years ago.

"I have to go back," she murmured as dread clogged her throat, but escape beckoned.

I go where you go, the young cat, Pizi, said, in actual telepathic words pinging through Levona's mind. These were the first words the small cat had sent mentally, rather than transmitting simple images trailing feelings, though Levona had felt a surge of hope from Pizi, too. She sent back love and felt it return.

The small female squirmed in the side-pocket of Levona's pack. She reached around and opened the flap and Pizi stuck her head out, rotated her ears, then angled her nose up to the sky. As if she'd be able to *smell* the spaceship.

Maybe Pizi could. Levona had sensed the power in the small animal when she'd found the young cat two months ago. But neither of them knew the cat's talents, and Pizi's eyes were crusted over, a continuing malady.

"Yeah, time to return to the city," Levona said aloud. Carefully, she adjusted the pack, her mind busy with the maps unfurling in her brain, one of her psychic talents. Once she saw a map, she always recalled it. She *made* maps in her head when she traveled. Right now, she knew all the folds of Coal Creek Canyon, Colorado, the twists of the river down to the plains and the city of CentralConglom.

I am tired of being carried! Pizi fussed, sending a barrage of emotions and images along with her demand.

"Okay," Levona grumbled, drew out the cat and attached a rigged-up harness so she could walk on her own. Levona let her mind interface with the small dust-colored tabby, so Pizi could "see" where they were going. The cat would slow Levona down, but there'd be plenty to think about on her — their — way back to the city. Like how to get accepted for the journey on a *starship* to a new planet.

Pizi lasted a full half-kilometer on her own before she wanted back in "her" pocket in the pack. That surprised Levona, and reassured her a bit that ... if anything happened to her, the little cat could survive on her own. Or at least find another mutant human companion to bond with.

The sun dipped below the western mountains as she and Pizi reached the bottom of the canyon. No more aircraft raced through the sky, but the road busied with traffic going toward CentralConglom. She figured the rare starship garnered a lot of attention from the gov types.

Quick spy eyes glittered over the city, zooming around, hanging mostly over the psi-ghetto where the ship must have landed. One spy eye shot toward the canyon and Levona flattened against the low side of the creek wall.

You do not SEE us! shrieked Pizi as the eye hovered near. The vibrations of the cat's mind hurt Levona's head. Then the spy sphere zipped up the canyon and back, all in the time it took for Levona to hold a long breath. She hoped she hadn't been noted. Didn't know if Pizi's telepathic blast had affected the eye.

They moved deeper into shadows and down a narrower ditch before Levona stopped and shared her standard meal of re-hydrated protein with Pizi. Closing her eyes, she visualized the snow run-off gullies winding to the scummy pond. Two years past, one rugged slope of the pond had held a hidden entrance to abandoned culverts and tunnels carrying lost streams.

I don't like those Images of Yours! Pizi stated. *All dark, dark, dark, no sunlight on My eyelids to show warm.* She sounded nervous and crawled into Levona's lap to curl up.

Levona took a large cap out of her backpack and stretched the knit thing gently over the small feline, making a warm and secure nest. Not weighing more than three kilograms, the fine-boned cat was easy to carry.

Keeping her thoughts steady but with an underlying buzz of anticipation, Levona replied, *The old republic made things to last, and the culverts did. Better than the corps and govs make now. It WILL be dark—*

And smelly! Pizi added.

Probably smelly, Levona confirmed. *But safe, the culverts will protect us. We will not be walking on the nanogrid and monitored. Won't be seen or sensed until we get near the cross-roads with the newer city water system. We'll have to watch out then.*

I know, Pizi said, though she didn't. She'd been born in the canyon, abandoned by her mother and littermates, and barely survived before Levona found her.

I've seen images from you, lots! Pizi stated. *Especially when you dream, the old tall, tall buildings, your neighborhood. How you got to the canyon and lived and later found Me.*

"A lucky day for both of us, to find a person to be a family."

Yes, Pizi replied with a spurt of love that Levona felt and returned.

Then her mind turned to the immediate future. *We'll have to be quiet, even in the tunnels. And keep our thoughts to-from each other on a private channel. There are some mutants who can overhear thoughts.* Or so rumors said.

Pizi sent an image of shadowy thoughts zooming back and forth between them, then something else, a silver bond connecting them heart to heart.

What's that? Levona asked, as she scanned their stopping place with her senses to make sure she wouldn't be leaving any physical, and only minor mental, residue behind.

Our friend bond, between our hearts! Pizi chirped.

"Oh," Levona said aloud, as her mind devolved into sentimental goosh. Yet, a chill flicked along her nerves. She had someone else to take care of, other than herself. What if she failed? Terrible.

Pizi stretched to swipe Levona's chin with a lick, then moved to the knapsack, found her side pocket and wiggled in. *What will Our starship be like?*

One starship here and available, and somehow Levona had to convince strangers to take her and Pizi away. More, she and Pizi had to stay out of sight of the state police, *and* out of any trouble while Levona found the people in charge of the departure. Now Levona had a beloved companion with expectations of her, an additional burden.

When will We leave in our starship? Soon? Excitement thrummed through Pizi, so much that Levona could feel her small body vibrate in the backpack.

Anxiety splashed in Levona's gut, but she kept her emotions free of it, laced anticipation through her telempathy with Pizi. *Yes, probably as soon as possible!* No one involved with the starship would want to hang around. The longer they stayed, the more likely the gov would try to stop them, or confiscate the ship, or stir mobs against them. And every mutant in the psi barrio already had a target on their forehead, marked ready for a laser to fry their brains.

Pizi didn't know this and Levona would strive to keep her companion innocent as long as possible.

It will be FUN! Going to another place.

"Yes," Levona muttered.

Where My eyes will stay clear. We have not had enough rain or snow lately.

An eyewash of collected rainwater in the canyon had dissolved the gunk for hours and allowed Pizi to see. But creek water didn't do the same. Levona didn't know if city water, with all the additives, would work, either.

They stopped at the pond's culvert opening, dense in years-thick brittle grasses and weeds, enough to keep them warm.

Before she went in, Levona added force rings to her fingers. Made of hard plastcal, they would hurt any attacker with each blow. If Levona grabbed on pressure points, she'd disable an attacker long enough for Pizi and her to escape. Her parents, both practitioners of martial arts, had taught her their skills, and how to use the rings, worked with her, until they died.

The rings wouldn't maim or kill. She hadn't devolved to match feral humans living underground, common criminals, psi-hater mob people, or fanatics.

Her energy stayed edgy as they trekked through the ancient waterways, the culverts and ditches and tunnels. Pizi chattered a bit, then the darkness got to her. She curled tighter in her pocket and slept.

Levona told herself she preferred it that way.

Finally the night lightened to dawn, spearing sun through a series of broken street-drains, and Levona knew they neared the intersection with the newer city tunnels.

She stared at the end of the culvert, a rockface, and the barely-person-sized hole halfway up the wall to her left that led to the CentralConglom systems. If she'd planned on staying here in her hometown, she'd have considered hiding that breach entrance.

Careful climbing ahead, and she sure didn't want to bang her pack or Pizi. So she opened Pizi's pocket and woke her.

Yay, I get out!

"Mind your steps and your jumps and stay close, no exploring," Levona muttered.

I will!

Levona placed the cat on the top stone of the hole, used their psychic link to string another sensory thread between them, watched as Pizi hopped down and began nosing around. Then Levona clambered through the opening.

Treading softly in the two-person wide and poorly lit tunnel, avoiding the patchy nanogrid that would mark their passage and alert security, they made it several kilometers before a watery rush hit Levona's ears. Pizi hopped around. *Water! NEW water? That can help my eyes?*

As she scooped up the cat, Levona minded her step as she moved to pipes along a wall. A stingy, dim yellow century bulb protruded from the wall, surrounded by mesh to stop vermin.

With a squint, and actually moving her lips, she read the gov symbols on the wall near two marked pipes leading into CentralConglom. *Filtered Fresh,* no doubt heading to the upperclass neighborhoods and downtown high level gov suites, and *Water Intake*, a much larger pipe for everyone else. Both had out-take spigots with handles.

Levona could maybe steal a trickle or two. Fill up a small bottle for Pizi. By the time the guards discovered the theft, it would be long done and believed minor. She reminded Pizi of the grid, but thought the cat's weight wouldn't be noticed. Near the pipes the grid became pressure-sensitive matting. Levona could reach the handle with the long-grip piece of the multi-tool she kept in her bag.

She lowered her pack, took out the multi-tool and the bottle, lit the tool and extended thin rods on both of them. Holding her breath, she tried the *Fresh Filtered* handle. Stuck.

Pizi mewed.

If Levona had been alone, she'd've given up. But she didn't steal for herself. For her cat and friend, Levona would do pretty much anything.

Try again. Fail. Settle into her balance and ground herself, breathe correctly. One more attempt without using the additional step of lubricant that might set off an alarm.

The handle turned. Levona filled the thin bottle the

length of her hand, 225 milliliters of excellent water. No hesitation, no drips, no spillage. Good.

Her fingers trembling, she shut off the flow and turned off the multi-tool's light and put it away in her pack, burying it at the bottom of the main compartment.

Sit, she ordered Pizi mentally.

The little cat did, lifting her head trustfully.

Levona dampened a clean rag with the water, gently wiped Pizi's eyes until the crusting dissolved. With mountain precipitation, the glop would soften quickly and remain gone for about six hours. Levona didn't know what this water would do, but since Pizi didn't squeal like she had from creek water, Levona thought it might be safe.

They waited a good five minutes before Pizi blinked and opened her eyes wide. *I can see! SEEEEEEE!* she broadcasted.

Levona flinched, not knowing whether Pizi could be heard by anyone else or not.

You are very pretty! Levona thought Pizi purred but couldn't hear her.

Thank you. Levona knew herself to be attractive enough for a twenty-two-year-old woman, had never had trouble getting sex partners.

I like your eyes, they is green like Mine!

A bluer green than Pizi's, and Levona's eyes contrasted with her dark hair and Asian-Latina heritage too much for her own liking. *Time to go. Be careful of the grid.*

I can see and whisker-sense the grid!

Step in between the squares if you can. Vary your pattern, weave across the corridor.

I will! You do not follow My steps.

I won't.

The air thickened with scents of tech and water and humans instead of dirt and weeds. They moved deeper and deeper into the CentralConglom system's tunnel webs under the dull light of the century bulbs every twenty meters.

Heading into the city churned emotions in Levona. For the last couple of years, she'd lived mostly on her own, with little contact with others ... and none at all with psi mutants ... in the mountains and canyons of Colorado.

Still as she sensed life buzzing above her, she acknowledged that she did miss the city, her hometown. She liked the feel of many people around her, the bustling human energy.

They wouldn't go as far as the innermost city. Too many traps there, and too watched, even in mostly forgotten tunnels. As light as she was, Pizi would set off alarms. Ancient Denver itself functioned under an atmospheric dome raised to protect people when humans poisoned the Earth. For the last century, they'd been clawing back to create a cleaner environment, but Levona still thought it touch-and-go.

They turned a corner and *Zzzzapp!*

The electric bolt hit the wall next to Levona's ear.

"Halt!" A woman in a rough onesuit held an electrozap pointed at Levona.

Not a guard, a tech. Outside Levona's reach. "Run, Pizi!" she shouted. Pizi screeched, and the woman glanced away.

Levona leapt, grabbed the woman's electrozap with her right hand, snatched it away. Levona's left hand applied pressure with the ring on the woman's inner wrist.

The tech yelled, her fingers opened.

Levona thumbed the electrozap setting level from highest to lowest and shot the woman below her ribcage. Her scream cut off, and Levona awkwardly lowered her to the ground, hearing her own panting.

Standing and trembling, Levona studied the electrozap. Illegal, and with a political sticker on it reading "Go forth and kill mutants." No way of telling whether the weapon included a geo-find nanochip, but the woman probably had such an implant.

Great.

As Levona got out a cleanser and wiped away her fingerprints, she noticed Pizi place a paw on the woman's forehead. *Forget,* Pizi whispered and sent a vibration into the woman's skull.

Levona jerked straight, let the weapon fall into a trickle of water crud in the narrow gutter in the middle of the tunnel. "That's wrong. We don't do that, Pizi!" She flinched as her high-toned words bounced loud off the stone walls of the passage.

Pizi turned her lambent yellow shaded green eyes to Levona. *It's done. She won't remember Us. She wanted to KILL Us. We don't allow that.*

All right. First time Levona experienced pragmatic cat behavior. What to say? *We are friends and companions. Please consult with me if you want to do something like that again.*

Big eyes. *Something like what? Telling a person to forget? That helps Us and doesn't hurt them.*

Levona wasn't so sure.

Tell You when I want to touch peoples, too?

No.

Not hurting her. Pizi stood and flicked her tail. *I will tell if I will hurt someone.*

That sounded like a concession, but Levona doubted the statement. Pizi did what she wanted. She gave up. *You want to ride in the knapsack?*

No. I will watch My step.

We need to exit as soon as possible. We'll backtrack and come up a different way at a place farther than I'd planned.

Okay!

Shouldering her pack, Levona called up the map in her

head and retreated to a tunnel along a twistier path that would keep them as hidden as possible.

We don't know what made the tech come looking for us, whether the faucet alerted, or the grid, or videos, or sound. She might even be a latent mutant and sensed us. And we don't know if she's on duty or not, and if so, when her shift ends. How soon someone will come looking for her.

I will move FAST! And Pizi zipped ahead, much quicker now that she could see, and along the route Levona had visualized. Maybe fast enough and light enough not to trigger the grid.

Throughout the couple of hours it took them to find the opening of an abandoned culvert, Levona kept her extended senses on high alert, felt herself sweating through her shirt and jacket. By the time she reached the broken concrete exit and crawled through dirt into a gully in a park, her nerves had frayed enough that she curled into a ball and breathed until her heartbeat calmed. She closed her eyes but heard Pizi's commentary.

Stranger, shorter grass. It's softer on My paws! Ooooh, toys! Pieces of paper litter, chased, pounced upon and shredded. *Yuck, doesn't taste good.*

Fur sliding by her nose. *Are you ready, Levona? We should go, into the lights and the streets and the peoples.*

They'd hit the city in the early hours of a Saturday evening. Yeah, people would be out. Levona rolled to her feet. Time to change her appearance so she could fit in, from mountain survivor woman to city dweller.

As an outsider she needed to hook up with a contact of the psi-mutant community to learn the news, what areas of the city were more dangerous than usual, and when they anticipated the next mob attacks on the ghetto. Most of all, to figure out how to get passage onto the starship for Pizi and herself.

She'd been self-indulgent in taking that break. She couldn't afford many more moments like that. *Think* next time.

Moving to the darkest shadows of evergreens, she stripped and used a cheap cleanse-cloth to wipe down.

She dressed in her other set of clothes, slightly newer, more citified. Used lingering febrile energy for a psi-spell to gather humidity from the air and clean her previous clothes of dirt and grime and sweat and chemicalized mud. Another spell to whip them dry.

She undid the string tie holding back her curly hair and fluffed waves-curls-friz. She wore her hair long to conceal her features.

Levona clamped her forged id bracelet around her right wrist and activated it, stood still to see if the update would out her as an illegal. The band held a warning spell that discreetly heated if anything went wrong.

All okay. For now. She'd make sure just to lurk around, not go anywhere or do anything that required the id to be scanned or shown or verified in any way.

They moved out. Levona and Pizi slid from shade to shadow and blackness to shade ... through quiet neighborhoods of people afraid to come out during failing sunlight and falling dark. Strolled to a busier area of a city, not quite the closest one to the psi barrio, but one where mutants had always kept a low presence.

People sauntered on the street, glanced at her and away, and she realized her clothes appeared out of fashion and downright shabby. Nothing to do about that right now. No one seemed to notice Pizi, a relief, but Levona wondered why not. She and the little cat were still discovering Pizi's psychic talents. As far as mutations went, Pizi had jumped a few generations, was an outlier.

And Levona's own gifts expanded with the interaction of the cat to prod them.

The heavy smell of too many people, too much tech, filtered into her lungs, the rise in ambient noise thrummed in her ears, and the pure psychic buzz of people both irritated her nerves and excited them. Instead of being in the mountains alone, she'd joined other humans in a large city. She swallowed, realizing that though she had no family and no good friends, she'd *missed* people, been lonely.

Finally she reached the small business district and the correct street. Here she could find out how to connect with the psi mutant resistance. The mutants had bought the ship, she and Pizi were mutants, and she wanted on board.

As a safety precaution for both of them, Pizi split off to wander on her own and thrillingly *look around.*

Because Levona didn't know how many previous images the gov might have of her in their databases, she took out a floppy brimmed hat — always in fashion to confound the gov cameras and observers — and let it droop around her face, with a carefully constructed upcurve that didn't block her vision.

With each rambling step, she *pushed* anxiety into the ground so she'd appear casual. Stopping at a food window, she dropped a bill for coffee, getting a standard disintegrating paper cup. From the nearly burning heat, she figured she'd be able to finish this block, cross to the other side of the street, and reach the far corner before the cup fell apart. Meanwhile, she had an extra prop to obscure her face.

In the back of her mind, she kept track of Pizi, who behaved like a regular stray cat, though, as a stray, she could be shot by any passing military or police. The cat intently explored the gaps between the shops, and portions of the alleys behind, crossing half a block ahead of Levona in a dark area.

Levona stayed one step behind a clump of people her age — early twenties — like she was part of the group and lagged behind, head angled down as if focused on her coffee so she'd finish the drink before the cup fell apart into soggy paper.

The three-meter-tall graffiti wall began on her right, and she strove to remain relaxed. Cameras would be recording her, and some of the street musicians or dancers would be gov agents.

With a sidelong glance, she gazed at the gaudily decorated concrete that the mutant psis — as well as other outcast groups — used for coded messages. Drawings and street art; words, phrases, and scribbling by many hands in a swath of tints and patterns swept across the surface, or pinched tight in tiny spaces, dazzling with intense emotions and the pop of color.

Now to look for the secret message of where and when and who she could meet from the underground psi resistance to ask about the ship.

She sent a splash of *power* across the width. Nothing showed up in the designated location.

Had to stop, now, within scan distance of the part of the wall behind her. She stumbled, dropped her coffee, swore when the cup hit the ground and splatted into paper strips, expensive liquid spreading across the pitted sidewalk. She squatted to pick up the sodden cup shreds. The lovely scent of lost coffee brought tears to her eyes that she couldn't afford if she had to search the wall for information.

Levona turned her head and summoned enough energy to pulse mind power at the wall behind her. Nothing.

Her heart began to beat faster, louder in her ears than the electric violin across the street, and the shuffling of dancing feet.

Had she been too long away from CentralConglom? Too out of the loop of tenuous connection with the mutant psi folk? Probably. Get moving. With one last swipe at the gritty sidewalk with an equally shredded tissue, she gathered the final strip of cup, and stood. Walked slowly to the next recycle canister, muttering to herself, straining to keep the psi flow at the wall. Finding the right message from the right group shouldn't be this difficult.

She slumped, scuffing the ground, acting peeved for anyone who watched ... and felt a tingle ahead of her near the top of the wall, *not* in the previously stipulated spot. Pausing to stare at the concrete slab, pretending to study the beautiful Arabic calligraphy at her eye-level, she saw what she'd hoped to discover. One black glyph of the manipura chakra, then the glowing-psi symbols of a green lotus and a quick flash of ... not the green triangle she expected but a brown knot.

The mutant contact tonight would be at The Frigid Rush coffee shop. Date and place known. The knot indicator of the *person*, Levona didn't parse. And didn't know if names or symbols had changed or whether this was a new liaison in the last two years.

She had old code phrases, of course, but the real identification of one mutant to another was flashing a bit of psi power.

If she didn't recognize the go-between ... she didn't know what she'd do. Have Pizi sniff the person and hope Pizi could sense honesty? That Levona herself could?

Not hesitating in stride, she walked past the end of the wall, touched the popular "lucky spot" with her knuckles like most everyone else, and continued on. When she reached the end of the small neighborhood business section Pizi joined her as the buildings became bungalows and night settled into the city.

Where We going? asked Pizi.

Levona visualized a map with The Frigid Rush marked on

it, no more than three kilometers away. *You pick the route,* she told Pizi mentally.

If someone watched them by chance, Pizi's choice of path might throw off a person. Or their wanderings would not seem purposeful to cameras and keep them under observation. As long as Levona hadn't been recognized as a mutant.

Whee! Pizi gave a hop and shot Levona a happy look from clear eyes and trotted to the yard of what looked like an empty house and back to the alley and north and ... thirty-five minutes later Levona entered the darkened coffee shop and Pizi slid in.

Levona glanced around the dim place and figured only those with psychic power that heightened their sight would be able to see well. Several couples groped each other and two pairs sexed in different corners.

I feels him! The one We is to meet! Pizi sent excitedly, and a 3-D room-map flooded Levona's mind, along with dim sparks and one large yellow glow fading and brightening. Levona pinpointed the table, nearly sighed as she recognized the man by the flickering of a candle in glass, Bartek Coval, a contact for the psi mutant resistance. About a decade older than her, once he appeared wiry, now he looked skeletal.

He is sick and dying, Pizi stated matter-of-factly.

Levona flinched. Grief and pity and anger surged through her. Life hadn't been easy for Bartek.

After ordering at the counter, and inwardly grumbling that she had to spend money on a second coffee, and more here than previously, she took a circuitous way to Bartek's table. She noticed nothing unusual in the dark and smelled coffee and a whiff of weed, and human sweat and sex.

"Hey, Bartek," she said, slipping down in the chair opposite him, waiting for a shock if he didn't want to talk.

Skinny black brows went up. "Levona Martinez."

She clenched her teeth that he'd said her full name, even

in such an undertone it came over more telepathically than through actual breath.

"You haven't been around lately," he said.

"Can you talk quieter?" she mumbled.

A brief smile showing gleaming teeth. "Gov cops and military can't listen in. Rats take care of any spy bugs."

Levona got the impression of a psi-gifted person running those rats.

"Just like your cat is dribble-pissing on a new ankle-height camera dropped off an hour ago. Cameras go bad in here for a number of reasons. Though, if I were you, I'd run a zip-zap for bugs or spells when I leave."

"I'll do that."

"Why're you down from the mountains?" Then he lifted his hand. "No, don't tell me, I can guess. You saw the starship."

"Yes, I want on."

"You and nearly everybody else with a hint of psi." He paused, then shook his head, and his black hair nearly as long as hers swung. "Can't do it. Our starship that's sitting in our ghetto can be staffed — crewed — by our mutant psi community here in the city. Seven hundred positions, and they filled up in a week. Should have come down from the canyon eight months ago, sweetness."

She found herself grinding her teeth, desperation to get off the planet swirling inside.

"And we're lucky we got a starship. Was supposed to go to the mutants in the AfriqStates, but they're down for the next wave of colonists." His words ended on a mocking note.

Their gazes met. A next wave wouldn't happen.

"No room aboard the starship." She forced her own words through stiff lips.

"No. Especially not since the ship really showed up and landed." He sent her a narrowed gaze. "The folk in the barrio have been clearing the whole upper half of our land for the ship for months. Those who did the work, an' those who've strong links in our resistance, and those who have—" he rubbed his thumb and fingers together in the old gesture of money — "all those are in. Also anyone Geek Class. The rest of us are OUT."

"But you're—"

"—more useful here, on the ground, in the resistance, talking to freaks like you than on their precious ship, they told me."

Something in his tone rang like he'd heard words not like the ones he reported, but statements he couldn't accept, so his mind twisted them. Probably words about his health.

"I'm sorry about that," she murmured.

He stared. "I believe you're sincere. I'm sorry about me and you and your little cat, too, sweetness." He paused and curled his hand around his thick pottery cup, steam rose. "Don't suppose you found lost treasure in the hills, a gold mine, perhaps? Made your fortune, got rich?"

"No."

"Might have found space for you and me and the cat, if you had. Perhaps even a cryonics tube."

"Cryonics tube." Levona's mind scrambled to fit an image and definition to the phrase.

"Those who bought the ship are traveling in style. They don't want to suffer the years like the rest of the generational staff."

"Years," she repeated.

"They think between seventy-five and a hundred and fifty. There's living space for a generation or three on-board, that's why it's called a generation starship. Those in the cryonics tube will be frozen and awakened after landing on the beautiful new world with no gov who hates mutants. Everyone will *be* a mutant."

"Especially after a couple of generations of breeding with each other," Levona murmured, but her brain clicked along. All right, she hadn't thought of a lifetime living on a starship — after she'd had the whole of the Rockies to run around in — or being frozen so she'd live on the planet. She didn't know what would have been worse.

What *would be* worse. She'd find a way to get on that ship with Pizi. During this passage through the waterway gulches and the stone sewers, she'd shut a stone door on her past life; the scraping by in the mountains, the danger of living in the city, hiding from the gov, on the outskirts of the persecuted psi community. Her existence always at risk. No. Never again. She'd get a better life for herself and Pizi.

Her future and Pizi's included the starship.

She didn't say so, instead she voiced another fear. "You think they'll make it off-planet?"

He looked at her sourly, sucked tea through a missing tooth. "Our ship, or the others?" He shrugged. "They'll try, but no. If you, or they, think the UStates gov will let them get away clean, you got many more thinks a-coming."

"Yeah," Levona said.

Sighing, Bartek stared into his coffee. "But we — they — might get lucky. The UStates oligarchy has to consult with the other WorldStates oligarchies, so that might delay any action against the ships."

"Huh," said Levona.

"Our leadership has been smart. They moved soon after the latest purging of the generals and military. Even in the mountains, you must have heard of that, about three weeks ago?"

"Yes. Why was it done?"

"The oligarch spouted that the generals 'overstepped their authority.' Where and when we weren't told, just the regular nonsense, so who really knows? It's shark eat shark at the top of the govs. We should be glad this dictator is more stupid than usual."

"True."

"I'm sure our mutant resistance leadership believes we can move faster than the new generals who are still scrambling to secure their positions. Those guys are probably risk-averse." A sardonic smile whipped on and off his mouth. "I'm sure our strategists, or one of our oracles, has calculated the timing of leaving down to the nanosecond."

"I hadn't thought of that." Levona paused. "No one who joined up is having second thoughts?" If she had after being told, others must.

Bartek drummed his fingers on the table, stared into Levona's eyes and she became aware how sunken his own were, surrounded by dark shadows. Pity twinged through her, but she kept it from showing. Plenty of times she'd seen pity on people's faces, especially after her parents died in the psi-killing bomb set off over the city two years and two months ago ... and when her neighbors stolidly watched the UStates gov confiscate her family home and all its contents. She'd observed from a hiding place across the street that night.

Some of her neighbors had sensed her, but everyone kept their mouths shut. After all, they hadn't been too far away from the psi ghetto, and no one who'd survived wanted to be labeled a mutant-freak.

"Perhaps some people did have second thoughts," Bartek said. "Not sure who has checked in. Everyone in the whole barrio showed up to gawk at the ship and mill around. Me, too. Since it didn't concern me, I didn't watch who might have reported as crew. Only the leaders are on the ship now, working. Provisioning will happen the next couple of days, and crew assignments after that. But I know there is a waiting list. Not sure how long the list is, but truth to tell, if you get on the ship and regret it, too damn bad. They're spacing from here. Perhaps they have some kind of sorting process, counseling, don't know."

He drank his coffee, then continued, "I hear that *Nuada's Sword*, the ship in NJNY, is larger than our *Lugh's Spear*, and they're taking on crew who aren't psi since the ghettos in the East have been decimated by fighting. There's a chance you and the kit could get on there, if you could make it to NJNY."

Levona tensed. "When's the takeoff date of the ship — ships?"

Another shrug. "Nobody's saying. The leaders told the govs *a* lift-off date, but I doubt anybody believes it. Sooner rather than later, though, for sure, within two weeks, perhaps a week."

She worried her bottom lip. "You know of a cheap way to get to NJNY?"

"Not a solid one. Sex with Geek Class pilots sometimes works, sometimes not. And, sweetness, what would you say when they ask why you want to go *there* and *right now*? You don't lie worth shit and would be outed as a mutant-freak."

Just the thought of it made her stomach clench, would set up trembles if she didn't squash her imagination. She sucked in air and nearly choked on burnt coffee, sex, and sweat. "Can you get to NJNY?"

"No, too damn important here, like I said, what they told me." Raising his cup to his mouth, he sipped, then said, "One of our local scientists gathered genetic material from every willing person in the ghetto. Our folk have my DNA in special storage for the new world." His lips twisted. "So I might have far-far-descendants someday. Our scientist even procured physical samples from ... other neighborhoods." He stared at her. From where she'd grown up, he meant. "If you left any DNA with anyone, or your parents did, both the gov and our folk have yours."

Her heart jumped in her chest. She didn't recall, but maybe when she'd been a baby her parents had trusted a doctor to do tests. She'd liked her childhood doctor, before the gov came for him. She wouldn't be surprised if her genetic sample was stored on the ship.

"We gathered DNA not only from this region, either. One of the more important rebels came from the East, with all of NJNY's sample. And, I think, with duplicate genetic material of the third starship's people, from EurAstates, *Arianrhod's Wheel*."

"My God," she breathed. Good for the colonists if they'd collected a lot of genetic code to take with take with them, saving all the different kinds of psi power, at least. Maybe a whole host of other kinds of talents and skills now suppressed by the govs, too.

If they'd done that with humans, they might have gotten DNA from animals, maybe all the extinct species, too, that couldn't survive on Earth as it was.

Distracting thought. Levona didn't want her genes to head to the new world, *she* wanted to go on this trip, this adventure that would save her life. Live without persecution, and take her cat with her. No one would have gotten Pizi's genetic sample, and that cat needed to be saved.

"It's not 'my God,'" Bartek chided. "We're not the True Religionists who follow one stern god and their beloved dictator. It's Lady and Lord, or Lord and Lady. Divine Couple."

"Huh?"

"Gotta build a community, our leaders have got that right, and from the minute they all step onto the ship, they'll have a new society. Maybe it'll stick down here, too, among the rest of us. Celtic-pagan culture."

"Oh." Levona didn't know what "Celtic" meant, and not much of "pagan" either, except that the True Religionists mob flung that insult-swear at mutants and freaks. Now the psi folk leaders had adopted it? Weird.

"Thanks for all the data." She stood and put her last big bill down on the table. Too much for his information, but she'd be able to survive one way or another without money and he ... couldn't.

"Good-bye, sweetness. Good luck." His hand swiped over the table and her seventy-five spot disappeared and he stared off into the room's dimness. "It's a wonder," he murmured. "The starship. Like I said, the buyers are calling our ship *Lugh's Spear*."

"Why?"

"All the names of our ships tie in with the new Celtic mythology." He shrugged off the explanation and focused on an inner vision. "It's a full kilometer and a half long. Beautiful, like a white plane, cylindrical body and angled wings."

Levona had seen that for herself when it had flown overhead, but she lingered, ears pricked for all the information she could get, and Pizi hadn't finished her rounds of sniffing the floor and everyone in the coffee shop. Levona hadn't grasped the size of the starship, except "huge."

"A wonder," he muttered, then, finally. "Someday one of my genetic descendants might walk on a new planet."

She bent and kissed him on the cheek, and he jerked, then patted her hand, but didn't meet her gaze again.

And she walked away.

Such a sickness could happen to her if she stayed, or worse, some nastiness could eat Pizi, starting with her eyelids.

Levona did a quick security zip-zap spell to kill any spy bugs and slipped out of The Frigid Rush, slinking along with Pizi in the darkest night shadows. Not many streetlights here, and like always, the murky atmosphere covered the moon. She'd loved watching the moon in the mountains.

Did the new planet have a moon? She didn't know and

shivered in the cool spring night. She'd been focused too much on herself and now regretted that. She'd left the city no more than a month after her parents' death. If she'd stayed she'd have connected more with the psi-mutant resistance and be on the ship for sure.

We going to Our ship now? Starship, starship, starsh—

The ship's called LUGH'S SPEAR, Levona informed Pizi telepathically, pronouncing it in her head the way Bartek did. It occurred to her that he'd changed his name-sigil on the message wall because of the — *their* — new culture. She hoped the Lady and Lord granted him peace, and found her lips mouthing that sentiment, a new prayer to a new god — *Divine Couple* — and how cool was that! And a new life for her and Pizi.

Levona was determined to get on that ship and get away.

The more she thought about the situation in the next hour and a half of gullies, stone sewer passages and hidden byways on the way to a secret entrance to the barrio, the more Levona believed the three starships might make it off planet.

The govs pretended to want the psi-mutants quarantined, and gone. The propaganda news stories preached that mutants caused a lot of unrevealed bad things to happen.

But the govs used the mutants to distract and scare the majority of the people from what else was going on. The UStates, particularly, not-so-secretly exhorted mobs, mostly the True Religionists, to attack the ghettos.

So the leaders of the resistance had publicly taken the govs at their word. They'd bought three starships and away they'd go. Levona figured the top elected mutant execs had been planning something like this a long time, and caught the govs by surprise.

Finally she and Pizi stopped at the hidden underground entrance to the barrio. She murmured the spellwords Bartek had told her at the barrier and it thinned enough for them to pass through without harm. Pushing through felt like walking through thick enveloping syrup. Naturally the above-ground fences set around the ghetto by the UStates gov didn't stop psis.

The minute they stepped across the boundary from city to restricted psi-mutant-freak-living-area a buzz filled her, along with more energy.

Pizi gasped. *I feels GOOD.*

Yeah. Levona had forgotten the power boost she got in the ghetto.

Fifteen minutes later they moved from underground to the surface exactly outside the expanse where *Lugh's Spear* stood. Only a few people of the barrio lingered to stare at the ship, Levona sensed everyone that had flown in on the vehicle remained inside.

Look at that! Pizi gasped and sniffed and rotated her ears. *FEEL that! It is WONDERFUL! Our new home!*

Obviously Pizi had no doubts that they'd be able to be taken on as crew, while uncertainty flooded Levona.

The beauty and the style of the ship impressed. Long, low landing runners had deployed from the underside of the standard plane shape to prop it up. In the middle of one side a ramp angled down with a closed door at the top, with civilian-type mutant guards stationed at the bottom.

The cylinder with wings angled back appeared more like a vehicle than a home, though it rose a good nineteen stories high and stretched a kilometer and a half long.

A generational ship — a spacecraft that people could live and pass their lives on and die. All pure white.

Just looking at *Lugh's Spear* made hope unfurl in her again. Hope that mutants would crew the vehicle, they'd get in and the ship would sail away into space to their new planet. A freak *psi* society would be founded.

That could happen. The resistance leaders were accustomed to strategizing, out-witting the gov and the mobs the gov agitated and sent against them. Used to fighting for every single thing they wanted.

And with the adversity of the last several decades, people's magic, their psychic mental powers, had increased, expanded.

So maybe they'd fly away, clean.

Time to break the bad news to Pizi. *We don't have a place in the ship.*

The little cat gasped, stopped and sat on Levona's feet and stared up at her with big eyes. *What!*

Levona paused, trying to find words.

Pizi stood, then hopped around. *What? What? What?*

I waited too long. All the living space filled up months ago.

You HAD to wait. For Me. If You came down here times ago, You wouldn't have found Me and We wouldn't be heart friends, she said with irrefutable logic that made the ends of Levona's mouth curve.

I don't think the people who own the ship will accept that excuse, she said, though with the prodigy that was Pizi, they should.

Pizi stopped her hopping and sniffed. *Then We will have to sneak in, like We've sneaked in many other spots.*

I guess so.

They are NOT leaving without US.

All right. We may get in trouble when we're caught, and we WILL be caught.

True?

Yes, the space trip will take a long time, we can't hide forever in the ship.

Not even in the walls?

Not even in the walls.

I hears. We will go and find a sneak place in, now.

Despite the four patrolling guards armed with long

blasters and two standing at the main entrance mid-ship at the bottom of the ramp to the doors, Pizi headed for the vehicle. No one seemed to notice her, a brownish cat slinking in the night, and she managed to reach the ship. Levona saw her put a paw on the landing runner.

Levona couldn't go into the starship, but if she walked around the vehicle, she'd get a good idea of the space and the structure, and how that space divided into rooms for sleeping and driving the ship or whatever. She didn't think she'd be stopped and questioned by the guards. She ran a little psi through her id bracelet so it glowed and they would know she fit the designation of mutant psi freak as well as they did. Besides, anyone would be interested in viewing the ship.

So she nodded to the sentries at the main doors, and circled the vehicle, noting its symmetry and figuring that it would reflect that symmetry on the inside. Tentative maps began forming in her head.

Three quarters around she heard a squeal from Pizi. *Here, here, here!* the cat shouted mentally along their private channel. *We can sneak in here, I think!*

Levona backtracked toward the tail end, and movement caught her eye, Pizi cavorting. Levona angled to see beyond the landing runner and under the ship. Yes, there appeared to be a small breach in the ship, a slight and jagged tear on the underside of the ship where the runner attached to the barrel. Hard to make out the exact dimensions in the shadows. Perhaps made when *Lugh's Spear* landed yesterday, and not yet fixed. Extending her senses, Levona didn't *feel* any special watch being kept on that particular section, nor any outside ship cameras.

With slow steps, she walked closer to the beautiful starship, as if she wanted to see the wings, or get a better sense of the size.

From the corner of her eye, she watched a woman

descend the ramp who turned to stare at her. The willowy blond appeared about her own age of twenty-two. The guards saluted this one, so Levona knew she was important.

Levona stopped her progress when the woman strode toward her, halted within a meter. They stared at each other, and their psi powers expanded, brushed, and Levona felt her own psi strength met and matched.

"Hi," Levona said, trying her best to look innocent.

The woman cocked her head. "You're a psi mutant, but I don't know you. I was born here in the ghetto, lived here all my life and served our community. I know everyone who lives in the barrio and most the local psi folk, particularly all who contribute to mutant society."

"Levona Martinez," she said, her voice serene but raising with a question about the woman's own identity.

Narrowing her eyes, the blond said, "There are two family groups with the surname 'Martinez,' but I know all their members."

"My father was Douglas Martinez, my mother Asaka Martinez."

The woman's frown deepened, then she glanced away, toward the shining ship. "I recognize those names as people who lived as normals but died when the gov exploded a sneak psi bomb over the city to ..." She stopped.

"To kill mutant freak rats hiding as good citizens," Levona ended tonelessly. "I was out partying with friends that night in old downtown Denver. The bomb missed me."

"A tragedy."

"The gov called it a triumphant cleansing of 636 people." Levona blinked back tears, not only of grief, but of injustice and fury.

"You didn't come here, to live in the barrio, after that demonstration of the gov's power," the blond said. "You didn't join our community."

"I went up into the mountains to grieve and heal. I came back because I wanted to see the ship," Levona replied, simply and sincerely. She turned to gaze at *Lugh's Spear*, wondering how much her sad history might touch this woman in authority. "It's a great piece of machinery."

"Fabulous piece of art," the other commented.

Levona flicked a hand toward the west. "I saw it fly overhead and wanted to take a peek."

The woman gave her a skeptical glance. "Just take a peek. Uh-huh."

Best to confirm as much info as possible, and maybe try and spin a bond between them by asking questions. "I heard there are three starships?"

"Who told you?"

"Bartek Coval at The Frigid Rush tonight."

Her expression formed into pity. "Ah. Poor Bartek."

"Yeah, looks bad."

After a sigh, the woman answered, "The leaders of the psi-mutants purchased three starships in total, all of them built at least thirty years ago and decommissioned and warehoused. Only *Lugh's Spear* will leave from here, taking our colonists."

Levona jerked a head at the gleaming white vehicle, old but beautiful. "Aren't you going?" She could tell by the woman's clothes that she came from a richer family than Levona herself, might even have enough money to buy a place in the cryonics tubes instead of being one of the crew. She smelled clean, with a touch of pretty floral scent that might be perfume.

The woman glanced at the ship wistfully, shook her head and met Levona's gaze again. "Someone has to stay and fight. For liberty, for the rights of mutants like us."

Levona dipped her head. "I hear you."

"But you don't agree, do you?"

Clearing her throat, Levona didn't answer but said, "You know who I am. I don't–"

"You don't know me, and you would if you identified with us as psi mutants." With a dip of the head, the woman said, "Karida Bonfils."

"I'm sure you have a title," Levona said.

"Senior liaison between the CentralConglom psis and the leadership of *Lugh's Spear*. "I'm a ..." Her face twitched into a smile that was more of a grimace. "Negotiator."

"A politician."

"Maybe. But you shouldn't be here."

Levona opened her eyes wide. "Just looking."

"Uh huh." Karida snapped her fingers. "Let's see your I.D. bracelet."

Suppressing anxiety, Levona detached it and handed it to Karida, who accessed the info and shook her head. "Minerva Starshine."

Levona shrugged.

"Smart, using the surname of the only old and powerful mutant family in the city." Karida weighed the bracelet in her hand as tension tightened in Levona. "A family with many members and several offshoots. But I don't think they'd approve of your use of this." She tucked Levona's only ID in a pocket of the expensive trousers.

"I'm a psi mutant freak," Levona stated. "I'm here and I believe in your – our – policies to keep our freedoms." She especially believed the best chance for every psi on the planet was to *get off* Earth.

Karida's lips firmed. "Our main policy is to protect ourselves. There will be more of us born."

"Oh, for sure. If the govs don't kill us when born," Levona said, "Or, better yet, prevent us from being conceived or born."

The liaison shuddered. "We have to fight that, too."

Levona shrugged. "The gov keeps secrets. Who knows what they do to our bodies in hospitals if we go there for pre-natal care, or to give birth? I won't take that chance." Her parents had lived in fear all of their lives and still had died from a weapon aimed at psi-mutants.

"You say the right things, but I believe it would be best if you come along with me as I walk you off the landing field."

"Or?"

Karida said, "Or I hand over your ID bracelet to our head of ghetto security, and we ... ah, detain you, until the ship leaves."

Fear spurted through Levona. Hide the emotion, hope Karida didn't sense the panic. Terrible to be locked up, stuck on Earth and in the barrio. No, that must *not* happen. Retreat, and *think*, and figure something out.

Pizi squeaked.

"What was that?" Karida demanded.

"My young cat, my animal companion," Levona said. Pizi raced from the direction of the field behind them, stopped and mewed. Levona stooped down to pick her up.

YOU NEED AN ANIMAL COMPANION! Pizi shouted.

Karida gasped. "I *heard* her." The other woman lowered her voice, "Telepathically." She held out her hands. "Please?" It *was* a plea.

Levona set Pizi in Karida's hands.

"Her fur's so soft," Karida said, and cuddled the cat against her cheek in a gesture revealing her inner child, one with a spark of hope that she yet felt, and contrasting with the thick jacket over personalized body armor.

Another little yeep from Pizi. *I know where there is a nest of young Cats, some nearly as smart as Me!*

Karida's caught breath matched Levona's.

Not very far from here. Pizi gazed at Karida with big eyes that probably glowed in the dim light. *They need human companions to help Them be all They can be. Come with Us and I'll take you to Them.*

Karida's jaw set and she looked around suspiciously. "There are only the two of you?"

Yes, Pizi and Levona said at the same time.

"Not distracting me so someone can sneak in?"

"No. And you have patrol guards on the grounds."

"Mostly to give alarm if the gov incites the mobs against us again. Not so much to guard the ship, and not military trained, just doing their duty to pay their passage as crew."

"Yeah," Levona said. "No one having second thoughts now that they see the ship where they'll be living in the rest of their lives and maybe that of their children's and grandchildren's?"

Karida hesitated. "Perhaps."

"Some of the singles, maybe, 'cuz they'll have to find mates from the folk on board?"

Another pause and a hard look at Levona. "Perhaps."

More hope unfurled inside Levona.

Pizi revved a small purr, touched Karida's face with a paw. *You need an animal companion. And someone needs YOU!*

More wistfulness emanated from Karida, but not aimed at the hope of the colonists, a new planet of their own, but yearning for a living being, an animal friend, here and now. She held the cat in front of her, and Pizi dangled. "You say these cats are like you?"

Not as SMART as Me, but ...

"They can talk telepathically?"

A teeny bit. Images, but still can be a true companion to You. Bond with You.

"Okay," Karida said. "Let me instruct the head sentry and we'll go."

She handed Pizi to Levona, walked over to the one on the right side of the ramp, and began talking. Levona petted Pizi with shaking hands and wondered if there was any way to finesse the situation and elude Karida and get on the ship. Or at least get her ID back. Levona's mind spun with thready plans, more hope than real. She couldn't give up hope.

Soon Karida joined them and Pizi leapt from Levona's fear-damp grip down to the ground to lead the way to the other cats.

They walked off the field and traversed several blocks in silence, all three of them female psi mutant-freaks, accepting of their gifts and themselves, but the humans wary of each other.

In a few minutes they reached the darkness of an alley off a street of small restaurants that made Levona's mouth water and stomach grumble — she hadn't wanted to try the dubious food The Frigid Rush served. There Pizi led them to a cat stink corner holding a box and stained cloth scraps. All the while she mentally broadcasted, *We come with food and love and love and food for YOU!*

Two skinny gray tabby cats, smaller and younger than Pizi herself, hovered over a heap of rags. Their muscles tensed as they readied to spring away and bolt from the alley.

"I don't have any food," Karida whispered.

"I do," Levona said, louder. "Radiate love and acceptance."

Yes! Pizi agreed.

"That's simple to do," Karida said, and the whole alley filled with reassuring, positive feelings, most from Karida, with a good amount from Levona and Pizi.

The cats relaxed and turned toward them, sending a yearning *need* back, until Levona's stomach rumbled with their hunger. Tentative hope flowed from them to Levona and Karida.

They don't know where to go to find peoples like Us and human companions, Pizi said.

"I didn't even know cats like these existed," Karida muttered.

It is good You all know of each other now, Pizi insisted.

"Absolutely," Levona said, shrugging off her pack and opening a long pocket containing food bits she kept for Pizi. With a spellword, she rehydrated and heated them and the beef smelled tasty.

A chorus of mews erupted and the cats stropped their ankles.

"Here, hold out your hands," Levona said to Karida. When the woman did, Levona dumped most of the bits into her hands, and Karida hunkered down to feed the felines.

Yowls stopped abruptly.

They're WONDERFUL, quite, quite, incredible, Karida said mentally. Levona sensed that the woman's throat had closed with emotion too thickly to talk.

The cats ate greedily, licking Karida's hands.

"They're hardly more than kittens," Levona murmured, squatting to offer her hand with some bites, too.

They is much younger than Me, Pizi said, though she only neared her four-month mark. *You should give Them ALL my treats. They need it more than Me,* she ended virtuously.

We'll get more for you, Levona said on their private channel.

Of course. Pizi had no doubts of that. She licked Levona's hand, then sauntered around the alley, lifted her muzzle and sniffed loudly, tilted her head.

There are more out there. The dam of these and the sire and others!

"We should bring them in, all of them, and take them to people who'll appreciate them," Karida said.

She meant folk in the barrio, and no doubt Karida believed in her community, but Levona had followed her parents' example and not stayed where she'd be specifically targeted for her psychic gifts.

Karida called out loud to the cats, and two more short-haired grays poked their heads around the alley wall. One trotted forward. Karida sat down right there in the alley, and projected a hypnotic mental song that stilled Levona, too. *Come to me, cats. I will find you homes with loving people who will cherish and respect you.*

Pizi nipped at Levona's thumb and she jerked from the trance, frowned at the summoning, and said, "You need to use less words and more images, and definitely send emotion. That way they'll *feel* that you're sincere and not wanting them for ... experiments ... or whatever."

Karida glanced up at her. "Right." Holding her hands flat, she inhaled and *drew* on her power. A moment later raw hamburger lay on her palms.

"Translocation," Levona breathed. "An impressive power."

"Yes, thank you." Then Karida turned her head to stare down the alley that opened into a rubbled space. "You have good maps in your head, that's one of your gifts."

"Yeah."

"Then you probably know all about the routes into the ship." She cleared her throat. "Into *Lugh's Spear.*"

"Maybe."

And once We get into the ship, We will FEEL it, and know all its passageways, too! Pizi burbled.

Levona grit her teeth at Pizi's revelation.

Karida wiggled, settling into the spot, body angling away from Levona and Pizi, as if dismissing them to go their way. "I believe that having semi-intelligent animal companions like these cats is very important to our cause here on Earth." She sighed, then reached out when another late-kittenhood feline zoomed toward them. The little black tom leapt and attached himself to Karida's jacket, crawled up to snuggle against her neck. "Lady and Lord," Karida murmured. "This one is *mine*!"

"Lady and Lord? Oh, the Divine Couple."

"Yes, a very good religion to forge a community, generous and with the tenet to do no harm."

"I can believe in that," Levona said.

The cat revved his purr. The soothing sound filled the alley. Levona sensed he, too, sent out a telepathic call.

"Better get going," Karida said.

"Yes."

"There's another cat," Karida whispered.

"They are psi mutants like us," Levona said. "They must be nurtured and cherished."

And become heart friends to peoples! Pizi put in. *We will alls help each others. Here and there and everywhere.*

"That sounds good to me," Karida said.

"I want one of these little cats to go to Bartek," Levona said.

Karida nodded. "Done, and I'll keep an eye on him." Her mouth flattened. "Quite a few of us are keeping an eye on Bartek. I'll watch out for him and the cat."

"Good."

Levona recalled words painted on the graffiti wall. "Blessed be."

"Blessed be, go with the Lady and Lord," Karida answered. She dug into her pocket and tossed up Levona's fake I.D. bracelet, didn't watch as Levona caught it.

I will do nothing to frustrate your ... plans, but I do not condone them, came Karida's whisper in Levona's mind. She turned squarely away from them.

The tom rumbled his purr even louder, using psi magic.

Show off, Pizi grumbled as Levona tip-toed out of the alley. Her purr had always been rather thin.

They found a cheap food window and Levona parted with a few singles for a veggie smelling handpie filled with stuff that promised to be nutritious if not tasty, and treats for Pizi.

They had to get on *Lugh's Spear* as soon as possible, before whatever good will Karida had for Pizi and Levona dried up. Sneaking on wouldn't be as difficult as hiding until the ship launched.

So they waited in the darkest of shadows through long hours with fear and anticipation rising and fading, but keeping Levona's teeth on edge and sending Pizi running under the long ship front and back.

In the earliest hours of the morning, even the relief guards nodded sleepily. Mouth drying, Levona crept near the tail of the starship, there she fell to her belly and crawled the last twenty meters until she was partially shielded from sight by the runners. The scent of winter grass and odd ship tech smell rose from the dirt around her.

Then she walked carefully, step by step over frost-crunchy grass for several meters, senses strained for any shout of alarmed discovery.

She stopped where Pizi indicated and drew out her multi-tool with the focused beam of light. Her tool showed the crack, smaller than she'd thought, and at a difficult angle to get in. Pizi assured her that she could fit.

Levona sucked in her breath and drew on all her power and jumped up and *in*. Pizi pushed with her power, too.

With much squishing of stomach and breasts along with bruising, Levona wiggled through the outer skin of the ship and lay panting and rubbing her hurt chest, trying to recover not only physical, but her psychic energy.

Pizi ran off to explore.

Levona lay in a space between the walls, maybe a service area. The intense darkness gave no clues about the blueprint of the vehicle. She would wait until she got her breath back before standing and sending out her psi senses to determine a rough map. Meanwhile her nose told her of old dust collected in the walls, and oil and fuel.

After a minute she sat and flicked on her tool-light, but

she couldn't identify some of the materials of the ship. She stared at a girder that looked — not really solid — touching it, the material felt like metal, but made of tiny cavities.

So she didn't know as much about the ship as she should have, desperately ignorant of everything, the crewing, the structure, the timeline ... Yeah, despite her loner tendencies, she should have come down from the mountains months ago and joined the psi-mutant community, in the barrio or out.

Before she'd interacted with Bartek and Karida, Levona hadn't truly realized how isolated she'd been from her own kind.

But she couldn't regret lingering. Pizi's trailing mew sounded in Levona's mind and a flush of love swept through her. As her cat companion pointed out earlier, if Levona had returned from the mountains earlier, in time to be accepted as part of the crew for *Lugh's Spear,* she'd have missed saving Pizi.

More than ever, Levona decided the cat was special, of the utmost importance. A genetic switch had flicked to make Pizi The Prodigy. The young cats they'd found that night seemed generations behind Levona's own animal companion. Pizi was a genius savant, and a higher priority than Levona herself for the gifted community.

She let the dimness of the ship, the odd smells and the *feel* of the atmosphere wrap around her, settling her emotions from the last few days. She and Pizi had arrived and accomplished their goal. So far.

As she calmed and became fully aware of her surroundings, she understood that more than her hope sparkled through the air of the ship. The vehicle itself carried the vibrations of the psi leaders who'd bought it, who'd already traveled on it, those of the ... pilot and the colonists.

Hope.

She felt comfortable here. For the first time, she could accept living her life on this ship, with these people.

If they ever accepted her.

At that moment Pizi traipsed back into sight. As soon as she saw the glow light, she trotted toward Levona, who opened her arms.

Pizi flung herself at her and Levona cradled the cat tight, closing her eyes, feeling the softness of her fur, smelling the dust and mountain tang of her cat and more, a coating of psi from the ship lingering on her fur. Slow and steadily, she petted her friend for long minutes. Pizi vibrated with her quiet purr.

I love you, Pizi, Levona sent mentally.

I love you, too, Pizi said, then *I have found a place I like, a little nest where We can stay.*

For now, Levona said. *We WILL be discovered at some point in time, probably when we go out for water and food.*

I know.

We are trying to hide until after the ship takes off.

"Yessss," Pizi hissed audibly.

"Yes," Levona muttered.

Follow me. Pizi hopped from Levona's loosened grasp, and moved from the web of metal pillars to a short corridor with metal panels, tail waving.

Keeping her steps as soft-footed as possible, Levona trailed her cat, who turned from a passage heading to the interior of the ship to one running the length of the ship, and too dim.

As they walked, Levona kept her hand against the inner wall, fingertips picking up dust and grime, but her mind drawing maps as they went, correlating with what she'd seen outside — a symmetrical vehicle top to bottom and side to side for four-fifths of the ship. The last fifth of the ship, the nose, angled to about three stories. From the *feeling* of that particular space, Levona thought the pilots and other crew who controlled the ship had their own living space there.

She frowned. The most important ... most intense and heaviest feeling came from mid-ship, several stories above the wide entrance doors. A phrase about ships floated to her mind, *Captain's Quarters*. Yes, several tiny rooms with thinner inner walls between them.

The nose had one large room ... for the pilot? But others with bunks. The ship contained fewer long dormitory rooms than Levona would have thought, more little rooms on each side of the main hallway. Because people liked privacy? She thought so.

Interesting, though.

Here! Pizi said, and held a paw to a circular door hole with a cracked-open portal. Levona put her hand on the part that swung in, no hinges on the outside, only on the inside. By the time she stepped to the far side of the door, Pizi had disappeared. *Long, long up, but fun! And, I think, lots of nice smells along the way!*

A tube climbed at about a forty-five-degree angle, with staggered openings on each level, and rough hand-holds-footholds along the way. Pizi hopped up, and with narrowed eyes, Levona thought she saw the cat use psi power for a boost. Feeling stronger and safer, Levona created and sent a glow light before her little friend. Levona tilted her head and studied her cat ... and the flow of the atmosphere around them. Yeah, Pizi pulled extra psi energy from the atmosphere and used it. Amazing.

They climbed a long time, up sixteen levels, and each time they passed a portal, Levona pressed her hand against it and sent a whisper of her own psi down the space. She confirmed what she thought, the configuration of the halls, little rooms and gathering rooms matched exactly from one level to the next ... except for four floors on the opposite side of the ship.

A huge space full of ... dirt ... and the beginnings of growing things?

Another idea she'd never considered with regard to the ship. Of course they'd need to have ... crops? Maybe a park, even?

The idea occupied her mind until Pizi stopped and slunk through the opening of another metal portal. Levona widened it and did the same, followed the dust trail of her cat for a handful of meters, smothering sneezes on her arm from the rising dust, and another scent of ... other lands, she supposed.

Finally they stopped at a bulb of no walls and more girders.

Our nest. We can stay here, and near the other peoples, too!

That rang an alarm in Levona's brain, but also intrigued. Straining, she tried to sense people moving through the vehicle, and she could! No doubt her psi-gift got a boost from being in a high-psi environment, like Pizi's had.

Pizi helped Levona make their "nest," pushing rags into heaps while Leona muttered spells with her fading energy to clean the space as best she could.

Then she pulled out all of her clothes and the thin special-tech camping blanket that would keep them warm, if not cushion them. But as she lay down, she realized the temperature of the ship had been steady and comfortable. Her mind finally slowed enough to allow more sensory stimulation – for her to miss the freshening breeze of the mountains, the thin high-altitude air, fresher than city air, the rustlings of other life around her. No bugs or beasts below or above her, here.

It felt ... odd ... sleeping in a metal construct, like a city building far above the ground, especially since she'd been living outside the city for two years, moving from campsite to hut to old park cabins that one wealthy guy or another had been given by the gov. Usually the rich spent little time on one of their many estates, so the outbuildings or former visitor centers provided good shelter for Levona.

Shutting her eyes, she began to breathe deeply, a childhood trick to lure sleep, despite the strangeness of her new spot. Pizi snuggled against her and soon slumber took her away.

The next morning, Levona snuck into one of the rooms on the floor below to use the tiny toilet and sink. This single room with toilet-shower bump would be hard to live in for the rest of her life ... very hard, but she was determined.

She wondered if the rest of the crew had seen their living space.

As she walked back to their nest, she became aware of ... others.

Voices didn't quite "echo" through the ship, but both Levona and Pizi could tell when one person spoke to another, and definitely when the leaders gathered. She deduced about ten people currently lived on the ship. Levona left Pizi in their nest and walked along the wall until she found the conference room. She stood a minute before rationalizing that she must listen in because she needed to know *everything* now since she'd missed so much.

She learned that some of the mutant leaders — of all the ships — had prices on their heads from the mobs, the True Religionists, and the gov, which kept the top leadership tense. So far *Lugh's Spear* housed only one pilot, Netra Sunaya Hoku, but two more should be coming.

The meeting broke up and Levona was beginning to explore one level below in detail when Pizi found her.

Peoples are outside with many big crates and putting foods and drinks here in My Ship! Levona changed her clothes to the more battered ones. She also arranged her hair differently and tinted a streak of purple in it — something that mutant-freaks rarely did because who wanted to call attention to themselves? — and slipped out of the ship while no one watched to become one of the workforce. She kept her psi-gifts locked down and shielded as she carried boxes from trucks to a staging area up a ramp and into a bay that held what appeared to be scientific instruments.

Psi-mutant guards watched the trucks, and one of the leaders, a tall, thin woman with dark skin, opened some of the boxes to check the food and taste it.

Her intimidating manner made the drivers and people delivering the food nervous, and Levona figured the woman intended that result, so the psi-folk wouldn't get cheated. After all, the colonists wouldn't be here on Earth to complain to the suppliers, would they?

So the delivery guys thought Levona worked for the ship, belonged to the barrio, and the psi-mutant freaks thought she'd come with the trucks.

Pizi took off to see the cats, and visit them in their new homes, and came back now and then to "supervise." The ship folk noted her — how could they not with Pizi mentally shouting? Most of the psis could hear her telepathically — but didn't associate her with Levona.

Levona also saw a group of psi mutant Geek Class techs march under *Lugh's Spear* to fix the tear she and Pizi had used to sneak into the ship. Since they took hours she figured they were doing an excellent job. Her and Pizi's escape route was gone.

Trucks kept coming and coming, and so did barrio guards, especially after one of the drivers had run at them with a knife, shouting, "Death to the mutants!" He'd been wrestled down, his truck stripped immediately of the provisions, those thoroughly checked, and he and his off-loaders escorted off the ghetto lands asap.

It made everyone nervous, and Levona figured they all believed the launch date just got moved up before the gov could whip up a mob against them, or the True Religionists got drunk enough to storm the gates, or the gov ordered the military in.

Levona and Pizi ate a late lunch off-site, strolling the neighborhoods for, she hoped, the last time.

After finishing the afternoon shift, Levona hid behind a panel in the storage area while the last truck left. Then she and Pizi snuck back to their nest. They ate dinner packets Levona had purchased and while Pizi explored inside some more, Levona kept her senses sharp. Sure enough, an hour and a half later, the leaders living on the ship convened another meeting.

This time Pizi came with Levona as she huddled behind the main conference room wall to eavesdrop. A jumble of people talked over each other before a sharp female tone stated, "Speaking of the cryonic tubes, they've been retrofitted for this older ship, and we don't know if they will work."

"Couldn't we depend on the trials from the other ships, *Nuada's Sword* and *Arianrhod's Wheel*? The systems remain standard, though theirs are newer," a softer-spoken woman said.

"We *could*," said a male sarcastically, "if the other colonists had done testing of the life-sustaining systems of the cryonics, the 'freezing' and 'awakening.' But they haven't. NJNY is lagging behind outfitting the ship because of the pressure of the mobs and, unlike us, their crew is not entirely psi mutants. As for EurAstates, we all have agreed they will have the easiest time of getting away and are on a slower schedule to get their systems in place."

"Which means since we're the ones ready to do the trials on the cryonics now, we'll be the first," an accented male voice said in a clipped tone. "We've already heard all the pros and cons of testing whether our cryogenics system will freeze, and more importantly, preserve a person to be revived later. Whether we will live through the process. Our arguments have become circular. No one wants to volunteer for the experiments. I understand that and accept it, but believe there is no point in continuing to discuss minutiae of this situation for hours. With the exception of Pilot Hoku, our skills are replaceable."

"I wouldn't say that, Clague," said the rich voice of the one she knew to be the pilot. "You're our trouble-shooter. If something goes wrong, you'll be around to be upgraded to Captain to fix it, like Kelse Bountry of NJNY in *Nuada's Sword*."

A murmur or agreement.

"Ah, those of us who have led a mutant rebel cell. In that instance, I think you need to listen to me. Further argument is futile, we need to test the cryonic system immediately. It is a vital process that demands time and precision. Problem-solver or not, if we get into trouble, I must be around to be awakened to address any issue. So we must know the freezing and reviving works. I suggest we draw lots."

That had silence writhing behind the wall, then a burst of noisy irritated voices bordering on anger.

Pizi scrunched up her face, rotating her ears. Her mental stream sounded shocked and trailed such emotion behind it. *THEY is mad at each other! They shouldn't be mad at each other!*

That surprised and disappointed Levona, too.

"What's that? Who's there?" the sharp tone snapped from a woman. "Behind the walls, two of them, gov *spies!*" Her voice rose to a screech. Levona could sense the focused point of her finger aimed at her and Pizi.

Levona closed her eyes, she and Pizi hadn't been wary enough. She wasn't used to being in an adversarial position with psi-gifted people. Usually mutant folk could be trusted, especially those with "good" vibes like those who stayed in the barrio and beyond the city wall. She hadn't shielded herself or Pizi. Stupid mistake.

*WE IS *NOT* SPIES. WE IS *CREW*,* Pizi shouted mentally.

"I heard her!" the soft-voiced woman said, and she had an accent like the one called Clague.

"Me, too!" spit out ... everyone else, Levona figured.

Pilot Hoku shouted — and since Levona barely heard him, she realized she'd been *listening* more with her psi power than her ears — "We will meet you in the main corridor ... crew."

WE WILL BE THERE! Pizi returned.

We will meet you there, sirs and mizzes, Levona sent telepathically, letting them hear the clear projection of her words, an indication of the strength of her gift. Not many people could project telepathy well. Maybe that would count for something. But dread invaded her bones.

A half-hour later she sat, spine straight, in the room she'd been eavesdropping on, awaiting questions. Most of the time the ten other psi-mutants exclaimed over Pizi, having her speak to them as a group and individually on private channels. Pizi always included Levona on those, though she didn't think the others realized that fact. The psi-mutant resistance leaders encouraged Pizi to prattle on about anything and everything, particularly her life with Levona in the mountains.

The physician-Healer, the soft-spoken wife of Umar Clague — he in his late thirties and her only a few years older than Levona — checked Pizi out from top to toe. The Healer paid special attention to Pizi's eyes, and murmured that excellent eye healing herbs lay stocked in the medical storage room.

Yes, Pizi fascinated everyone. Levona got the impression

that if they could ditch her and keep Pizi, everyone would be happier.

An attractive man nearing middle-age and at the height of his power began her ... questioning — the pilot, Netra Sunaya Hoku. But the others pressed for the man of stiff military bearing, the trouble-shooter, to interrogate her. And their psi-gifts buzzed around her, tingling her skin as they gauged her truthfulness, probed into her emotions.

Levona answered every question in crisp detail as they requested, all too aware of her lower-to-middle-class upbringing, the fact that she'd taken off on her own to the mountains instead of working with the psi-mutant community, and that she sat with raggedy hair in shabby clothes with the fragrance of sweat and the underscent of muddy ditch water rising from them.

They discussed the breach that only skinny young people could wriggle through and which had been fixed that day. Levona closed her eyes enough to visualize any other tiny stress cracks in the vehicle and broadcast that information to everyone so they could work on those, too. She hoped that would demonstrate her cooperation ...

Finally Pizi protested that *she* needed food and her wonderful *heart friend*, Levona, must also. At that point, the black woman who'd handled the provisions delivery earlier — also showing a military bearing — left. She returned with a nice steaming heap of beef and greens on a plate for Pizi, and a small hot hand pastry of standard meat-like and cheese-like substance for Levona. No one else ate.

Probably because breaking bread still held connotations of hospitality and courtesy.

"I recognize you," the black woman said. "You worked all day unloading provisions." She paused, swept a glance over the other nine. "And she stood with me during the attack." A wintry smile. "I didn't need her help, but I believe she'd have entered the fray on my side, if necessary." She held out a hand. "Megan Dufort."

Levona took her hand and shook it. "Levona Martinez."

"I know." Megan faded back to lean against the table. "Levona worked hard today." Megan cast a glance at Pizi. "Unlike the cat whom I observed coming and going and playing around the landing site. I'm inclined to think well of Levona and support her in her bid to take an empty space if someone doesn't show."

"We have a full waiting list! She would take the place of someone who has already proven their worth to us! It is unfair for this person to take someone else's deeply desired position," the sharp-toned woman pointed out. A pale blond, she stood, tall and thin, with a small hunch of her shoulders. She didn't introduce herself, but others had called her Ava Quintana.

With a sinking feeling in her gut, Levona admitted the justice of the woman's statement. All the others radiated acceptance of those words, backed by emotions of ... honor.

While marching to the conference room surrounded by other gifted psi-mutants, Levona's brain had scrambled to find a way she could stay on the ship. Sucking in her breath now, she scanned the faces before her — Donna Clague, Megan Dufort and Netra Hoku sympathetic, Ava Quintana and a couple of others antagonistic, but most showed an impassive expression like Umar Clague.

All these people judged her.

She couldn't lose this opportunity. She *couldn't*. She met each chill gaze. "You need a volunteer for the cryonic process."

Pizi gasped, but Levona continued. "I will do that. I will volunteer to be frozen and put in stasis and later be revived. For a place in the crew, and for a tube for myself and Pizi, should one become available."

"All the tubes are bespoke," Ava Quintana said in a hard voice.

"But not all of those who paid for the tubes have arrived, right? If you have a vacancy, I want it."

"The cost is much higher than anything *you* could provide," replied Ava. She kept staring just past Levona's ear, so she must see something normal people didn't.

"Is that what my aura tells you?" Levona asked. "That I have little money? That is true."

BUT WE HAS SKILLS! Especially My Levona! Pizi yelled.

Most people winced at the sound blasting into their brains. "We can hear you, cat," Hoku said.

"She *does* have the cat," Donna murmured. "And the cat is extraordinary, a true psychic mutant. A cat with excellent psi that could show up in her kittens, if she bred. We need all the psi we can get."

"And Levona Martinez also carries excellent psychic talent in her genes, should she decide to breed on this voyage, rather the same situation as myself," Megan Dufort said.

Accent thicker, Umar Clague said, "We will not discriminate on the basis of psychic power. We will *not* refuse a person on our waiting list with ... marginal talent ... because we would prefer a stronger psychic like Levona Martinez. I refuse to accept this notion." He made a cutting gesture. "That discussion is closed."

I WILL be Mother of Cats. Of Heart Friend Cats and companions! Pizi put in.

Hoku rubbed his face. "Is there a way we can find a position—"

Umar Clague cut him off. "The situation before us is that we need to test the cryonics tube process — the putting a person into such a "sleep" and reviving them, *successfully.* Earlier this evening, none of us wished to volunteer, and we'd reached an impasse. Now we have a volunteer."

"She'll do it for a price," Ava spit out.

"This whole venture is being done for each of our benefits. We're all reaping a huge reward. We get to escape this world to a new one. That's a benefit few on this planet continue to have," Megan stated. "And we are paying, too. I put in every last centime I had to reserve a cryonics tube, I traversed a country to reach the gathering place and got on *Lugh's Spear* and flew here with the rest of you. I am offering my skills as a provisioner and a guard. I am offering my body and my future to find an acceptable lover and have psychically talented children. Every one of us has the same story."

Time to speak up again. "I *do* volunteer as a ... as a specimen for your experiment." Not quite the right word, but Levona pushed on. "As I understand, neither of the other ships have done a test of the cryonics procedure, either. I volunteer, you can use me as a sample. You can study me and report the results of the process to everyone else on all the ships who intend to travel this way. I will place my life in your hands." Another sweep of her glance to each. "In the hands of people who dislike me, but whom I trust to be honorable."

Honor. The word worked on each and every one of them. A word that bound them together in a community. All of them had gifts that others had feared or scorned or envied, that the gov had condemned.

When placed in the psi ghettos, they'd banded together, with so much more in common with each other than with people with more normal talents and gifts. They'd combined, and the glue that held them together was trust, and that consisted of honor, honesty. Courage.

Levona could live with dislike, as long as she respected the people who disliked her.

Donna Clague stepped forward. "Let's get this done, the sooner the better. *I* agree to your terms. For undergoing this process, we will make a place for you and Pizi on board this ship. If a person who has reserved a cryonics tube fails to arrive before the time it takes us to launch, you will be assigned the tube." Now the younger woman stared at her fellows. "Any further discussion?"

Her husband added dryly, "Anyone else here want to volunteer?"

Silence.

"I'll take to you the cryonics bay for the procedure," Donna said. The door opened at the wave of her hand and she left. Levona followed, her mouth dry and her stomach clenching at the thought of all this. Everything had happened so quickly. She wasn't ready! Though she couldn't change her mind. This is how she and Pizi would escape Earth. "Should I have fasted?" she asked.

With a smile over her shoulder, Donna said, "We'll clean you out."

Oh, joy.

Pizi leapt into Levona's arms and she cherished the warmth and breathing and *aliveness* of her friend.

Every single other person trailed after them.

Donna continued, "You will also enter a cleansing and disinfecting station, then we will prepare you for the cryonics tube. You'll lie down, we'll inject you with the drugs necessary for the process, the upper glass will close over you and additional gas will fill the capsule and preserve you." The woman sent her a reassuring smile. "Any questions?"

"I got the layman's explanation," Levona stated.

Nodding, Donna said, "Yes. Everyone who reserved a cryonics tube received an 800-page report of each detail of the procedure, the freezing, the stasis state, and the thawing or awakening."

"We got it, and decided whether to read it or not," Megan Dufort said. "I glanced through it, read a bit here and there."

Umar put in, "We know the procedure worked previously,

in other situations, as well as on other starships. We received communications from colonists on other planets."

"Once or twice," Hoku said. "Whether we continue to receive such communications no one here knows. The gov hasn't relayed that information to us. Not even those of us who recently worked for the WorldStates gov."

"Once upon a time, we went into space. Once upon a time, we colonized other planets." Megan sighed.

And suddenly the walk up and down the corridors, the travel by omnivator to another level, ended. They faced wide doors that opened in front of them, but showed only a vestibule and another set of doors.

"Sterilization chamber," Donna explained as she stepped in. Levona did, too, and though a couple of people hesitated, they all crowded together and the doors closed behind them. Pizi sneezed at the tech and psi-tech process that left Levona's cheap clothes in tatters and her feeling scrubbed clean to her last skin-cell.

Pizi hopped from Levona's arms to an examination table.

I WILL DO THIS TOO! The cat sat straight, tiny head lifted in pride.

Donna's expression softened. "Not this time." She glanced at Levona.

With fear zooming through her, Levona realized she could truly die. That might help the colonists regulate the cryonics procedure, but she'd be dead. Clearing her throat, she said, "Let me do this first, Pizi. They have, um, specifications for humans, but will have to work up amounts of the drugs and stuff for a cat companion."

A heart friend.

"Yes," Levona and Donna said in unison.

But We will go to sleep together in Our tube for the trip, Pizi insisted.

"I can do that," Donna said.

Levona stared at her, more, probed the woman for confidence and veracity. The physician believed she spoke the truth. "Have you had any experience of initiating and finishing the cryonics procedure?" Levona asked as she should have before.

"I've watched the procedure often. I know the chemicals and the timeline," Donna stated.

Levona wouldn't ask if she'd observed in person or participated. Too late now.

Ignoring everyone else's gazes on her bruised and scratched, too-thin body, she disrobed and followed each step of the process. Finally, she sat on the edge of the narrow pad comprising the bottom of the tube. "How long will I be ... out?"

"As long as we can test you for, but probably for no less than three days and ..." Donna glanced over to the others observing the process ...

"Not longer than a week," the smooth-talking pilot stated. *He* trusted Levona with information, at least.

She knew that the Geek Class would need at least forty-eight hours of full preparation before the ship launched. At least *Lugh's Spear* would. She hadn't figured out, yet, how their time tables interwove with the schedules of *Nuada's Sword* that would leave from NJNY and *Arianrhod's Wheel* launching from EurAstates.

She couldn't hug Pizi now, could only stare at her and emanate the huge emotion, and send telepathically, *I love You, Pizi.*

I love You, too, Levona, my heart friend, Pizi said from the firm grasp of Netra Sunaya Hoku.

She met his dark brown eyes, then switched her gaze to Donna. "You will take care of Pizi for me? You all must realize by now she's a very special cat, a true animal companion."

Everyone loved Pizi, and if they didn't need Levona to

come out of this experiment, she figured they'd keep the cat and kick Levona off the ship.

"We promise on our honor," several people said, more than half ... six. And since they replied in unison, she understood it to be a common phrase in the community that she would have to learn, and live by.

Dipping her head, and snuffling back her tears, she said, "Thank you."

"Look at me," Donna lilted.

Levona did.

TRANCE!

And Levona fell ... drifted. She saw more than felt the injections. Noticed the hot heat of the hands of a couple of the men who lowered her steadily to the sponge beneath her, straightened her limbs and head. The domed lid of the tube snapped over her and her heart leapt and blood surged in fear — but no. Her mind *thought* that should be happening, but her blood continued to slow along with the beating of her heart as the air chilled around her.

Fog clouded her eyes, or the inside of the pod, she didn't know. She thought she wanted to say something but her thoughts s-l-o-w-e-d and her lips froze like all the rest of her.

Down. Down. Down into muddy darkness, breaking chill thin-iced water in a ditch and settling on the bottom. Gray stones closed around her, curving over her like an old-time crypt tomb. She felt ... more enervated than they'd said, as if she sank into death and not a deep coma-sleep with a tinge of awareness.

She'd *listened* to the explanations, but ... this ... was ... not ... right. She *couldn't* let herself slip away into sleep because she was sure she would not wake again. She'd die, and that might not help anyone.

She wanted to be of use, she *wanted* to contribute, not to be a leech, or even taken along out of sufferance.

Yes, stone blocks bricked around her, pressed on her chest, sat on her head and if she allowed it, would infiltrate her brain and solidify it. Solidify *everything*. Not the preferred process. *Not.*

THINK! she screamed into her own mind. Tried to twitch her fingers, couldn't. That was correct, what was supposed to happen. Breathing nearly stopped. Correct. One last breath. *No! THINK.* What was going wrong? *THINK!*

Chemical equations danced before her vision, the various stuff slipped in to her blood. *CHECK BLOOD! FEEL BLOOD! Wrong. Wrong, wrong, wrong. Too much of ... too much of something.*

Fight. But stone encased her now, not just the slabs but layered over her body like inflexible armor.

THINK! Harder and harder to think. So *fight!* Fight for another breath because to stop would be to die. Emotional hurt to lose Pizi. Pizi would hurt, too. That gave her a spurt of energy.

Sniff the gas. Gas correct.

Only a little too much bad stuff in her veins. Or arteries. Or both. Blood.

If she could have spilt her blood, drained it, she would have.

Dark redness, blood.

Spiraling downward, away, away, away from the here and now.

NO! FIGHT!

Fight. In her head she sat up. The capsule had disappeared ... in the far distance she saw it waiting for her down a stone passage looking like some she — they'd, she and Pizi — had gone through on the way to the city. The way to the ship, to *Lugh's Spear.* The name of the ship infused hope that energized.

She *would* find her way back in her mind from this place

in the stone passages of the city to the capsule far away, one that represented safety and life. Arise from the cryonics tube of *Lugh's Spear*.

Already in her imagination, she did not lie flat, but sat straight, stiff in her stone, but with grit enough to fight. *Yes!* Hearing her own creaks, she moved one knee. Difficult. Slow. Heavy.

Taking too long. She could roll ... *NO! THINK!*

If she rolled off what seemed like a stone dais, she'd hit the stone floor and she would not get up again. The armor encasing her would trap her. For the moment it, and her body, still responded to the control of her mind. As long as she didn't sleep.

Stand up, get moving, keep moving. Like all of her life.

She'd find Pizi again, and ... and maybe friends, maybe a lover on the voyage for the rest of her life. She visualized a boat on the sea. It dissipated with the next thought. She imagined the starship moving through the vastness of galaxies. It popped the next second.

Just. Move.

Stone scraping stone she slid, creaked, toppled from the dais, caught herself. Tried to bite her lip instinctively. Couldn't. Crystallized lips, too. Her face was stone. Her eyes couldn't move, could see through a narrow band, maybe a rock helmet, too.

Didn't matter. Fight. Keep moving. *March!*

And she did, for an eternity, until she didn't know who she was or why she moved, only that she could see a sunburst far in front of her and she had to reach it because it would be warm, and purr, and the fur would soak up her tears when she buried her face in it.

Step, step, step.

Two arches stood in front of her. Both dark. She paused and would have slumped and fallen but the stone armor kept her upright. Right. The right arch, the correct arch, on the other side of the tunnel. She liked going to the left, less chance of being trapped. Less confinement, to the left.

Not this time.

Awake!

She shuddered in her stone skin. Not her voice, some *other* voice.

Heart friend!

Yes.

Step, stumble, *run!*

Levona opened her eyes and looked through clear glass. She'd awakened from the cold, cold, cold stone. Now felt many stares locked on her again. Time had passed, her body told her that, but she didn't know how much. Before she'd slid into the frozen stasis *they'd* said the test would last days or a week. But *they'd* miscalculated the amount of the damn chemicals injected into her body. *That* she knew.

The moment the flexible tube shield slid into the side of the platform, a small thump hit her stomach and a warmth traipsed up her body and nuzzled her under her chin. *You is BACK. You came back. I knews You would! You is strong and My heart friend! I will lie here on You and help!*

Yes, soft fur, the smell of Pizi and mountain dust and brown-yellow weeds and ... stars to come.

Tears spurted from Levona's eyes.

"Here, then. Here." A soft, soothing voice that matched the soft cloth that patted her face.

Her mouth ... moved. She could move her mouth. "Almost died."

A slight clearing of more than one throat. "Yes. We noted something went wrong almost immediately, but believed stopping the process would kill you." A different woman's voice. The first had belonged to the ... to Donna ... Clague.

This one, *not* snippy, came from Ava Quintana.

One of the men said, "We think the blend of the chemical mixture is off. Not sure why."

"Let's do a complete chem run, blood analysis, and other procedures," Donna ordered, and whipped a spider-armed medical robot over the bed. It looked more like a torture device than an aid for human health. Levona managed to lift her hand and pet ... no, just touch ... Pizi, who breathed warm and vibrantly alive, atop her.

"Yes," Levona croaked. "I felt ... something wrong ... one of the chemicals too much, I think, in my blood."

Umar Clague came into view behind his lady. "We'll debrief you and listen to your experience later." A wintry smile, accompanied by a shake of his head. "After you also survive the awakening process and all the medical tests in the world."

She'd have sighed, but even the small weight of Pizi compressed her chest.

"How long?" That seemed to be the last words she could speak.

"As long as we possibly could keep you for the test and still have a good idea of the results of the process, and report to the colonists on the other ships and keep to our timeline. This is dawn of the eighth day. We noted that you yet lived, and wanted to carry on with the experiment."

Because Levona was expendable.

"Because we are all depending on the cryonics process to live." Ava's voice held a note of steel.

A pause, another dip of the head from Umar Clague. "We'll be initiating the forty-eight-hour launch sequence at dawn tomorrow morning."

Tongue thick, Levona said, "You didn't give yourself much leeway to discover what went wrong with me."

"No. But we knew something went wrong and continued the procedure and analyzed it as it went along. And you *fought* to stay alive. We observed that, too. And you lived. *You* gave us life, too. Most of us, under the same circumstances, would have fought. So, all in all, a good result," Umar Clague finished.

The med-bot squeaked as it tried to work around Pizi. She hissed back.

"I'm sorry, Pizi, but we need to help Levona, help us *all*. I will be picking You up now," Hoku said. Levona hadn't seen him, but then her eyelids had fluttered shut. So exhausted.

"I fought for a week," she whispered. Didn't know if anyone heard her, then slid down a stone-lined hole to the darkness of sleep.

The rest of the day they pummeled her with tests, and she faded in and out of consciousness. Miserable except for the presence of Pizi. Later that afternoon she sat in the main conference room with the ten leaders, clothed in some soft undies, trousers and shirt, a donation from some unknown person that Megan had delivered to the medical bay. The clothes didn't quite fit. But Levona's pack sat propped against her chair legs, and Pizi purred on her lap.

"I'll tell *everything*. I think one of the chemical amounts was too much, at least for me." She blinked. "I could distinguish the problem. It showed up as one of the chemicals in my blood, not in the gas."

"That's correct," Donna said. She bit her lip. "I'm sorry that the process didn't go as smoothly as expected." She stood, hands on table, and scanned everyone. "But I am convinced we've found the problem and remedied it." With a smile at Levona, she said, "We relayed the fact we had a problem within the first hour to the leadership crew of the other ships and that prodded them to institute their own tests. Off-site for the NJNY crowd, they are still stringing along the local gov that the ship won't lift for another couple of weeks. And *Arianrhod's Wheel* did its own tests in its cryonics bay. All of their multiple samples proceeded perfectly."

"Multiple," Levona said.

"A total of six. Two procedures by NJNY and four by the EurAstates Resistance."

"Good. That's good," Levona said.

"We are all very pleased, but, naturally, you went into the capsule first and were the last to be awakened, so we have had the most complete process," Donna ended and sat.

Drawing in a breath, Levona said, "I knew one of the chemicals was too high, but I couldn't say so. I examined — as much as my ability allowed — the gas and other factors and believed only that one chemical in the mixture wasn't right." She grimaced. "Then I fought. I lost myself in the fight until you called me back."

WE called You back, Pizi licked Levona's hand.

Yes, she replied privately to her friend.

"I wasn't aware that a week had passed." Another big breath, she set her chin, then stated calmly, "I've fulfilled my part of the bargain."

Yes! Pizi leapt onto the table before Levona, defending her. *We've been Good! I could not smell or touch or lick My friend all that looong time. I did like You peoples asked. I will be Mother of Cats, and My Levona has skills and fight like You need.*

The stares, grimaces, and the expressions in the eyes and on the faces, showed reluctant acceptance.

Umar Clague inclined his head. "We are honorable folk. We do not make deals and renege on them like the government. You have earned your right to stay on the ship along with Pizi, and have been assigned a room with the crew."

Ava stood. "We have researched the files we have on you and your parents and your contributions to the psi-community — or lack of that." She bent a stern look on Levona who refuse to flinch. "We've spoken to other members of the community who know you such as Bartek Coval and Karida Bonfils, who give you good references. We are pleased with your performance so far."

"I volunteered for a procedure no one else would," Levona put in.

Ava's mouth soured. She shrugged. "We personnel managers have agreed that your crew assignment should be working in the ag section of *Lugh's Spear.*"

Levona's mouth fell open. That meant — farming? She could do that!

"As you may or may not know, the greenspace ag section comprises a full third of this ship."

Delight filled her. Not truly *outside* but, but, a greenspace!

Ava lifted her hand. "You will be assigned to the ag area at the most menial level. Currently that means planting seedlings under supervision."

Swallowing, Levona nodded. "I can do that." Feeling baby shoots of green in her hands. Wonderful.

Umar Clague rose and everyone else followed. "Be assured that now you have become a part of our community, you must follow our rules."

"Your ship, your rules," Levona managed.

"This is true. However, we are cognizant of our agreement with you and if someone who has reserved one of the twenty-two cryonics tubes does not arrive by the minimum two and a half hours before we launch, when we close the boarding doors, you and Pizi will be assigned that tube. As it stands, some of the former crew members have canceled their requests to join us on this voyage and we are working through our waiting list, but are not at the bottom where you were placed. We are making a position for you. Be thankful."

"I am." Levona snagged her bag and stood, too.

I am! Pizi hopped up and down, flicking her tail.

Ava said, "I will lead you to your room so you may note

where it is. The ag greenspace needs hands as soon as possible. Report to your supervisor for your duties and your schedule tomorrow morning at workbell."

"Thank you."

She reached her tiny room, put on a nightshirt and slid under the covers. Physically and emotionally weary, she wondered if she would fear falling asleep. If the drop into unconsciousness would remind her of her struggle in the tube and the testing that day. If nightmares would torture her. But she closed her eyes . . . and slid into sleep with her next warm breath.

A knock at her door awakened her, and the in-built clock on the closet wall at the end of her bed informed her that four hours had passed. Though the flat light and metal-tinged air provided no clues, it would be night outside. With a pang, she wondered if she'd ever see the moon and stars again. "Come in," she croaked, shifting on the bed too narrow for both her and Pizi, who lay on her stomach napping.

Nothing happened.

Are you awake in there? came a whisper to her mind.

Levona blinked. She knew that voice, though she hadn't heard it for a long time – since the first day she'd been in the barrio.

Karida? Levona sent back, then, *Come on in!*

The mental exchange woke Pizi and she extended her spine in a quick stretch before hopping down to the floor, sitting within petting reach and purring.

Carrying a box, Karida entered as soon as the door retracted into the wall. She stopped at one step and looked around, appalled. Levona gritted her teeth. She hated the narrow room, but would tolerate it – for the whole damn trip, if necessary.

"Hi, Levona." A false smile until she looked down into the box she carried that rustled like it held a lot of scrunched and old paper shreds. The woman offered Levona a lopsided smile, a sincere one not given to her before. "Since you're the one who introduced me to the concept of near-telepathic animals —"

Almost as smart as ME! Pizi put in, then licked a patch of fur near her shoulder.

"Almost, but none of the kittens can actually use words like you do to speak," Karida said with a grave nod at Pizi.

"No," Levona agreed. "Pizi is a prodigy."

"Anyway, I — and many of my friends — have been searching the city, all parts of the city, for such animals." Another smile. "We even found a puppy or two."

Pizi jumped to her feet, her tongue stuck out. *No!*

"Yes. I think we've rescued them all, and every psi mutant in the city, living in the ghetto or not, will be keeping watch for them. Everyone in the barrio who wanted a pet — an animal companion, has one."

"Bartek Coval?"

"He received a young tom, a fierce mouser."

"Good."

Karida nodded, then her voice became drier. "And some of our wealthiest people" — she paused to stare pointedly at Levona — "like the *real* Minerva Starshine, received an unrelated male and female pair to breed." Karida marched over and upended the box, and six small and squeaking kittens tumbled over Levona. "These semi-intelligent animals are now available for adoption by the starship folk."

Sudden tears overflowed Levona's eyes, no way could she control them. She sniffed hard, pulled a rag near her pillow to wipe her eyes and nose, and caught one black kitten before it fell off the bed.

"Thank you."

Karida inclined her head. "Since you first introduced us all to such animals, we of the psi mutant barrio community decided you should be the one to find these kittens new homes."

"Wonderful." Levona's voice sounded even gruffer from throaty tears.

Setting the box down by the bed, under Pizi's nose — and an odor of *cat* rose from it — Karida crossed back to the threshold of the open door. She stared at Levona, swept the room with her gaze and the corridor that began to fill with people.

Mentally, she sent, *So the ship leaves at dawn, the day after tomorrow.*

Yes, Levona confirmed telepathically.

Aloud, Karida said, "We'll all be providing cover for you, for the ship, milling around. Looking like we're working on it." She shrugged. "That will hopefully keep the gov from thinking you'll be taking off, so you'll all get away clean."

"Appreciate it."

"We psi mutants stick together." Karida gave Levona a half-salute wave. "Good luck to you, Levona Martinez. May you gain what you wish. Blessed be and go with the Lady and Lord."

Levona managed to gather the kittens so she could scoot back and sit straighter. "Good luck to you, too, Karida Bonfils. May you gain what you wish."

"I have." One corner of Karida's mouth turned up. "While I was on this animal hunt I met Apollo Starshine and we ... clicked. He's moving into the barrio to be my mate."

A sharp stab of envy speared Levona, but she summoned a smile. "Good, that's good to hear. You'll have children."

Karida patted her abdomen and grinned. "Oh, yes, we will."

"Great!" Levona meant it. "Go with the Lady and Lord. Blessed be."

With a last finger wave, Karida left.

Levona found a line had formed outside her door. More than six. As she continued to try and gather the active kittens in her arms, she knew she didn't want to give *any* of them away.

Pizi hopped onto the bed, stared at the people in the hallway and yelled mentally, *These Kittens only go to peoples who are NOT travelling in tubes!*

Many grumbled and left, but others tried to crowd through the door that wouldn't even accommodate two.

Pizi hissed, then shouted, *I WILL CHOOSE THOSE WHO SHOULD HAVE THESE CATS. LET ME THROUGH SO I CAN SNIFF YOU.*

The crowd backed up. Levona smiled.

In under twenty minutes the rambunctious kittens had been parceled out and Pizi stood on Levona's lap, staring up at her. *We go back to sleep now.*

And Levona allowed herself to be ordered by her animal companion, and shut her eyes.

An hour into her job the next morning, Levona felt the artificial sun's light on her shoulders and sighed. *She'd made it! She and Pizi were escaping Earth!*

All she'd suffered was worth it.

Most of the rest of the crew had trickled in while she'd been under. And Pizi walked the corridors, greeting newcomers, acting as an emotional support cat, being loved and petted. Neither Levona nor Pizi could determine how many people *didn't* show up as generational staff. Levona did keep an eye on the cryonics chamber.

Working in the ag sector, farming, soothed her beyond all understanding. She loved her home mountains, but working with the burgeoning green plants and trees and crops fulfilled her. Maybe she should have gone East after escaping Central-Conglom two years ago, spent time traveling through green forests until she reached her psi-mutant people in NJNY, the deadliest psi-ghetto in the world ... But she'd have missed finding Pizi ...

In any event, Levona understood she *could* live in this ship her whole life, even in her tiny, single room, since she'd be working in the green. Setting up the ag for the generations to come kept the anxious buzz along her nerves of *waiting* for launch under control.

Then the final hours passed and she and Pizi sat in their assigned spot, both strapped in with slings, three hours before the ship lifted off. Following the rules when a few others still roamed the deck, not wanting to be immobilized yet.

She and Pizi murmured together, Levona reassuring her cat that she totally accepted not being assigned a tube and they'd live and make friends and take lovers during their lives on the ship.

The lights blinked and the atmosphere changed and Levona sensed the starship's doors closing. She leaned back and visualized the plot she'd planted in the ag section, the feel of the dirt on her hands, the tender leaves of the seedlings, the ...

"Come along, Levona. Wake up, Pizi. We need to get you into one of the final tubes," Donna Clague said.

Relief, hope, shuddered through Levona and she couldn't stop tears from welling and sliding down her cheeks. She snapped open the web restraints and hurried after Donna who moved fast.

"Who's in the final tube?" Levona asked.

Donna threw a smile over her shoulder. "Me. I wanted to be able to take you to the bay if an opening happened. We're friends."

"Yes, we are. Thank you."

WE'RE GOING INTO THE TUBE! HOORAY! Pizi squealed.

To Levona's surprise, not many in the two rows of people on either side of the take-off corridor seemed to hear her. Of those who looked startled, one man raised his hand and called, "Good luck!" then muttered, "You couldn't pay me to get in one of those tubes."

And Levona's mouth dried at the recollection of the struggle for her life. What if something went wrong again? She banished the thought, and *would NOT* think of anything happening to Pizi. She'd gotten a brief report that other animals had survived the testing of the cryonics process. Not in *Lugh's Spear* but ...

Then she and Pizi were in the cryonics bay, being prepped. Neither of them had eaten anything for twenty-four hours ... just in case. Techs took Pizi away to prepare her, as others helped Levona disrobe ... as Donna Clague undressed, across the room near her husband, Umar, who already slept in a foggy capsule.

Donna sat and let needles pierce her skin and words came from Levona's mouth. "Thank you for being my friend, Donna. See you on the other side."

The woman chuckled. "You may not know it, but you're easy to be friends with, Levona. Later!" She lay down in the tube, looked over toward her husband, and Levona saw the love. A slight movement came from Umar as if he *felt* the love. Then the glass covered Donna and gas poured into her pod.

"Look at me," ordered the tech, and caught Levona in her gaze. Levona sat on the bottom of her tube and felt the sting of injections, scanned the room a last time and saw people she didn't know, but also Ava Quintana and Megan Dufort. They'd been friendly with her, too, had eaten with her at meals, like Pilot Hoku and Umar Clague and others.

Levona *had* made friends.

Then she let the techs and their hot hands arrange her,

put Pizi on her chest. The cat's eyes appeared half open. *I ... love ... You ... Le ... vona.*

I love you, Pizi.

We ... are ... Peo ... ple ... with ... Peoples who likes Us. Friends.

Yes. Finally Levona stopped running away and staying apart. She'd joined a community — and been accepted by them — and with them would forge a new world together.

HOMING STONE

RAND ASH MEETS HOM HOLLY

From the publication of my first book, ***HeartMate***, readers have been asking for the meeting between Rand Ash and Holm Holly when they were seventeen. That's when Ash worked as a blacksmith in the Downwind slums and Holly went through his death-duel Passages to free his psi magic-Flair. Here it is.

HOMING STONE

380 Years After Earth Starship Colonization of Celta, Druida City, Spring

RAND ASH SAT IN THE CORNER OF THE DOWNWIND BAR, waiting for trouble to walk through the door. Trouble for this joint, and maybe the slum itself, but an opportunity for him. He'd heard a rumor that a nobleman had cruised the taverns in this, the poorest part of town, last night. The guy hadn't broken up this bar. Yet.

Sipping bad whiskey from a heavy and not-too-clean glass, Rand kept his gaze moving. When it grazed across someone, man or woman, that person took another couple of steps away from him. A flimsy little table stood before him, one he could make splinters of with a single quick kick. Nobody sat near him and nobody blocked his way to the bar. If he went on the move, nobody'd block his way to the door, neither.

He was young and strong ... and obsessed.

And maybe lucky.

He'd soon find out if his prophetic rune reading that morning was right, and fortune favored him.

Vengeance simmered inside him, and he could use one nobleman, the nobleman Ash figured would come into this saloon, to get it. Ash *would* prevail against his noble enemies.

He smiled and his nearest neighbor scraped a chair closer to the big round table where the guy sat gabbling with friends.

Wait. Wait. Wait. Rand Ash had learned to be patient.

And trouble *did* walk into the bar.

More like swaggered. A huge black and white tomcat with tattered ears, Zanth.

"Hey," snapped the barkeep at the cat.

But Zanth, Ash's Familiar Companion, jumped and landed on the table before Ash with a solid thump. Rocking the little table, the cat squatted to keep his balance. No one laughed.

In fact, the room fell quiet. Except for Zanth's slurping of Ash's whiskey. His tail waved in time to his guzzle.

Ash's Fam projected mentally on their private channel, *You walked too fast.* A near grumble, as always.

Ash replied telepathically, *You dawdled.*

Zanth lifted his muzzle, whiskey dripping from his whiskers. *Stopped to kill sewer rat. Yum!*

There might still be traces of that rat, and rat blood, on Zanth's whiskers. Ash slipped his whiskey away from the cat. Since Zanth wanted the alcohol, Ash put it on the floor for his Fam. Zanth took up too much space on the table.

With an audible growl that had others glancing at them nervously, Zanth followed the drink under the table, tilting the furniture again.

Stay outta my fliggerin' way if I move, Ash sent.

Of course Zanth ignored him.

Patience. Ash did *not* glance at his cheap wrist timer. The runes had been interesting that morning--be sociable, no brooding on problems too great to master alone, a favorable change was blowing into his life.

Since he'd made the divination stones himself, he tended to follow their advice. Combined with the afternoon gossip of a nobleman in the slums of Downwind, prickles of destiny had slid down Ash's nerves. Finally it would be time to move against his enemies, exact vengeance, claim his lost title and power.

So he'd gone to the bar he'd calculated to be next on the nobleman's path.

Before Ash called for another drink -- an ale this time to save precious coin -- the real entertainment of the evening strode in and ordered the best liquor in the place, paid with a new and gleaming weighty silver coin.

People moved away from this guy, too. More due to his attitude than his height. With breathtaking arrogance, he turned to scan the room, study each person there while the bartender got his drink.

Probably seventeen, like himself. But unlike Ash, the man hadn't filled out yet. Ash's blacksmithing had already thickened his muscles. What muscles this guy had were strung over a lean build.

Ash stared, like every other person in the tavern, at the man with gray eyes and white-silver-blond hair. He wore materials so expensive that the amount he'd paid for his threads would clothe everyone in the place for a decade.

Most people saw a noble or two now and then, and most knew of noble fashion, and his was the latest.

Ash reflected on the books he'd read about noble Families. The volume he'd escaped with when he'd run away from the fiery inferno his home had become, destroyed by greedy Family enemies. The book remained his most prized possession since he'd been six.

And he thought of the lessons he'd paid to the old noblewoman living Downwind. That information about the great nobles, the FirstFamilies he'd learned. He frowned as early gossamer memories wisped through his mind as he examined the guy's aquiline features, noble features.

Yeah, Ash nodded, he could guess the identity of this guy. Ash sensed the fluctuations of great Flair, psychic magic power. That meant the nobleman suffered through the dreamquest of Passage. Long days when internal psi abilities would rise and a gifted person had to master them to control newly augmented talents ... power.

He looked flushed and nervy.

Most people with good psychic power endured three Passages, one in childhood, one about now at seventeen, and a third one some years later.

Most people suffered through the days of fevers and sweats and the emotional turmoil to free and conquer their Flair in the safety and comfort of their home, among their family.

Most people weren't a member of the fighting Family of Holly.

The Hollys didn't stay home when Passage hit them. Legend had it they went out prowling, looking for challenges. Fought death duels.

And Ash was here to help this nobleman in those fights and death duels, get the guy in his debt.

Yeah, Ash could guess the man's name and pedigree.

Holm Holly, heir to GreatLord T'Holly himself. Holm Holly-Heir, he'd be called. If Ash cared to address him by name. Ash's lip curled and he put his hands quietly on the table. No doubt he'd see what stuff the Holly was made of.

Zanth grumbled from under the table, privately to Ash. *Man stinks like hunting Cat. Can smell on his clothes from here.* Zanth sniffed. *Stupid female hunting cat who rubbed against his boots.* Another sniff. *TAME Cat.*

Don't matter. Shut up, Ash sent to his Fam.

Zanth did worse, he left the shadows of the table and sauntered a couple of steps, then leapt onto the bar, stuck his nose in the prime whiskey before the Holly could curve his hand around the glass and lift it to drink.

That was all it took.

Holly flinched, yanked the short tumbler from the Fam, spilling liquor. Zanth opened his mouth to yowl, then the rest of the drink was flung at his head.

The cat's piercing shriek hurt Rand's ears.

Holly picked up the cat by the scruff of his neck, whirled, and threw him at the first escaping customer. Turned back and grabbed the barman. "Wha' the *fligger* is *that*?"

Ash stood.

ALL FOUR PAWS FLEXED, ZANTH BOUNCED OFF THE shoulders of the man he'd hit. Springing back toward the Holly, all claws primed, Zanth hissed so loud the sound rose above other cries of erupting fights. Locals settling slights and scores.

"Stop!" Ash ordered and everyone froze, just the way he liked. These Downwind folk knew his voice, wouldn't disobey. At the same time he reached out and snagged his big cat out of the air, a one-Word spell blunting Zanth's claws for a minute. Ash let the cat wrap around his arm, and strode up to the bar and the Holly standing in-balance and easily, ready to move in an instant, offense or defense.

"This thing is my Fam," Ash said, displaying a toothy Zanth. "I'm Ash, Rand Ash." He narrowed his eyes, wondering if the man would recognize his name.

"Nice catch," the Holly said. Eying Zanth, the man grunted. "Fam, huh?"

Stupid. Stup. STUP, Zanth snapped mentally.

"Yes, I have enough Flair to hear you, master FamCat." Holly's nostrils widened in disdain, maybe because he smelled a whiff of sewer rat. "You ruined my drink, and I wanted it before I started my fun."

Zanth growled.

The Holly's eyebrows twitched and Ash could *feel* the Flair-psi-magic rising in the man, the need to fight.

"You want payback, talk to Zanth." Ash jerked his chin toward the door. "Take this outside." Testing the guy's control, Ash turned his back.

He'd only moved a step before a crash of glass came, the sound of blows, a smothered oath, then a rich laugh.

Whirling, he saw three men surrounding the fighter, and another down and skidding across the floor to land under a table. *Fligger.*

"Gotta have pockets fulla gilt," said a brute even bigger than Ash. The *stup* smiled with broken teeth, but couldn't match Holly's gleeful grin.

The night had gone to hell. No doubt in Ash's mind that the Holly would continue to wipe the floor with every man who challenged him, which screwed with Ash's plan.

Off me! he raised his arm.

FIGHT! Zanth yowled and leapt for the skinniest guy in front of the Holly.

Ash took a step and grabbed the third guy by the collar and flung him away, heard the crash of a breaking table.

His ears picked up the hiss of a blade being unsheathed. Knife, thirty centimeters, inferior steel. As a blacksmith, Ash knew.

"Behind you!" Holly yelled.

Ash dropped to the floor, rolled out of the way of the man with the knife.

The barkeep -- the owner of this joint -- clapped his hands and an illegal *BOOM* spell thundered through the place. Everyone crumpled.

Ash's ears rang but he felt no liquid like blood running from them. He opened his mouth to breathe as if that would ease the concussive noise still rattling around in his head.

Glancing around with blurred vision at the rest of the patrons who lay sprawled on the floor -- at least he'd been down before the boom -- he saw some pale and unconscious, some twitching madly, and the Holly's face red with fury as he rocked to his hands and knees, already up. Just. Great.

The Downwind thug bigger than Ash still clutched at the nobleman's ankle. A plus for being so large.

Ash swam his hands and knees in position, pushed up. He'd been through a boomer before, but didn't know whether the Holly had, and the only thought in Ash's head was to get the man indebted to him.

Then the first sounds filtered to his ears. Zanth of course, was shrieking, and the owner yelling at the big man grunting on the floor. With a nasty snarl at him and the Holly, the barkeep shouted, "Take it outdoors or I do it agin', an' nobody lives to tell about it. Got body cleanup guys, I do, no questions asked."

Ash believed him, he swung his head back and forth until his gaze lifted to find and focus on Zanth. The FamCat had been through a boomer before, too. This time he'd attached himself to the scarred wooden-wheel light-fixture in the center of the room. Upside down he hung, all his fur stuck out, every hair, and his mouth opened wider than Ash ever thought it could, the better for the high-decibel screeching.

Get moving! Zanth demanded in a mind-shout as forceful as his scream. *Come under Me so I can drop on you ...*

Ash didn't think so. That cat wouldn't be careful with his claws. So he tried to ignore the beast.

Managing the jump from hands and knees to squat--practiced that thousands of times--Ash slowly straightened his legs to stand tall, stride to the Holly, kick the large thug's hand away from the nobleman's ankle, and grasp the rich man's biceps.

And realized he'd be leaving filthy, sweaty fingerprints on the whitest fabric he'd seen since he was six years old. The most sensual cloth he ever remembered touching. So he might have gripped harder than he meant and the Holly swung body and fist. Rand followed the man's full body movement, kept his balance, blocked the blow.

"I'm on your side." He touched the guy's expensive HouseRing, hiding it from everyone, so no one could see it and want it and track them through the Flair. The nobleman, scanning the rest of the room, didn't seem to notice.

"Let's go." Ash dropped his grasp from the man, gestured for the noble to leave, Ash would guard the nobleman from the rear and the room's inhabitants getting up.

Meeeee! shrieked Zanth.

Land on the big guy, Ash said carelessly.

So Zanth did, smashing the large man back onto the floor. Then the cat hopped back onto the bar counter, and the owner swiped at him, snapped a towel. "Get out. Don't come back never again, *cat*! Be watchin' for ya! Trap ya!" the barman yelled.

Holly seemed to glide away from the wooden bar, with a

last regretful glance at its emptiness of glasses full of liquor, and Ash followed.

They weren't, quite, the first ones outside and into the street. Some of the scrawnier, tougher folk made it before them. Those born and raised Downwind for generations.

And word had spread about the brawl and the cause of it--a rich man ready for the plucking.

Folks jumped at them, and those who missed lunged at others they might want to get even with. The whole narrow street filled with fighting.

The nobleman slid away from the first bunch, made it three strides before more toughs circled him.

ASH MUSCLED HIS WAY THROUGH THE CLUMPS OF BRAWLERS to the largest group skirmishing. He pushed into the center and the nobleman. "Back to back!" he shouted to the Holly, wondering if his faith in the man's fighting skills was correct. He'd soon find out.

And he did when a sinewy back slammed against him. More yells and taunts at his battle companion.

He heard the rasp of a good blade being slid from an equally excellent sheath, a wild laugh from the Holly.

More joyful dares, this time from right behind him. The nobleman slinging filthy insults at his opponents.

Uh-oh. What had Ash gotten himself into?

Yeah, the press of people came toward him. For an instant, in the flash of a lightspell, he thought he saw the three-club symbol of the noble house of Rue.

No. Ash imagined that because he lusted for vengeance. Craved payback against the Rues for killing his Family. His mind lit with images as he recalled the fire, the flames consuming T'Ash Residence. Himself at six years old running away alone ... into the slums Downwind ... followed by a string of three-club images.

FAM MAN! came Zanth's mental screech, along with a cat yowl trailing from inside the tavern to shrill even louder outside.

Here, Ash replied steadily, shoving a man back into his friends. He recognized the guy, some jerk with a grudge because Ash wouldn't mend the man's piece-of-shit sword. He saw the gleam of a blade in the man's hand, a good, long main gauche. Unusual.

But he'd bet his own sword was better than any in the courtyard, including the Holly's.

FAM MAN!

Human screams as Zanth made his way, tooth and claw, to Ash. The cat thudded onto Ash's shoulder, then turned his ass toward the knot of men surging toward them.

With a quick spell Word, Ash coated himself with a deflection spell, and when Zanth sprayed, the piss didn't stick to either of them or the Holly behind them.

Zanth yowled in triumph!

A terrible stink rose.

The clutch of men faded back, choking.

One said, "Gettin' outta here, gotta clean up *now* if'n I don' want piss-smell-clothes for the next damn year."

Others grumbled but followed. The crowd dispersed.

"Cat piss as a weapon," came the muffled snort from the man stepping away from Ash. The cool spring air chilled Ash's sweat and smells arose. Good clean fight sweat from Ash, spicy herbs from the noble young man.

Another memory punched Rand. His mother bespelling his clothes so they'd release herbal freshness instead of little-boy grossness when he sweat or fell into a mud puddle ... or the fascinating pig pen.

He and the Holly found themselves alone on the stingy

sidewalk curbing the equally small lane. No vehicles, expensive gliders, ever came here. The very thought just stopped and fizzled in Ash's head. The original colonists might have made streets for vehicles, but population did *not* burgeon as they'd thought and Downwind streets held foot traffic only.

Me hero! Zanth leapt down from Ash's shoulder, a relief to both of them, and sauntered back toward the bar's entrance.

A roar came and the burly owner standing on the threshold of his place pointed at Zanth. "Lookit your piss everywhere! Nasty cat. Never come back! Told you before, an' I mean it. You neither, Ash." The irate man clumped into his bar and returned in seconds with a large pitcher. He flung the contents at them.

Zanth shrieked and bolted down the street. *A drop! A drop of ale hit Me! Yowwwwwwllll!*

The deflection spell continued to work, Ash and Holly remained dry. Though the ale added a layer to the indescribable stench rising from the cobblestones.

"Cat!" yelled the Holly.

Skidding in his tracks, Zanth stopped, looked back. *Yes?* he put a sneer into the loud mental tone.

The nobleman bared his own teeth. "My Family keeps hunting cats as big as you. I know how to handle you."

Zanth spat. *Tame Cats*.

"Where's the next good fight?" asked Holly, rolling his shoulders. Then he said a spell Word that cleansed and polished his blade, impressing Ash who'd developed such a spell after months of work.

Zanth's tail flipped up, the tip flicking back and forth. *Follow Me*.

The cat would lead them down to the worst of the old docks ... where the most vicious sewer rats lived, both four-footed and two-legged. Oh, yeah, this was probably not the best idea Ash had had lately.

The man turned to him, scanned him up and down and Ash jerked himself straight and to his full height, some long and excellent centimeters over the nobleman. Definitely wider than the guy, too. Ash had plenty of muscle.

"Hmm." Then the nobleman nodded, offered his arm for a greeting grip. "Holm HollyHeir."

Ash grunted, clasped the other's strong forearm, felt a tight grip and release, then they both stepped back. "Rand--"

Come ON! mind-shouted Zanth.

Holm Holly jumped at the loud telepathy, laughed, and took off after Ash's FamCat.

Ash loped after, scrambling a couple of times as his foot hit slime and threw him off balance. He felt dull and stupid and staid.

The benefit would be worth the effort.

Probably.

TIME TICKED PAST MIDNIGHT, EVEN PAST THE SEVENTY-minute septhour after Transition Bell when most deaths occurred. Thank the Lord and Lady, Ash hadn't died tonight.

His whole body ached. He figured he'd hurt even more later in the morning, and all through the grueling day of work at his smithy. Yet he trudged after a near-dancing Holm HollyHeir toward the next tavern, watched the man swagger inside with a cheerful wave for the drinkers.

The "fun" of clearing out a couple of dockyard joints hadn't lasted long before the Holly wanted "something more sporting than brute force."

Zanth had abandoned them to stalk a celtaroon snake back to its nest, and Ash was on his own with the nobleman. Ash stubbornly held on to his plan, especially since he'd already put in one miserable night. Holly owed him, and Ash would collect. The FirstFamily heir would have to help him.

Vengeance would be Ash's. His enemies would pay for killing his entire Family -- yes, Family with a capital "F," he was a FirstFamily -- and Ash would get back his lands and his title and rebuild his Residence.

He licked his lips, tasting not the flavor of sweet vengeance, but the salt of fight sweat that had run down his face to his mouth.

Shouts hit his ears as he opened the tavern's door and entered. Saw three-fools-on-one-Holly. All right. Coulda been five-or-six-on one. Had been earlier. Ash paused to shake out his limbs, check his blade. Nick free, clean, ready.

"Hey, Ash, get your fliggerin' friend outta here afore he breaks up my bar. I don' care if'n he leaves a trail of gold gilt coins behind him. Would rather keep the place as is than work hard to clean it up ..." shouted the owner from the short gallery above the taproom.

Closer, near Ash's jaw, came another, "Hey, Ash." Murmured by a well-endowed woman he'd partnered in bed now and again. Never paid for as other guys had, though. She liked big men with a bit of finesse. "Ash, take the pretty man away and come back soon, why don't ya?"

No plans to do that, too long of a night and a full work day to follow, but he jerked a nod and said, "Later," headed toward the Holly. Ash timed it perfectly, a final sword-pommel-to-the-chin and the well-trained noble freed himself of his last opponent to scan the room for more.

Before the guy could spew insults, all of which Ash had heard several times previously during the lengthy night, and many of which applied to him, too, he used main force to haul Holly back outside. Cool air, misty with spring humidity, carrying the slight odor of the ocean.

Ash handed the Holly fighter a softleaf. "You're not

looking well," he said. He'd planned the comment to distract the noble, but now that Ash really considered the man, Ash saw he spoke the truth. The guy's face appeared pallid, and he smelled like a whole shed of herbs had been dumped on him.

"Huh," Ash said, tapped the wooden lightpost near the door, and the crystal he'd carved, powered, and set himself, brightened to illuminate the cul-de-sac. "Look downright wasted." He paused. "And not just from drink." The rich man had been more interested in fighting than drinking, and had made his contempt of the quality of liquor Downwind known.

"Done, I'm done," the Holly gasped. His spine curved a bit as he scrubbed his face. "I'm done for now." When he looked up, he graced Rand with a crooked smile. "I'm only done for the night, not for my death duels Passage."

"Hear you," Ash said.

HollyHeir squinted. "Downwind, am I?"

"Yup."

"Interesting." He frowned, rubbed his face again. "Just how many guys did I kill tonight?"

"None that weren't trying to kill you," Ash replied. Four. He'd killed two bad characters himself, but he had to live here. The six wouldn't be missed by no one except to have their stuff taken by their ex-friends chuckling at the windfall.

"That's fine then." The Holly leaned against the door beam and his breath rattled out in a long groan. Ash just watched and guarded, shook out his limbs so the aches might not set in and hurt so much.

When the nobleman opened his eyes, he said, "How many times did you save my life?"

"Hard to say," Ash replied. "Saving was mutual."

A lopsided smile from the Holly. "I don't think so." Then the nobleman pushed up a sleeve, revealing a wrist timer that would keep a Downwind family of four all of their lives. It glinted gold and Ash's ears caught scrabbling near an alley mouth.

He jerked the noble's shirt back down. "Don't flash that 'round here!"

"Ah. Oh. Past Transition Bell."

"I know."

"We both lived through that."

"Know that, too."

"Time for me to go, though." He squinted up and down the narrow lane that looked like dozens of others Downwind, shrugged as if he gave up trying to understand his location. "I'll be back, friend Rand." He tried buffeting Ash's back, but when he lifted his arm to do so, he began to crumple and Ash had to haul his body up to his feet. If the guy fell, it would take Flair to get him up off the slimy street.

He propped the guy against the slightly cleaner saloon wall.

The nobleman rested a couple of minutes before continuing, "I'll be back tomorrow night, I'd imagine--"

"Tonight," Rand said. "Don't wear nice clothes, *don't* wear timer or jewelry, nothing expensive on ya." He nodded at the man's gleaming HouseRing that earlier he'd masked with a spell.

Holm HollyHeir's spine went rigid. "You want me to leave my best weapons at home, too?" he sneered.

"You can if you want," Ash sneered back. "I could give you a sword or main gauche or dagger or two." He drew his sword. "You won't find any better than this."

Holding his weapon so the light slid down the long and heavy blade, chased with elegantly inscribed spellrunes, he showed off his work, then shoved it back into a plain black sheath.

"Wait, I want to see that. Wait--"

Ash clapped a hand on his acquaintance's -- no matter

what the Holly said, they weren't friends -- shoulder. "You 'port home." Ash winced at his downwind shortspeech, the way he'd talked since he'd been six. Clearing his throat, he practiced the words and accent he'd paid a noblewoman to teach him. "You should teleport home now, HollyHeir."

"I would, my friend Rand, if I could. Head is muzzy. Dizzy." He began to slide down the wall.

A distant timer tolled Four Morning Bells, three septhours before Ash started work. Irritation flashing, Ash slapped the man back against the wall. "Stay up or leave you to die," he lied.

HollyHeir blinked. "Those are quite harsh words."

"'Zactly what'll happen." Rand scowled, thought what he could say to make the guy stay upright. "You Holly, control self!"

Holm jerked, his boots began slipping in the slime, he caught himself on the lightpost for balance. Remained on his feet.

"Good," Rand said. He reached into his pockets and pulled out a stone. Good stone and good work on his part with his Flair, but he considered giving it to Holly an investment, like the rest of the whole night. Lord and Lady knew that Family held such generational wealth that no one Holly could ever spend it all.

Tapping the round black stone embedded with silver sparkles, Ash put it in Holm's tunic pocket. "Think of home or person and there you get. Called a homing stone."

"Oh." Holm unwrapped one arm from the lightpost, leaned his whole body against it, then patted his free hand against his pocket. "Good Flair. Yeah, think this'll get me home."

"Go, then."

"Thank you, for everything." The nobleman counted

down his teleportation beats, wavered, then disappeared. Leaving Ash in the dark and quiet stink of Downwind.

Ash sheathed his sword, wiped his arm across his forehead. The nobleman had impressed him. Not only with his fighting ability, though he demonstrated moves Ash had never seen before, was the best fighter Ash had ever known. But Holly's cheerfulness, and his ... honor ... Holm Holly hadn't pulled any dirty fighting tricks. He hadn't had to. His reputation remained ... clean. Yeah, remarkable man.

All Ash's hurts throbbed, and he walked slowly but with extreme precision back toward his home, hand on sword hilt, forcing his senses to acute wariness. Couldn't let his guard down. Some tough might be watching.

HollyHeir would probably soak in herbal soothing waters, have all his aches banished by an expensive Healer, roll into the softest of beds between the best of linens. Maybe even have some Family members, women even, cluck over and tend to him, wrap him in loving affection. Dream noble dreams.

Ash would plod back to the street level lean-to he rented behind his forge. Zanth, who'd stayed at the docks, might or might not show up that night, bringing the stench of himself and sewer rat or celtaroon guts. Ash would fall on a cot and dream of fire and fear, smoke and running ... and death.

HOLM WOKE THE NEXT MORNING WITH A WRETCHED headache. Probably from passing out and staying in one position all night. Other echoes of aches indicated that he'd had cuts and bruises all over his body and more than a few strained muscles, but had been Healed.

"Initiate lightspell," said FirstFamily GreatLord T'Holly, Holm's father.

The small lightspell, modeled after their sun, blue-white Bel, glowed on and circled the ceiling.

His father, the greatest fighter in all the world, fixed a sapient gaze on Holm. "Second night of SecondPassage done," he stated gruffly, but Holm could feel the relief and the love. "Glad you made it back home again. Your mother prayed all night long to the Lady and Lord in our chapel."

"We still weren't able to track you after you teleported away when your fever hit you, and we're hoping you remember *something* this morning." T'Holly paused slightly.

"I think so," Holm ground out in a gritty morning voice.

A creak came from the other side of the huge wooden bed, the Heir's ancestral bed, and Holm's G'Uncle Tab, the owner of The Green Knight Fencing and Fighting Salon, rose from a groaning chair. "Obviously challenged others to death duels. I heard of nothing with regard to fights with any noble houses."

Holm sat up, found himself naked, didn't care. He scratched his head, flakes of green herbs fell from his scalp and hair. He must have soaked in the bathing pool, but didn't remember.

He didn't recall much. Rubbing his temples, he frowned, pulling out dim memories, mostly images, and, yes, definitely dark-hued. "I didn't stay here in Noble Country, not even in the main Druida City proper. I went Downwind."

Both his relatives sucked their breaths in between their teeth.

"Then I'm a'thinkin'," Tab said with that seafarer's lilt from his past, "you had help."

"Yes, I did have help with my fights." The young man's swarthy face swam before Holm's mind's eye. "Rand. Not sure I got his last name." Holm frowned. "He looked somewhat familiar. He's about my age, and heavier."

Another mind-pic, this one gleaming, "Had a fabulous sword."

"Sword?" both men asked, leaning forward.

Holm shrugged, worked those back and shoulder muscles. He needed to seriously limber up before Passage fever yanked him by the balls again, flung him into mindless death duels.

G'Uncle Tab buffeted Holm on the shoulder, he hadn't been braced, and had to use his core strength not to topple over. "All right, good reflexes, but need to be better if you're heading for Downwind again tonight."

"We'll prepare you all day," said T'Holly.

Which meant sparring bouts and surprise attacks and three-on-one fights with GreatLord Holly, G'Uncle Tab and Holm's younger brother, Tinne. Joy.

Holm had rather thought he could rest and maybe try to meditate, though that tended to slip around his active mind. He'd soak some more, be massaged top to bottom, eat well ... but no.

Tab hauled him out of bed. "Dress and put on your training robes. Meet us in Sparring Room Four in half a septhour. I'll pick out some clothes appropriate for Downwind tonight. You don't want to go in looking rich and noble."

"Too late," Holm said. "All the bars Downwind know me, or know of me, I believe."

"We'll school you in wariness today, then," T'Holly said.

"And the dirtiest street fighting," Tab added.

Fabulous, just how he'd wanted to spend the day, actively preparing for an exhausting night. For an instant his friend's face -- any man who'd saved his life more than once Holm considered a friend -- swam into his mind again and he wondered what Rand was doing, easy work, maybe.

Then Tab kicked Holm's feet out from under him and they began the day.

ASH ROSE LATER THAN USUAL, AFTER SUNRISE, AND STARED at his papyrus schedule tacked to his flimsy bedroom wall. No one he knew could afford the gilt or psi-power Flair for a calendar sphere construct that could be programmed and alert a person to upcoming appointments. Not that full workdays needed to be noted.

Naturally, he had commissions, but not as many as he liked. He'd worried about that -- last month. Grunting, he continued staring at the papyrus, his thoughts seeming to form slowly, as he considered his blacksmith work.

His sword, hell, all his weapons, were equal or better to what the Holly carried. Ash'd shown his sword to the man, who'd been interested in the quality, right? Yeah, just before the guy teleported home ... with the homing stone Ash had made. Another piece of good work.

Could maybe sell weapons to the nobleman, get gilt to live on and for the Vengeance Stalk to find and destroy his enemies -- first the Rues, then the Flametrees who'd given a terrible spell to the Rues.

Nothing to worry about right now, today. Holly liked Ash's sword, would commission a weapon, Ash felt it in his bones ... his increasingly warm bones and he hadn't stoked the forge yet. Even selling a dagger to the man might keep Ash and Zanth in food and rent for ... maybe for a year, even! Calculations sludged through this morning, even financial totting ups that he liked.

When his unmarried and miserly master had died from a sickness that ravaged Downwind two years ago, Ash had taken over the forge and business. He'd claimed the tools, had even discovered some good metals and a tiny cache of gems.

That was past. Now, he blinked, thinking of the simple

knife to finish by the end of this eightday, two days from now. Next week two sets of pretty eating utensils as a marriage gift were due. Ash would work on the knife today since he'd be spending all night long for the next-however-many-nights with Holm HollyHeir in his fever dreamquest of SecondPassage.

Ash's body had folded into a slump, so he straightened and stretched, glanced around his room. No Zanth. Frowning, he considered if his FamCat been a real benefit in the night before. Probably. Didn't matter, Zanth would want to "play" tonight, too.

Ash let out a shuddering breath, once again aware of all his throbbing aches, a couple of slices, even. He'd tend to those, then head to work.

"Fligger!" Ash swore as he stepped away from the anvil and the knife he'd been forging.

You burnt Yourself, Zanth said, sauntering in close to Noon-Bell. He leapt to a shelf Ash had put up when he'd reinforced the walls of this rental for his blacksmith space.

"I know that," Rand growled at his Fam, using both Flair and Healing ointment to treat his hand. He'd stripped down to his raggedy trous, coating his body with a strong protection spell. He could work naked if he wanted, if his forge hadn't bordered on a busy Downwind lane where he'd attract more attention and sexual offers than usual.

That shielding spell shouldn't have caused the heat surging through his body. Or made his fingers tremble when he worked, his hand jerk to burn himself.

"Fligger!" He realized the problem. Holm's death duels had triggered his own SecondPassage. He should stay home tonight, prepare his lean-to, business, and self for however

long it would take for the dreamquest fever to move through him.

Couldn't. Ash hadn't promised Holm HollyHeir they'd meet, but Ash figured the guy would expect him. The nobleman had called Ash "friend," and he'd pondered that as he worked on the knife. He didn't have any good friends, but looking back, he'd liked the man more than Ash had expected.

Maybe they could go beyond exchanging saving-each-other's-lives ... The notion had seeped into Rand's brain that HollyHeir, Holm, *his soon-to-be friend Holm,* would probably consider a hands-on approach to helping him. Would fight with Ash on the Vengeance Stalk, that could include a number of duels, or the initiation of a formal feud.

So he and Holm might not only be fighting this night, but for ... months. Until Ash punished the Flametrees for selling the firebombspell to the Rues and yanked his properties and wealth back from the Rues, got his title restored. Yeah.

Despite how he felt, he had to ignore his own onset of SecondPassage and *work* through it to support Holm during his death duels.

Ash stared at the knife. A few more folds of metal to make and pound, then the finishing and polishing and honing.

When he turned to put it away for later, he tripped over Zanth.

Yowl! Zanth hopped back. Hissed. *You look bad.*

My Passage starting. Ash narrowed gritty eyes. *We can't afford to NOT help Holm HollyHeir tonight.*

Zanth sniffed. *We want Our gilt and Our title and Our new Residence with good pillows.*

"Yeah," Ash croaked aloud. "And Holly will help us get that."

Prowling around Ash, Zanth said, *Maybe You should sleep now, wake later.*

Not feeling up to replying aloud, Ash sent mental words to Zanth. *Lie down to sleep and I won't get up.*

With a growl, Zanth said, *Don't want you to die tonight.*

Really don't want that neither, Ash replied. Brain continuing dull, he thought of stimulants he might take. That could be good.

Get good herbs, Zanth said, echoing his thoughts. He zipped away too fast for Ash's fixed gaze to follow.

Yeah, Ash said, pummeled his brain some more about what he should do to weather Passage. No one around here to talk to. Any Downwinder with good psi-power got out of the slum.

Holm HollyHeir, Holm, displayed great Flair which led to extreme Passages. Because he was a FirstFamily son, inherited psi talent from a long line of people. All the way from the original colonists who'd funded the starships and the journey from Earth to Celta, who colonized Celta.

Ash, though he had no title or wealth or property, had the blood of the colonists running through *his* veins, too. Great Flair leading to extreme Passages.

Fantastic.

Zanth swatted his calf, huffing, *Here is medicine pouch.*

The leather bag lay on Ash's feet. Being a saving sort of guy, Ash only used medicinal herbs as a last resort. Hadn't occurred to him to take anything this morning for his bruising aches, for instance.

And being a planning sort of guy, he'd intended to have his room ready and his forge closed and himself prepared before his SecondPassage.

That hadn't happened and now the event hit him. But he'd thought he'd suffer through the dreamquest during the month *of* Ash. The month assigned to the Ashes as a Great-House FirstFamily ... and that month would start at the end of next week at dark twinmoons. He'd anticipated having plenty of time.

He looked at the wall timer, an outline of a round clock he'd made of iron with actual moving hands. He had about six septhours before sunset and the arrival of an impatient Holm.

First, Ash must close down the fires of his forge, bank them completely. Tidy the forge manually with broom and cloth, no cleansing spells. He sensed he'd need all the Flair he could get during the death duels. And he wouldn't be able to count on his usual well of psi-power, Flair, since it notoriously fluctuated during Passage.

He moved slowly and found himself standing blankly, shuddering with fever, and only being brought out of it by the prickling of Zanth's claws in his flesh, and Ash figured he'd need every one of those six septhours.

TAKE HERBS! yelled Zanth, right in Ash's ear. The FamCat had hopped onto his shoulder -- his now shirt-clad shoulder -- and his room looked good, his bed prepared for him to crash, and on the side table a stack of foodbars and a large cauldron of water along with a chipped mug.

He opened the door to the forge and it smelled ... clean, looked fine. No fires.

I'll check to make sure the fires are out in the forge, he sent to Zanth, who swatted him on the ear. "Ouch!"

You check on fire THREE TIMES now.

Oh. He paused, saw that two septhours had passed since he'd begun preparations. *What else do I need to do?* Maybe the Fam would know.

You making sign.

Oh.

Here! Zanth leapt down to the bed and sat, crinkling a sheet of papyrus gray from multiple uses. He wiggled his butt and around the fat ass, Ash saw a "Closed," sign in words and symbols and pictures. He took a corner of the sign and yanked, tumbling Zanth over, but not ripping the papyrus. Sturdier than he'd thought for such an old piece.

He went through his forge to the outer door and onto the narrow sidewalk, walked carefully, one foot placed after another, to the wide and barricaded door of his forge, found the nail head sticking out, and shoved the papyrus onto it. The sheet flattened, spread thin and stuck.

Oh. He'd used too much Flair. Or too much Flair spiraled out of him.

"Ash, you don't look well," said an older woman dressed in layers of clothes, peering at him from under a scarf-shawl and the low brim of a hat.

No use saying "Passage." Downwinders, the lowest of the low, most with pitiful Flair, wouldn't believe him if he gave that excuse.

"Sick," he said instead, raising his arm and wiping it over his sweaty face. Smelled not-too-bad, not work-sweat or fight-sweat, but Passage-sweat, with a sweet note. Helluva thing.

She hesitated, dug through her tunic layers for a pocket, pulled out a button of plant-material he recognized as prime Healing herb with a spell for fever and clear thinking. Better than anything he had in stock. "Here."

"Pay you back when better," Ash offered.

With a smile, she sighed. "Yeah, later."

"Later." He eyed the thinned and stretched sign. Looked odd, but definitely announced "Closed." Good enough. He'd lose custom, but he'd rarely been unavailable, and never for sickness, so no one would bother him.

Zanth rumbled a loud purr. The woman dipped her knees to pat him on his large, round head, then walked away.

With another thwack on Ash's ankle, Zanth said, *Follow Me inside. You sit and eat and drink herb water. When close to sunset Me make sure you wake and take good herb-tab and get ready for fun tonight!*

"Fun," said Ash and sat in the one battered chair in his room near the antique no-time food storage unit and the little eating table.

His vision darkened and soot-smoke swarmed around him with flicks of bright cinders for a long time.

Wakie! Zanth sat on his lap, angled his head and licked under Ash's chin. He shuddered out of a stupor, took an old cloth and wiped his head and neck down, sniffed at his armpits. Not terrible.

Take pill now! The FamCat snapped his paw down next to the herb disk that the old woman had given Ash. So he did, and initiated the Healing spell, too.

After a couple of minutes, Ash rose and began to move, ignoring the fever aches in head and body and old bruises from the night before. He stood and flexed and lunged, warming his muscles, making his blood course through his body, hoping to give the herbs a boost.

He buckled his sword sheath around his waist, then pulled out his weapon and did passes as Zanth hunkered under the bed. As the spell and herbs mitigated the fever and his body moved better and his mind cleared of fog, his determination grew.

The advantages to helping Holm still outweighed the effort, particularly if Ash received some short-term benefits, too, like selling his work to the man. Yes, risk his life in the death duels tonight, and maybe by the end of the night he'd have a real friend, not just one in name only.

LONG MINUTES PASSED AND GLOOM FILLED HIS ROOMS AS HE waited for the the time for Holly to come Downwind. Ash didn't waste energy in turning on a Flair-tech light or summoning a lightspell

Finally, he left his lean-to, wanting to be well away from his home when the fighting started. No need for Holm or any dockrat thug to know where he lived. He trod the winding streets toward the main teleportation pad straddling lower-class Druida and Downwind. Maybe the nobleman wouldn't want to explore the depths of the slum tonight. Ash wouldn't mind following the Holly to bigger, less slimier streets. To less dangerous bars holding people who fought to hurt, not to kill.

And when the correct shade of twilight neared when Holm Holly arrived the evening before, Ash listened closely for his spy's alert. Zanth had a network of informants and this time they'd report to Ash.

He is HERE! squeaked the faint mental voice that belonged to a young feral tom. *My favor paid, Zanth. Me go back to My new home in temple!*

Zanth stopped and turned around in the street to stare at Ash.

"I heard," he said.

Did you SEE place where noble is? Zanth flicked a ragged ear.

"No."

A sniff. *Follow Me.*

Ash's mind had cleared to close to normal, and his determination solidified to help the Holly in his Passage death duels.

Zanth and Ash wound through a maze of twisty little passageways. As he and his Fam closed the distance toward Holm, Rand sensed the homing stone he'd given to Holm to help him teleport. The man carried it and the fact he did pleased Ash.

But as they walked, he caught the muttering and murmuring and ... *scent* ... of something stirring of note to Downwind folk. Not just this Holly noble who'd shown up for a third night running, but other outsiders lurking around where they shouldn't be.

Ash slid soft-footed around the crumbling corner of a gray brick building. Across a dirty open rectangular space -- cleared because buildings fell down, not planned like the rest of Druida City -- a man in dark green stood arrogantly. His hand rested on the hilt of his sword -- blade too long for the guy, looked too thin, too. Since such a narrow sheath could hold it, a rapier for noble duels, not a broadsword for fighting ... Rand stopped thinking of the quality of the weapon and stared at the man he'd seen twice before in the worst moments of his life.

His gorge rose as terror flashed through him, then subsided into a burning anger. The man was older, of course. Not a young man now, but in the prime of his life.

All the better to hate. Since his mouth went iron-blood tang, Ash knew his emotions affected all his senses.

His breathing sped to rapid, his brain sharpened. Felt no fever now.

This terrible man, awful enemy. *He'd* been the one to oversee the killing of the Ash Family, the destruction of T'Ash Residence -- an intelligent house -- with a firebomb spell. A horrible fire that ate everything down to nothing once it caught.

Ash had watched his Family die, his beautiful mother turning back to be with his stricken father and his trapped brothers. He'd been six years old.

A few days later, he'd seen this man when his underlings had tracked Ash Downwind. With Zanth's help, Ash escaped.

This man with the surname of Rue. The son and heir of the GrandLord Rue.

The Family who had claimed all the estates and riches the Ashes had held.

Now this enemy returned Downwind.

Maybe the Rue had followed the Holly, hearing rumors of the young man's death duels and maybe even that Ash had helped Holm. Maybe the Rue wanted to kill the Holly for evil purposes of his own, his Family's.

But Ash figured the Rue'd want to use fights to destroy the last Ash. An Ash who was supposed to have died with the rest of his Family a decade ago -- Rand's being alive a secret only he and Zanth and the Rues knew.

Yeah, use those death duels to kill Ash.

But the last Ash could damn well turn tables on Rue and do the same. Use the fights as cover to remove an enemy.

Ash found himself smiling with bared teeth. He wasn't six anymore. He'd grown big and strong, and practiced blacksmithing more than crafting little jewelry pieces. Eying the evil man, Ash figured he would have no problem breaking his neck. No, too quick. Breaking his spine. Maybe a femur or two ....

Zanth hissed, swatted Ash's leg, *BAD Man who tried to hurt Me long ago.*

Yes, Ash sent back mentally.

We will get HIM this time! Zanth sounded as bloodthirsty as Ash felt. The cat padded forward on quiet paws, slunk around the buildings forming the edge of the rectangular area. Ash wasn't certain whether the FamCat could actually kill a human or not, he'd discouraged that. The notion appealed, but not quite as much as dueling with the man.

Though this Rue would be only the first on Ash's Vengeance Stalk. One of the main players, like GrandLord Flametree who'd created and sold the firebomb spell, but Rand Ash must take down both Families, neutralize the whole GrandHouse Rue, as they'd done with his.

Take back his property and his wealth and his title.

Patience and strategy.

With a shriek, Zanth launched himself at the man, who

jumped away. "What the hell is *that*?" he cried out.

"Cat," said a man who'd blended into the shadows.

"Some stupid Lord and Lady bedamned feral Downwind slum cat," the Rue sneered. "None of our concern. Let's talk, you can tell me what you learned this evening." With a gesture the noble commanded the other, probably a minor member of his Family, to accompany him as he strode across the open space to the nicest tavern Downwind.

Zanth sat on the stone flagstones, tail thrashing. *He doesn't remember ME?*

Doesn't sound like it, Ash said mentally. The Rue's mistake that Zanth would correct sooner rather than later, Rand figured.

Meanwhile light laughter drifted from a more-than-shabby nearby saloon a few doors down this side of the rough square. Ash already recognized the mirth of Holm HollyHeir.

Ash shrugged. Time to help the Holly, and Rand would have the noble's aid in dealing with not only this Rue, but the whole clan.

Even as Zanth slunk after the Rue men, Ash sauntered into the Pewter Celtaroon, better known as the Putrid Roon, and saw Holm holding his bared sword, his chin jutting out. Had probably just delivered a string of insults.

"Greetyou," Ash said, and it emerged like a growl from his throat, his residual anger matched heat with his Passage fever burning through him, taking the sharp edge of his mind away.

A sea of whispers rose throughout the room, and men close to the Holly, and to Ash, faded back to leave the long length of the bar to them. The barkeep looked pained at the desertion of drinkers.

"Greetyou, friend Rand!" HollyHeir switched his sword to his left hand, though Ash had already determined the man could fight perfectly with either, thrust out his arm for a manly elbow-clasp.

Yeah, Passage fever showed in those eyes, no doubt spiking even more recklessness than usual in the nobleman. Ash found his own energy rising, decided that repressing it took too much caring. "Hope you had a better day than I, Holm," Ash found himself saying, a little surprised. He didn't complain, never spoke about his personal life.

Holm heaved a breath. "Pounded on by my brother and father and G'Uncle to prepare me for tonight." He still sounded jaunty, and unlike Ash, didn't smell like Passage-sweat but the best herbs. No doubt had them inside and out. Lucky guy.

A commanding cough issued from the barkeep. When Ash glanced at him, he jerked his head toward the door, mouthed "Pay you gilt later. Go, now."

Ash felt agreeable, since he wouldn't put it past Holm to instigate another brawl right here. He angled his head, asked the Holly, "You really wanna break up more furniture? Hard on the body."

The man pivoted on his heel, his grip easy but firm on his sword. People shrank back to the walls. "Bunch of cowa-- "

Ash grabbed him before he could finish. "Out, Holly."

He'd done that enough the night before that the noble didn't fight him, merely blinked, then followed Ash's push to the door.

He reached it first and held it open.

"Grateful!" called the barman.

"Later," replied Holm brightly.

As Ash stepped behind him, drew the heavy door closed, the noble frowned at him. "Call me Holm. You haven't used my name, and after we fought together all last night." Settling into his stance he stared at Ash.

"Holm," Ash said.

"Good, that's good." He looked around the rubble rectangle, and Ash couldn't tell how much he saw, how good his night vision was. Ash suspected better than his own sight, part of the man's Flair.

"Maybe we can go into Druida City proper," Ash offered. "Find some wrongdoers." Might take all night looking for fools up and down the streets, but better that than fighting every minute of the whole night. Might even get back to his lean-to before dawn.

"Aren't there folk you want to score off of in your part of the city?"

"I can settle any slights with ill-friends -- should they dare to challenge me -- in bouts at The Green Knight Fencing and Fighting Salon." Holm's words came casual and cheerful, not with the arrogant spin Zanth would have put on them. Holm flung his arms wide, sword tipping downward, then reeled. Ash propped him up first with his torso to keep Holm standing, then with an arm around his shoulders. As their bodies brushed, Rand realized the Passage fever sparking in Holm's eyes revealed the least of the man's biological and emotional changes. Holm's third night of Passage outstripped Ash's first evening by far.

If Rand felt off-kilter, barely able to think, Holm must be operating solely on instinct. Ash's respect for the man grew. Yeah, Rand's protestation of friendship could become real with a man like this.

He'd always heard the Hollys practiced Honor and Loyalty, the two most precious personal qualities as far as Ash was concerned.

"I hear you, friend Holm."

"Go back to Druida City instead of staying Downwind? Perhaps. There are usually troublemakers at the gates of the city," Holm stepped away from Ash to sheathe his sword. "Think I heard ruffians are bothering the southgate guards. We can go there first."

Teleport clear around the walled city, to each of the three

gates, maybe stand on the western cliff north of the docks and Downwind and look at the ocean? Hop over and lurk around Landing Park outside the starship *Nuada's Sword?* Holm could probably do that, Ash couldn't, not by himself.

But if SecondPassage gave Holm the same kind of energy now flowing through Ash, Holm could probably haul Ash around with him. Ash said, "Let's get to the working teleportation pad three streets away." He gestured toward the right direction.

Holm knocked away Ash's arm, sank into his balance, gaze quartering the empty rough space, all his cheer flickering gone and looking like a feral ... person. "No. Take too long to go here, go there, *talk* with guards, whatever. Gotta *fight*."

Fligger. Scrubbing his face, then letting his hands drop, Ash dredged up the next option he'd thought of while he *could* still think and grunted, "'kay. Come with me. Time to clean out a thieves' den." He rolled his shoulders to release heat and energy and tension. "Murderous thieves who wait 'til the darkest time of night to hunt and kill. Take clothes and silver slivers." Ash scowled at Holm. "You be worth decades of good gilt."

Holm grinned, drew his blade and sliced it around in a fancy pattern that would have carved a man to bits if there'd been one in front of him.

Impressive.

At that moment, Zanth swaggered up. *Me got them noble mens, one and two. Shredded theys boots, then rubbed good-stink of sewer rat guts into them.*

Holm choked a laugh. "No such thing as good-stinking sewer rat."

Zanth sniffed. *Maybe not to fancy human, but to Other* --

"Beasties," Ash said.

Others of US, there is good stinks. They rich mens cough and cough and swears. Zanth glanced up at Ash. *They don't swear as good as You, neither. Then they 'port away like pampered pussycats. They will remember Me, now!* he finished.

"Nobles? Who are the mens -- men?" asked Holm, sounding diverted.

Ash snapped his teeth shut. "Rues. Rues sometimes come Downwind." Looking for him.

The Holly's brows winged up. "Rues." Then the same mobile brows dipped over narrowed eyes. "Rues ... social climbers beyond their intelligence, abilities and Flair ... Some old rumor I heard. Don't recall, but ... nasty bunch. G'Uncle Tab banned them from his fighting salon. Never liked them."

Me, neither, Zanth added virtuously. *Gone for tonight, now.*

"With boots needing to be replaced." Holm snorted, then slid his sword back into its sheath, did some sort of exercise or fighting pattern clear across the square, ending with tumbling that would have cut up Ash's hands. Zanth pranced along, keeping pace with the man. Ash trudged behind, rolling fever-dried eyes.

Holm stood and stretched, clothes pristine, hands clean, and sword kept tidily in its sheath next to his leg. Rand felt dull and stupid.

"Rand, let's go clean out the den of thieves." Some of the flushed color had left Holm's face with the activity.

"Sure," Ash said.

"Good man."

Dull and stupid but loyal and honorable.

Reaching out, Holm squeezed Rand's shoulder, frowned. "Wouldn't think we had anything in common, but I get along with you very well. Better than most guys of my own age that I know."

We is good people! Zanth announced. *We make good friends. Friends with good hearts. Friends with hearts like Yours.*

"Perhaps so," said Holm. His hand slid into his trous pocket, pulled out the homing stone, let it sit on his palm, gleaming in the dim twinmoons light. "Friends." He smiled down at the stone. "I can get as lost as I want 'cause this will help me teleport home." He inclined his head to Ash. "Thanks."

"'Welcome,"

Then Holm swept a hand before him. "You know these thieves, FamCat?"

"Yesssss," Zanth vocalized.

"Lead the way."

Ash watched a patch of white on Zanth's tail wave back and forth as they wound through walkways.

And found the large but falling-down huts of the gang of robbers who prowled Downwind and preyed on the weak.

Holm HollyHeir kicked in the door. "Surprise!"

The ten men went for knives and swords. Poor steel.

Zanth screeched, Holm went in swinging ... and Ash simply cleaned up. To Ash's disgust, the fight with the thieves was short and brutal. It would have taken longer if the gang had been smarter or less drunk.

When the walls began to splinter and tilt, the ceiling to groan and break, Ash yanked Holm from the place, and ran away from the collapsing hovel, uncaring that some of the gang escaped.

"Not much fun," Holm grumbled when he caught up with Ash. Herb-smell wafted from him, of course -- this time Ash's nose twitched from soothing scents. To calm the man? Ash didn't know. He *did* stand close to the guy and inhaled deeply to get the smells into his own lungs. His mind cleared a bit and he stood quiet enough to let his heart rate steady.

But as he breathed, Holm cleansed his sword with a simple spell, turned and headed back into the narrow Downwind warrens.

Ash lagged behind the Holly, as usual, and Passage fever swarmed through him.

A few minutes later, his nostrils caught smells of fried food ladening the air and his stomach growled. He didn't recall when or what he'd last eaten.

He followed Holm as the guy slipped into a man-wide walkway between two buildings leading into a small cul-de-sac with a good cafe that stayed open late.

A woman's scream came from the small roundish courtyard ahead. Shouts, slamming doors, Ash rushed through the crack.

The clash of sword on sword. Good metal.

Whooshing of outdoor grills, of a *bonfire* somewhere near.

His fury merged with the fever and the atmosphere took on a thickness where smoky air seemed to clog his lungs and he moved slow. Too slow to survive.

The swings of his sword arm lagged behind his instincts, as if waiting for a foggy brain to direct blows instead of *acting*. He lumbered around with no grace as if pushing through fluid instead of air. But hot. Feverish. Billowing blinding clouds of soot.

He'd open his mouth to speak and nothing emerged but a quiet hiss or grunt.

Meanwhile he *heard* fighting, the shuffle of Holm's quick steps, his fast but even breathing. A fighting Holly, no one would beat him.

Then he cried out.

So did Zanth. *TRAP. AMBUSH.*

As if the back of Ash's brain hadn't known that. Ash pulled his dagger, weapons in both hands. Blindly waded in, slashing, keeping his sense of Holm on his right, the ambushers on his left. One stride, two.

Viscous. Vis-cous, molten lava, pushing through air like that.

Vicious. Vic-ious. Cruel men attacking, ambushing, firing T'Ash Residence, killing all Ash's Family.

Yes, that torched Ash's mind, and sharpened it.

Fire, smoke, soot, all things that reminded him of the worst night of his life, fears he'd have to face and triumph over during this SecondPassage.

Terror-sweat rolled down him. He'd be too late to save Holm, as he couldn't have saved his Family. He'd be somewhere else than where he needed to be.

Thinking TOO MUCH! ACT!

He ran forward, blinking hard, clearing the fog-fever film from his eyes, jerking his head to fling sweat away. Hell, he had a spell couplet for that. Through hot-cracked lips he shouted it.

Smoke smothered him and he couldn't tell whether it was behind or before his eyes, pressing against his nostrils and filling his lungs, or already inside him, swirling from fires set by his enemies to confuse and destroy.

Maybe. Maybe all the fires flamed in his head.

Who knew? Passage.

Fire. He feared and hated fire.

And worked with fire every-damn-day.

He let flames burn through him.

The forge of his fever.

The forge of his Passage.

The forge of his Flair.

Heat seared, burst from him in one massive spell, more an inchoate shout than Word. "Fire!"

A huge ball of flames exploded into existence, hung like a low sun, brilliantly exposing all in the courtyard.

Holm Holly against a wall, sword flashing.

Four men on him ... three Rue guards and one mercenary.

A man of the Rue Family, young like Rand and Holm, mouth stretched in a feral grin, raised a blazer gun and aimed at Holm.

With one leaping stride, a sweep of Rand's blade, and the

Rue would die. Rand flexed to jump. Heard a shout from Holm, two paces away, saw *all* the other men pressing him. Holm took two blows—one to his swordarm that would paralyze nerves; the other to his head from a sword pommel.

Vengeance or friendship?

Couldn't hesitate more. Ash leapt, plowing into two villains to the left of the Holly—who'd grabbed his blade with his left hand, and thrust and parried more from instinct than thought.

Ash hitting the group pushed all of them back. Holm spun away naturally, out of swordlength, and Rand concentrated on kicking and striking to damage as he staggered to keep his balance.

The young man who'd planned to blazer Holm leapt before Ash, weapon still raised. Rage flashed through Rand and he beat it back, loosened his teeth that had clamped together. This time *he* would kill.

His hated enemy. Without thought Ash lunged forward, stabbed. His good sword went slick through poorly bespelled armor. The blade hit the boy's heart and Ash jerked back, blood dripping from the fuller groove in his sword.

Blazer and boy crumbled, the weapon made a sound, the dead boy did not.

The older Rue glanced away from Holm. He yelled, shattering that fight and three leapt at Ash.

He spun, whirled, gave himself to the fury-smoke in his head, *acted*. Let his body rule, hoped the Holly could work around Ash, 'cause he wasn't thinking at all.

At spellwords from upper windows, a quick wind whipped through the cul-de-sac, smoke vanished. Water followed, drenching the courtyard, fires hissed dead.

Ash used the soaking water to cool, blinked to *see*.

Ambushers down. The Rue his age dead. The mercenary's throat cut, dead eyes staring up at the night sky.

Two Rues on Holm. One with a clawed cheek slashing at Zanth.

A flash of Holm's knife blade caught Ash's eye before it buried itself into the heart of the oldest Rue guard. The man fell dead, and Holly occupied himself with a sword duel with the younger guard.

The Rue targeting Rand whirled close from his left, stabbed out with a long blade, a main gauche, caught Ash in the side. He felt the cold bite of the knife. Heat-ice-pain only spurred him to fight *harder*.

This Rue laughed as he withdrew the knife with Rand's blood. Ash staggered back, muttered a melding spell that worked better on metal than on flesh, but would do for now.

He locked gazes with the shorter Rue man, the one who'd ordered the deaths of his parents, his brothers, who torched T'Ash Residence with a firebomb spell while Rand watched and wept.

The worst Rue. The one Ash wanted to kill the most.

And the fever and fury came back and filled his head and he shouted and held his weapons deadly forward and charged.

"Stop!" shouted HollyHeir.

STOP! screeched Zanth in his mind. Rand found himself squatting, looked over to see Zanth nose to nose with him, the Holly standing and frowning down. Felt blood on his hands and looked down to see a multitude of punctures in the Rue who'd killed his Family.

As Rand watched, the spark of intelligence, of life, drained from his eyes, and death came to him all too quickly. Rand had moved too instinctively and efficiently to prolong the Rue's suffering despite the four stab wounds around his heart. One each for Rand's parents and brothers.

Zanth revved his purr until it echoed with Flair throughout the cul-de-sac. *Me love You, FamMan.*

"I love you, too, Zanth."

Ash rose from his crouch over the body, cleansed his knife and his sword, then took a sweat rag from his trous pocket and wiped his face. He thought he'd lost a few minutes, not sure how long, of the fight and aftermath.

"They drew us here to ambush us," Holm HollyHeir said. He paced around the small circular courtyard. Ash noted people at the second story windows, watching from behind curtains, but he didn't think the nobleman did. And those folk wouldn't come down until they were gone.

Holm's lip lifted in disdain. "I recognize these colors and sigils. The GrandHouse of Rue, like you said before. Stups to come dressed in your own colors to ambush."

"Five Rue guards. They thought they'd win," Rand said. "Leave no one alive to talk."

ME would talk! To everyone. To city guards even! Zanth insisted.

"I suppose the decent thing to do is to send them to Deathgrove instead of letting the bodies be stripped of their wealth," Holly said.

Their wealth stolen from the Ashes, but Rand didn't mention that.

Holm touched the point of his sword to the young man their age. "Rue to Noble Deathgrove." The body disappeared.

Interesting, Zanth said. *Me watch.* And the cat did, as the man made each enemy vanish. Ash didn't know how such a spell worked. The Downwind thugs they'd killed they'd left for the regular scavengers.

Finally, when nothing remained except bodily stains, Holm walked toward Rand. A pace away, he stopped, shuddered, suddenly sagged.

Ash hopped forward and caught him.

"Passage finished. Done for." His head turned slowly back and forth and for the first time in two nights, Rand saw piercing intelligence in his eyes. "Not dead."

"No."

"A blessing." His gaze fixed on Rand.

Rand grunted.

"I'd imagine I owe you some thanks for saving my skin tonight, and more than once." Holm pushed away from Ash. Swayed on his feet, hunkered into his balance and found it.

Then he slowly straightened his knees and rubbed his hand through his hair. Nice smells came from the strands that Rand thought might be because of sweat-release smells. Nope, the nobles of Celta never smelled like regular people.

"You're my friend, Rand?" he asked, a new note in his clear voice.

"Yes," Ash affirmed.

"We've become friends." Holm tilted his head, studying Rand.

"Yes."

"But now that I can think, I believe you found me and joined with me to help me with my death duels because you had an agenda." Holm's eyes narrowed.

"Yes." Ash held his arms wide, they trembled with the heat of his own SecondPassage. Legs shivered, too. Whole body shuddered. Showed himself open and vulnerable to the suspicious Holly.

Then he offered his arm for a friend's clasp.

And Holm stepped forward, his fingers curving around Rand's forearm near the elbow. Ash set his hand on Holm's arm, squeezed.

When Holm stepped back, Rand wobbled.

"Wait," Holm said, silver-blonde brows lifting in a pale face. He flicked a gesture at Rand. "You're leaking."

Zanth sniffed. *Leaking blood.*

Ash grunted, pressed his hand against his side, pushing what little mending and making and Healing Flair he had to his wound, irked at having to use so much power, and the fact that some of his good clothes now had holes in them and bloodstains on them.

"Let me see that." Holm took a pace to him, braced Rand's shoulders with one arm, yanked up his tunic and his shirt.

Rand sucked in a painful breath.

"No vital organ hit," Holm said. "Just through muscle."

Rand grunted.

"Primo Healing patches before and behind will take care of this without going to a HealingHall. Want those or a HealingHall?"

The words circled in Rand's brain. "Don't care to go to HealingHall." Maybe the other Rues would find him there, trap him there. But he didn't know where to get primo Healing patches, neither. As far as he knew one patch would cost him about five years of business profit.

Then Holm poked at Rand's wounds and said some cleansing and anti-bacterial spells and two Healing patches were being slapped none-too-gently on him.

Rand gasped with pain, doubled-over to pant through it and maybe stay on his feet.

"You'll do."

"Thanks." He meant the word to be sarcastic but it came out as a whisper.

"You're welcome. Now, what was your agenda?"

"Rues. They here for me, the last Ash."

"Ash! The Ashes were wiped out by an unknown enemy, a firebomb spell that took out T'Ash Residence and the whole Family!" Holm's voice rose and echoed around the courtyard. People slammed their shutters closed. They didn't want to hear this, get involved in FirstFamily feuds.

"Rue killed parents and Nuin and Gwydion. I escaped, here, Downwind."

"That was years ago!"

"Eleven. I was six."

"How did you stay alive?"

"Was a big kid, and I found Zanth."

Me found him and helped him. We Fam companions. Friends of the heart.

"All right." Holm nodded. "I can understand that."

"I want my Family's murderers punished. I want justice! Want my title and estates back." He gestured to the drying bloodstains on the flagstones. "Rues came to find me, kill me and all the Ashes gone. Maybe kill you, too."

Holm nodded. "I'm understanding that, too."

We killed THEM, good start to make them pay for Bad acts! Zanth spat.

"Rues fools to come Downwind and try to take me, take Zanth. Take *you,* Holm."

"Yes, very foolish." Holm's voice hardened to arrogant noble. And Holm's gaze -- clear from Passage death duel lust -- fixed on Rand. He smiled and his pewter eyes took on a gleam of anticipatory joy at another fight, this one featuring a multitude of nobles and lasting months, if not years. "You and your Family deserves justice."

Zanth sauntered up, tail high and waving, a few flecks of blood still on his whiskers. *Me deserves a Residence.*

Rand felt his face go to stone. The basis of the intelligent house, his Residence, still lived in its HeartStones, secretly hidden. He didn't have the gilt, yet, to build a new house -- rebuild his home. He would.

He felt the sizzle on his right biceps of the god-given tattoo for the Vengeance Stalk. He lifted his fist. "We will win."

"Yes. I'll stand by you," Holm said.

We will win. Life is good, Zanth said.

FRACTURED STONE

This story needed tightening and polishing when the Covid 19 virus hit. Like most people, I felt helpless in this time of pandemic, and I also wanted to give back to those who were staying at home. So I posted *Fractured Stone* every day, page by page, and included the cut scenes while trying to finish the collection. I put up the story on my website and my blog. I also posted on Facebook with a daily photo I hoped illustrated the scene. So *Fractured Stone* became my Staying At Home story, and one people got to see in all its flaws.

This story follows the events of ***Heart Duel****, as requested by a friend. Holm Holly has been disinherited and lost his family, status, and basic identity. Now he must make a new life in Gael City with his HeartMate and their Familiar companions.*

FRACTURED STONE

Gael City, Celta, 403 Years After Colonization, Summer

HOLM HOLLY—*NO, NOT HOLLY*—HOLM APPLE STOOD ON the wide sidewalk in the small and bustling town of Gael City and stared at the modest building. He'd thought he'd been coping well with his disinheritance, but from the churning in his gut he realized he'd lied ... more to himself than everyone else, he suspected.

This step, the renting of this building as space for a fencing and fighting salon, naturally to be the best in the city, would turn his life in a different direction. A final acknowledgment that he no longer belonged to the Holly Family. That his status as HollyHeir, a man who would become a FirstFamily GreatLord, the highest of the high, had vanished.

"Maybe we're moving too fast and I shouldn't have brought you here yet," said the woman beside him. The absolute best part of this new life, his HeartMate, Lark. She murmured the statement more mind-to-mind with telepathy than the whisper he heard.

He unlinked their fingers and put his arm around her waist, savoring the feel of her pliant body against his own as much or as more than the brush of her mind, and their emotional connection. "No, you're right. We must get on with our lives."

He'd lost himself, and though he pretended, he hadn't really made a new self. He'd made plans without expecting them to happen. Now he had to follow through, *become* someone else. Grow.

Drawing in a deep breath of air not-at-all like Druida City's, he smelled the dust of a smaller town, the earth of the mountains to the north, a fresh water river instead of a nearby great salt-ocean.

"I think this building will do well," he croaked, and stepped up to the one-story structure that showcased large shop-like windows in the front. He'd have to protect that glass with strong Flair, psi magic, and definitely allow *no* training to spill over into the front room. Write a stipulation in his contracts with clients that any breakage would be paid for by the culprit.

Lark moved with him, then up to the door. She murmured passcoded spellwords to drop the psi shield and allow them in.

They stepped over the small ridge of threshold into the space, redolent with the scent of cleanser and wood polish.

To Holm's surprise, the entry room comprised the full width of the building but only extended about three meters deep, making a wide but shallow foyer. The pale blue smooth upper walls accented the dark wood wainscoting on the bottom.

The near wall in front of them sported a pair of double-doors. When he pushed them, they swung back and forth easily on their hinges. He strode into a large, empty room with floor-to-ceiling mirrors on the left wall, and the right wall interrupted by two doors, one reading "Men's Dressing Room," and the other, "Women's Dressing Room."

The shining wooden floor felt hard and new beneath his feet. "Your father doesn't own this property, does he?"

"Not that I know of, but he did refer me to it. Actually, I think he consulted with your G'Uncle Tab who runs the salon in Druida, and asked what was needed."

"Oh. Good."

"Father's note said this had been an exercise space for dance and theater artists."

Holm stared at the mirrors and figured they'd have to be specially shielded for his business.

At that moment his and Lark's FamCats, young orange tabby brothers, tumbled into the room. As soon as they all had arrived in a glider, the toms had leapt from the vehicle to run around the building and check out the yard behind.

Our space! the young cats yelled telepathically. Meserve, lazier and fatter than his brother — Holm's kitten who'd been pampered and spoilt by the Holly Family — cuffed Phyll. *My space. *I* am Trainer Cat.*

The cats rolled around wrestling, breaking away, pouncing on each other as Holm prowled to the mirror wall, placed his hand on the glass. He sensed no spells, simply glass. Nothing to protect the wall from flying bodies.

Shocking.

The mirrors needed shielding at the very least. Better would be coating spells that could set various types of walls over the glass — wood or plaster or permacrete — to be cycled as Holm needed.

And that would be expensive.

His brain stopped. He had no money, no gilt, at all.

His father had confiscated Holm's personal account as belonging to HollyHeir, as it had. Holm hadn't separated his own noblegilt salary, the money he'd received from the Councils for any quests they sent him on — minimal — from any other funds.

He'd rarely given personal money any thought. Anything he'd needed had been charged to the Holly Family accounts.

He'd always worked ... for his father, GreatLord T'Holly, learning how to be a good lord, how to handle their affairs and property. He'd also worked at the Family enterprise owned and run by his G'Uncle Tab, The Green Knight Fencing and Fighting Salon, training and giving private lessons, taking part in melees, whatever G'Uncle Tab needed. And done his annual noblegilt duty.

But Holm had never actually been paid by his Family for HollyHeir duties. Or had a bank account not linked with his Family. Had never had to consider whether he could actually afford to purchase something.

He'd been so blindsided by the disowning, so emotionally staggered, that he hadn't considered his "individual" money ... Well, he'd never considered any of his gilt personal. All went into the Family coffers, and he charged whatever he needed to the Family.

Now he had nothing.

Where would he get the money, the gilt, to pay someone for the shields? And they wouldn't be the *best* shields, because the best practitioners with the most Flair, psychic magical power, lived in Druida City. If he wanted the best, he'd have to bring them down ... and he had no idea how to pay them.

"What's wrong?" Lark asked, and Holm realized he'd folded over, hands braced on knees, panting as if he'd fought several hearty bouts in a row.

"I have no gilt," he ground out.

Laughter rippled from her, and it speared him that she didn't share his consternation. She patted him lightly on the back, and sent him a wash of comfort ... tinged with amusement. "That's all right, I have plenty. Not only the noblegilt the Councils pay me for my services, but a very nice salary for being the new head of the Gael City HealingHall."

"Good," he said through stiff and cold lips. Before he could straighten, both young cats hopped on his lower back, crawled up to his shoulders. *Fun!* said Phyll.

We don't cost much! Meserve's whiskers tickled Holm's right ear. Holm wondered how his Fam knew about gilt and expenses, where he'd learned of it.

Slowly, Holm straightened and his HeartMate continued to rub his back in a soothing manner. Easy to recall that she'd been estranged from her own FirstFamily GreatLord father, married a commoner and lived with that commoner husband outside the Family Residence while they both worked at HealingHalls.

Lark had handled all the details of this little family's move. So she'd help him get through this, and teach him.

He stiffened his spine, but kept his knees loose and ready to respond to any threat. Plucking Phyll from his left shoulder, he handed the Fam to Lark. With a controlled pivot, he scanned the room. "This will do very well." But he wondered how much it would cost to shield the mirrors, and the expenses of getting a business up and running. Another thing he had no notion about.

Lark nodded. "A good and simple space." She patted Phyll and his purr filled the room, augmented by his Flair-magic. So Meserve purred too, in competition, bouncing the warm sound off the mirrors.

"Enough!" Lark laughed and put her cat down on the floor. Holm dropped Meserve, who landed lightly.

But the three of them had worked together to ease his anxiety, and the very fact that they *knew* he was anxious irritated him. Reminded him of the recent past.

He'd thought he'd gotten over having to be perfect as the golden boy of the Hollys, the HollyHeir, fulfilling all such expectations of that status.

Perhaps so, but he'd discovered a new and unwelcome negative emotion seeded inside him.

Feeling useless. Worthless. Like his father had made him feel when he'd been disowned. His whole life and purpose ripped away.

Yes, he'd have to follow plans he'd made but hadn't accepted at an emotional level. He'd have to accept help just to survive, let alone flourish, and do that gracefully. He'd have to grow and *become* Holm Apple.

Also accept he'd create his new life here, in Gael City.

Sucking in a deep breath, he cast a final glance around the main room. He'd check out the dressing rooms ... and the plumbing! ... later.

"Yes, I think this will do very well." Holm forced a smile. "I'm sure The Green Knight Fencing and Fighting Salon started out small, too." Though the beginnings of that generational Family enterprise was lost in history and legend.

"I'm sure," Lark smiled at him, and he felt her supreme confidence in him. He swallowed.

Tag, you're IT! shrieked Meserve and hit the door with enough acceleration to go through and his brother zoomed after him before it swung shut. The front door slammed open with Flair.

Lark shrieked, "The street!" and bolted after them.

Holm hurried out. Not much glider traffic here, but antigrav hauling sleds and beasts and carts from the countryside, even on this last day of the weekend. Holm figured the Fams could dodge or teleport or—but tell that to a Healer who often saw the worst.

So there they stood, all three, on the sidewalk with Lark shaking her finger at the cats and them ignoring her.

Holm dismissed the lightspells in the building, locked up with key and passcode, and left. Then paused and looked at the small, ordinary structure he hoped to rent and build a business in, somehow. He wondered whether he *could* make a successful enterprise with only himself as proprietor and single trainer. The task seemed overwhelming.

And how long it would take. A month? A year? Five?

HOLM TOOK LARK'S HAND TO WALK HOME. TIME TO experience the city where he'd be living. Since she'd dismissed the HealingHall glider, they sauntered through the sunshine of late summer through the compact area of the city's downtown business sector — Holm's studio was not on one of the two main streets — and past the Temple and the round green across from it. He *sensed* the slower and more casual atmosphere of the people around him, sensed more open friendliness.

Let out a breath.

They reached the home Lark's father had given them to live in until ... perhaps their whole lives. The young cats scampered to the overgrown side yard high with plumed grass, where they could hide and pounce on each other.

Lark tugged on Holm's hand and they circled the two-story pale goldish stone house to the back and the smooth green grassyard bordered with fully mature splashy flower gardens.

She hummed with pleasure and set her arm around his waist. He felt her pleasure at the floral show and she smiled up at him, stroked her hand down his chest as if checking on the tenseness of his muscles. Yes, returning to a new private sanctuary eased him.

Pulling away, Lark translocated a basket and a ritual knife, walked over to a thick patch of ivy and murmured a prayer, then cut several stalks, sealing the wounds with a touch. Ivy — in the language of flowers, wedded love, fidelity, friendship and affection. All of which she sent him down their bond, and he returned. Then she crossed the yard to the rose garden.

He turned and stared at the modest house, *not* a huge intelligent Residence modeled like an Earthan castle like he — and Lark — had grown up in. The dimensions and proportions pleased him. A two and a half story house of pale yellow stone stood, showing four windows on each side and one above the double door. All of the windows on the upper story had small greeniron balconies that echoed the tint of the roof.

The half story revealed one large center multi-paned window and two small dormer windows on each side. Each included a fancy molding frame that repeated the arty rectangular designs along the wall under the roof.

He smiled, glanced over to Lark who sat on the ground deftly fashioning a wreath from the herbs and flowers she'd harvested, being climbed on by the young cats. Another pleasing picture.

As he watched, she wove in white heather, a symbol of her mother's Family, meaning protection.

His brows dipped when he sensed she made another wreath for *him*.

Then Meserve shot over to Holm, pounced on his boots. *Train, we haven't done a drill today!*

"You're speaking for yourself, cat," Holm said. He'd done plenty of fighting patterns, katas and drills, today. Morning exercise ... though he'd missed the opportunity to test out the floor of his new space. Too broody.

A fighting pattern — including tumbling — would banish dark-thought cobwebs.

He gauged the space needed and backed up. Deciding on a rarely practiced set of springs and rolls and falls, he began, keeping an eye out for the leaping Meserve.

When he ended, he did feel better. Meserve seemed to be toning up some ... without Holm's Mama and other Hollys slipping him table tidbits.

Holm looked over to his HeartMate. She'd tidied up her work, and now stood.

With a deep breath, she flung out her arms and spun, and Holm felt the heavy scents of the flowers mix in the wind, then wrap around him. He let the fragrance fill him and eased into his emotional balance.

But when she finished spinning and faced him, her expression didn't show exaltation, but narrowed-eyed Healer consideration. Uh-oh.

Walking over to him, she placed the wreath on his head. The sturdy green frame of ivy mixed with sprigs of white heather, but deep crimson roses intertwined with that. *Mourning.*

The wreath hurt. Not the negligible weight of it, and no

woody stems poked his scalp, but among the heather and the ivy were apple leaves, and despite the roses, that was the odor that stayed in his nostrils.

"Mourning, truly?" he asked.

She opened his arms and stepped against him, stroking his face. "There are hurts within you that must be acknowledged."

"Ever the Healer." He sighed, closed his eyes and let sweat cool on his body, smelled the apple wreath, and the lingering floral breeze, and the herbal spell of his garments that wicked away sweat. "What hurts do you mean? I'd rather deal with them here, outside, than in our home."

Her head nodded against his chest. "Very well. It's an abscess that needs to be lanced."

"Excellent image," he muttered, *not* wanting to visualize some big yellow pus sack inside himself.

"But we can speak of our new home first," she said with a faint smile that showed she wanted to give him a nice feeling before ...

"I like it very much," he said, "Your father obviously worked on this piece of property for us."

"With mature gardens for me. I like the house, too, but it seems he anticipated what kind of dwelling you'd prefer. Of course, he's lived in a tall gray stone castle Residence all his life just as you have."

Lark had not. She'd been estranged from her father, lived outside the sentient T'Hawthorn Residence first as the wife of a commoner, then as a widow in an actual apartment building.

"I like the house," Holm repeated. Opened his eyes to look at it's good proportions and symmetry, then reached up to touch the dark red roses. "Nothing to mourn for there."

"No. It's a lovely house. But you must mourn for your Residence, the home you miss, *as a being*. It was as much a member of your Family as the rest of the Hollys. And you must mourn the loss of your Family. You lived with your parents and brother and cuzes all your life. You will have missed seeing your Family at meals, or ..." she made a hesitant gesture "training—"

"Sparring with my father and brother and cuzes and G'Uncle Tab." The words came out roughly as the *missing* surged through him, whipping him raw with memory-images. He had to sink into his balance, and she came with him, steadied him, his HeartMate, as he shuddered, breathed through both nose and mouth as the grief stormed. Couldn't ignore that he wouldn't be returning to his Residence at the end of the day, or the end of the next day. Whatever Hollys still supported him, he wouldn't see often. They lived north and distant, across mountains.

He drew in a shuddering breath and stretched cramping muscles. The beautiful wreath fell to his feet. He kicked it to fly and disintegrate. Then flinched. He'd destroyed a gift from his HeartMate. He turned to apologize, but she placed her fingers on his lips.

"The wreath served its purpose." Linking her arm with his, she began strolling toward the house. "I want special food from the no-time. Feast-day food, from Samhain celebrating New Year and new beginnings."

Samhain was over two months away, in the autumn.

Holm grunted, "Fine. I need to take a waterfall, I'll join you in a few minutes." He hoped there weren't any more pockets of pain within him that she'd feel needed dealt with.

Accompanied by both cats, he trudged through the back door. As soon as they entered the small tiled entryway, light-spells came on and not only in this room, but throughout the house.

A welcoming place. This place, this house would eventually become a Residence over a couple of centuries, if greatly Flaired people lived here and made it—loved it—as a *home.*

So far Holm had only addressed the house once or twice as "Residence" and asked for something, then stood a few seconds waiting for the being to respond before realizing he'd have to take care of the chore himself.

A fresh energy, maybe a whiff of a scent he couldn't place, seemed to imbue the atmosphere with not only that trace of odor but a ... a delight, a cheerfulness.

Lark stopped, sniffed. "What's that?"

He found his shoulders dipping in relief, a smile touching his lips. "I think it's Clam." Now he moved quickly, through the back mudroom into the kitchen, then down a short hall to the mainspace where a large salt water tank held Clam — really a pearl mollusk — and the sea life he preferred.

The changes of tanks, underwater scenery and the move had invigorated Clam. He'd produced several stunning pearls in various forms that Holm forwarded to his friend T'Ash — jeweler and blacksmith. Clam Apple, an artist who fit in well with all the other creative Apples.

The notion curved Holm's mouth. Holm had always considered Clam a ... neutral or pessimistic being, but the move had brought him joy that he shared with his Family. Holm thought it to be the location in the busy mainspace of the house, but for all he knew, there'd been new nutrients in his tank.

As Holm considered this, he could only pray to the Lady and Lord that this new environment of Gael City would be rich with nutrients for him — students, friends, experiences.

Focus on the positive. He *had* managed to cobble together a self made out of essential experiences: he'd won his HeartMate, he had good friends in the highest status that he'd made himself, as well as a former brother and G'Uncle who loved him.

He vowed his new life would be positive.

HER HEARTMATE CAME TO BED, AND LARK ROLLED TO hold him. Unlike nights before, his body and mind didn't hum with tension, and she sensed a slight positive note. She matched her resting energy with his, let her calmer thoughts cycle to him.

And a few moments later, he slept, and, she thought, settled into the first good sleep since their move.

So she allowed tears for him, warm and silent tears, to fall. And banished the wetness as it crept down her cheeks.

Who would have thought that her father, once the greatest man on the whole of Celta, would have been more forgiving than Holm's father?

Now and then she caught Holm's expression of complete confusion.

Not defeat, not desolation, not despair. Utter shock.

But then the feud had been terrible. Her father's hubris in believing he could win against the Holly warriors. The terrible accidental knifing by her nephew of Holm's mother. The loss of her estranged brother, her father's revenge ... blood red events tumbled through her mind.

Finally, her father, T'Hawthorn, had come to his senses and surrendered to the Hollys, reconciled with his remaining relatives. Worked at being a good and loving man.

Her thoughts turned from that awful feud back to her newly discovered HeartMate, her beloved Holm. She had no doubt he'd master this new world he'd been thrown into because he'd already proven how incredibly he could grow, by changing enough in this very lifetime to become her HeartMate.

Life tested him, her Holm ... Apple. But she'd stand with

him. Help him as much as she could, *push* him to deal with his issues, but he'd have to continue to do hard emotional work himself — to grow.

And when she felt him fall into sour dreams she woke him with a sure and passionate touch and stoked the fire between them until he took her fiercely like a warrior.

THEY FINISHED BREAKFAST, THEIR THIRD MORNING MEAL together in their own home, and Holm liked the healthy and nutritional food. So did Lark and her young cat, Phyll, but Holm's own ginger tabby grumbled at the mixture of meat and greens with no human table scraps as he'd gotten before.

Continuing to solidify habits in this new life, Holm stood and went to Lark's chair to slide it back for her, and she took their dishes to the cleanser. He'd cleaned his plate. Little by little, he'd begun eating as much as he had before he'd been disinherited.

When she came back, she wrapped her arms around Holm, hugged. He sensed she wanted to rock together so did that — otherwise she couldn't move him. "My first full day as Head of Gael City HealingHall, I'm nervous," she murmured.

She fudged the truth. She'd applied for the position months ago, had been planning on changing her life in a large way before the Hawthorn-Holly feud, and anticipated the job with rising satisfaction. If he hadn't been disinherited, she'd have lived with him in T'Holly Residence with the rest of his Family and continued her career at Druida City HealingHalls.

So, though her life had altered dramatically, she welcomed it more, and the move, too. Altogether more sanguine and serene, his Lark. He stepped even closer until their lengths pressed together. She'd become his anchor in the storm his life had become.

Then two young cats landed on Holm's shoulders, draped over his and Lark's. *We are going to the HealingHall today!* Phyll, Lark's cat said. *We will be Healing Cats, I will teach Meserve more.*

Meserve hissed and leapt down, his brother followed. They tussled from the kitchen to the main space where they stopped and stared at a wall. *Hello, Clam!* shouted Meserve. *Hello, Clam!* echoed Phyll.

A watery sense of satisfaction wafted through the house. Greeting enough, Holm supposed. He stepped away from Lark, took her hands, inhaled deeply and said, "I'd like to sign the rental contract for the building housing my studio salon and get started on refurbishing the space. Can I draw gilt from your account?"

Her head tilted, her eyes softened and welled with tears.

Holm squeezed her fingers. "What?"

"I know that cost you in pride. But you asked. You are my HeartMate, we are partners, now and forever." She clasped his fingers tightly, the golden bond between them cycled with deep love for several moments, smiling at him as she did no one else. "I added you to all my accounts at Cascara Bank the evening we acknowledged we were HeartMates."

"You did that for me?" He'd had no such thought for her.

Her brows raised. "Of course. We're HeartMates, linked emotionally, we could not betray each other."

"No." He couldn't even grasp that concept. Not when he'd lived with his HeartMated parents who stood as a solid unit. "I'll ride in the HealingHall glider with you, and walk to City-Center to sign the lease for the building."

Standing on the walk outside Gael City HealingHall, he kissed Lark and petted each FamCat, watched as they entered the place. Then Holm walked to the office of the owner of the building, and spoke with the man's assistant. At no time in his previous business life had he dealt with an assistant instead of the principal of a business. But everything went smoothly and he left detailed notes about how he planned to shield the windows and mirrored wall at his own expense. He'd gotten a recommendation for such an expert and made an appointment for the afternoon, then transferred gilt from Lark's — their — account for a deposit and three months' rent.

A deposit and three months' rent. The amount, two months ago, would have felt insignificant. Today, when he had no gilt, doling it out made his gut churn.

The first gilt spent on his own business. He didn't feel excitement and anticipation, but low-level anxiety.

Despite emotional and spiritual work, Holm still loathed failing. Creating, growing a successful business — something totally new he could fail at.

He wondered that since Gael City boasted no good training studio, academy, salle, fencing and fighting perhaps others had closed, as had the exercise and dance facility previously in his building. Other people might have failed in the same business, people who'd *wanted* their own businesses. Even failed in his new space. Terrible idea.

He'd work hard. But the success of a business didn't solely depend on him, did it? It depended on people wanting to train, be taught. He had to find and keep clients and finding clients might be difficult.

Yes, he'd work harder at this than any other thing in his entire life. Just the thought made him sweat.

If he failed, he wouldn't lose Lark.

But he'd lose self-respect, and gilt *she'd* made.

He already felt as if she gave more to their partnership than he. Another stupid idea, she didn't tally giving and receiving, and neither had he ... before. Now was a whole different matter. The feeling of unbalance settled under his skin and itched.

Holm reached home a few minutes before Lark was due

to arrive with the FamCats — an emergency had her running late, and he'd stayed to discuss the shields with the slow but thorough expert a lot longer than he'd anticipated.

Flopping down into a chair in the mainspace, he rubbed his aching head. Making decisions about gilt had never taxed him so before. But this was *Lark's* gilt, and a finite amount. He should have done a budget. He knew how, but he hadn't before. Something to tackle this evening.

Talk it over with Lark, make it a *sharing experience*. Fligger.

The scrybowl chimed like clashing daggers. Holm jerked upright, the sound of a call from The Green Knight Fencing and Fighting Salon in Druida City. Either his G'Uncle Tab who owned the place, or Holm's brother Tinne, who *would have* taken over that business if he hadn't now been promoted to GreatLord T'Holly's heir.

Stupid for his heart to leap, for him to think Tab or Tinne scried because Holm's father wanted him back as HollyHeir, but that notion hit his emotions and his brain first.

Then pain struck, because GreatLord Holly would *not* admit any error. He'd been a wonderful father, until that last irreconcilable difference, shocking Holm.

And now Holm had to definitely change. Had he thought his father would come around? Perhaps. Thought more that his Mama would work on his father to revoke the disinheritance of his first son and heir? Yes.

Even after weeks, he'd believed that. Fooled himself.

Continued to think with his heart and his gut instead of his brain.

Striding over to the scrybowl, he circled his finger around the edge of the bowl to accept the call. G'Uncle Tab's face formed in the water droplets hanging over the bowl. "Greetyou, Holm Apple," he said.

Holm's abs tightened, though he didn't think his expression changed. And, yes, G'Uncle Tab would understand Holm continued to hope his status as a disinherited son would change, despite everything.

"Greetyou, Tab Holly."

His expression hardened. "You call me G'Uncle Tab, you hear?"

"Yes, sir."

A headjerk of agreement. "Now, I went back and figured out how much I could pay you for your help in The Green Knight Fencing and Fighting Salon this year."

"You don't need to—"

"I *know* I don't *need* to, but you worked for me, and I paid your father for your services." Tab's face creased with a grim smile. "I told him I wanted my money back." Tab chuckled. "I insisted. It warn't me who disinherited you. I presented him with an accounting of what you'd cost me for the whole year, since Samhain last."

"Nearly ten months," Holm choked.

"That's right. He bills me yearly, so I asked for your fees and got them." Another smile, this one almost cherubic, an odd look on a tough, old warrior. "And I billed him for the absence of services of his new HollyHeir owed me—"

"Tinne!" Holm's brother.

"Who was *my* heir who T'Holly took away from me. I had to use cuzes to fill in all the classes and private lessons and whatnot, and I still don't have an heir yet." Tab stared penetratingly at Holm.

"I ... I can't." He swallowed. "I don't think T'Holly would allow that, either."

"I am the master of The Green Knight Fencing and Fighting Salon," Tab said. "But it would be awkward ... right now. Gotta tell you, though, I don't think your disinheritance will last." He lifted a hand. "Holm senior is very hardheaded, and I anticipate that breaking their Vows of Honor — always a terrible thing — will work on him and your mother, so you might be looking at some years there in Gael City. But eventually, he'll come around."

Hope hurt too much. Hope, then crashing betrayal of that faith hurt more than anything else in the world. Holm didn't want to hope. *Didn't* hope with his head, and his heart would learn soon enough and stop the cycle of pain.

"Anyways, I sent payment to ya through T'Reed's bank there in Gael City, and they'll be holdin' the gilt for ya."

"Enough ... enough to coat a wall of mirrors with an anti-breakage shieldspell?" Holm would like Tab's view on the deal Holm had negotiated.

"How big a wall? Tab asked.

"About four meters tall and a quarter of the length of the main fighting area of your salon."

Tab nodded, "For sure." Another cool smile. "You were a highly paid commodity. Excellent fighting skills."

"Thank you."

"So the check is large."

"Nice to have some gilt," Holm said.

Tab chuckled, just as Lark had. "Yah. Prob'ly never thought about gilt a'tall, did ya? Not like the rest of us who've worked for our livings outside the Family."

"That's right." Holm tried an easy smile and didn't think it formed too oddly on his lips. "Hell of a shock."

"Imagine so." Tab scrutinized him. "You'll do, Holm Junior. You got grit enough. You and Tinne showed that when ya walked from the northern mountains back to Druida City." Another firm nod. "And ya grew enough to find and claim your HeartMate. You'll do well."

"Thank you."

"And how is your Mayblossom Larkspur Bella Hawthorn Collinson Apple—" all the long names of his HeartMate rolled well off the old sailor's tongue, "—doing?"

"We're very well."

"Also good to hear. Merry meet."

"And merry part," Holm said. It was almost true.

"And merry meet again. Later." Tab cut the scry and the water above the bowl stopped holding the colors of his being and dropped down.

Holm stumbled back to his chair. He could pay Lark back, cover all the costs he'd laid out today. Move his share of *their* funds from T'Reed's bank, a noble patronized bank, to Cascara's, that more middle-class folk used.

So he'd have enough gilt for now, to take care of the building and perhaps a few months of startup for his business.

That didn't mean he, or his fighting salle, would be a success. In his head came the vision of a sandglass, with grains of gilt in the top that simply drained away.

Until he had to use Lark's money again.

THE NEXT FEW DAYS PASSED AND HE THREW MORE GILT AT his business. The process moved apace. Holm figured it was mostly because he paid for services at the time of the contract, though the fast turnaround might also be due to his former name and status. Or because Lark, as T'Hawthorn's daughter and Head of the Gael City HealingHall, dropped words-or-two in certain ears. Or perhaps the fact he still had good contacts with important nobles of Druida City.

He purchased shieldspells for the front windows, three kinds of coating spells for the mirrors, and in a hopeful surge of optimism, visited the Gael City Merchant Guards Guild. There he sparred with other professionals, and took down names of those he could call in to work if he got busy.

Holm's Training Studio—a name he finally settled on — would open the last business day of that very week.

He couldn't figure out whether that was good or bad.

KOAD DAY, THE LAST WORKDAY OF THE WEEK, AS SHE walked hand-in-hand with her HeartMate down their drive to where the HealingHall glider waited on the street, Lark studied Holm.

His night had been restless, typical for any new business owner opening the next day. They'd made love several times and slept in between bouts. She grinned. They'd been noisy enough the FamCats had left in a huff to bed down in the mainspace and the soothing presence of Clam.

Now Holm appeared energetic, with a buzz of Flair running under his skin. Ready and revved for the day. She, herself, felt tired and hoped no emergency came up that she'd have to handle, or use great Healing Flair.

But Holm would do very well today

He lifted the glider door for her and the Fams, greeted her usual driver, then slid in and made casual conversation on the way to the HealingHall. His body, too, seemed as natural and poised as it should be. Though he didn't remind her driver that the salon was launching today.

Holm must get over his inverse pride. She understood that he refused to trade on his FirstFamily name, wanted his work to speak for itself, for his clientele to come from excellent word-of-mouth. Still, he hadn't said anything, not even a subtle hint, that he was *the* Holm-former-Holly. She'd had to push him to put a single announcement of the startup of his training salle in the newssheets.

Naturally, he couldn't use his former name, Holly, but he'd originally planned on calling the salon The Green Man, a direct reflection of The Green Knight Fencing and Fighting Salon in Druida City run by Holm's G'Uncle Tab Holly. *Tab* hadn't disowned Holm and would have approved of the name. But Holm had switched to "Holm's Training Studio" out of sheer embarrassment. He'd said The Green Man sounded pretentious.

Now they'd arrived at the HealingHall. He exited and held the door for her and the cats. To keep the Fams out of his way, Lark would be taking them with her today, and they followed her happily out of the glider and shot toward the Healing Grove behind the Hall.

Holm swung her into his arms and their golden HeartMate bond wound them close. All she sensed was him, his hard, strong body, his need for her, emotional as well as physical. That met her own needs for him. An honorable man she could always rely on. So sexy.

His scent wrapped around her and she dimly noted it had changed when mixed with the air of Gael City. Then she didn't think at all, only felt his lips on hers, tasting then penetrating, and she gave back the kiss.

One last taste for both of them, and they broke apart. Lark noted their female driver looking envious. "HeartMates," the woman murmured, shaking her head.

"Oh, yeah," Holm said, then lifted Lark's hand to press a tingling kiss in her palm, fold her fingers over the slight dampness. "A kiss for luck."

"Looks like some damn good luck." The driver glanced at Lark.

"Not for her," Holm said with a devastating smile. "For me."

That got him a long stare.

"You will be fabulous," Lark stated, sending positive energy that *should* diminish his doubts. If he let her words into his stubborn head and heart.

She turned to her driver. "Please take Holm to his place of business which will be opening in a septhour, Holm's Training Studio, 300 Caer Street."

"Sure thing!" The woman beamed and punched him on

the shoulder with congratulations and an airy statement that she'd drop by sometime.

And as Lark watched the glider slip away, Holm casual in the back, she recalled that he'd spent many years training in The Green Knight. He'd probably realized this would be more familiar to him than anything else, lately, including having a regular lover and HeartMate.

He must have missed the work, as she would have miss hers.

Absolutely, he'd be fine. She'd only check their link every few minutes or so.

When the emergency alarm sounded, Lark ran to the Hall, focused on her own work.

WORKBELL RANG AND THE STUDIO OPENED FOR BUSINESS. Holm stood, feet braced, on the polished wooden floor of his new fencing and fighting salon, awaiting students. He swallowed hard, hoping people would respond to his simple announcement in the newssheet.

Now, he waited. He'd opened the doors separating the main training room from the entryway, and propped open the outer door to the street, too. He'd wanted to stand near the outer door and welcome people in, but though that felt right to his notion of hospitality, it also felt desperate to be a success.

No Holly — hell, Apple — should ever be desperate under such ... commonplace circumstances as opening a business. Unexpectedly launched into space to circle the planet then fall back down into untracked mountains, yes. Sinking in quicksand and dying, yes. Not standing alone in a room and looking at the huge block of sunlight stream through the open outside door and waiting for students.

He'd placed a sidebar at one end of the entry room and stocked it with caff and cocoa and a pile of freshly baked pastries. Holm waved a hand and sent delicious smells wafting out the door.

What if no one came?

That would be a blow to his minuscule pride indeed. He'd been considered the second most skilled fighter in the whole world, after his father, FirstFamily GreatLord T'Holly. Hopefully his reputation drew clients.

He had the skills and knowledge to train others, he just didn't know if he had the talent to teach. That took different kinds of abilities, like patience and understanding. Ah, he'd work on those aspects of himself to bring the best to his clients.

If students came to Holm's Training Studio. And if students didn't appear, he'd be humiliated as well as pretty battered. His shaky sense of a new self would explode again.

What would he do if the fighting studio didn't work? He didn't know. He had few other skills.

"Ahem," a man coughed, pulling Holm from his thoughts. When he looked up, the middle-aged guy faded back, nearly stumbled. Holm stopped himself from smiling in relief, that would look bad, as if he laughed at the guy's lurch.

"Greetyou, Sir." Holm bowed and prowled toward the atrium. "Welcome to my studio. Would you like caff or cocoa?" He gestured to the set-up.

The tall and gangly man who didn't move well, didn't seem well-seated in his body, eyed the drink and pastries. "Better not. I'm, uh, here for a lesson and probably best to eat afterward?"

"Indeed," Holm said. At The Green Knight Fencing and Fighting Salon one of his cuzes who staffed the reception desk would step forward and get all sorts of particulars, schedule a training course, set up sessions, whatever. From the man's nerves, Holm didn't think he dared activate a simple calendarsphere.

He held out his forearm to clasp. "Welcome, again. I'm Holm ... Apple and I offer hand-to-hand fighting training that will help you with your balance, as well as weapons training. That is, knife, dagger, main gauche, short sword and rapier, broadsword and others of that like, as well as blazer pistols."

The man paused in his step to clasp Holm's arm, swallowed, then narrow fingers curved softly around Holm's arm and the man withdrew. Holm raised his brows.

"Oh, ah, Allspice. That is, newly GraceLord Allspice. Pime. Pime Allspice."

"Greetyou, GraceLord."

"Greetyou, GrandSir Apple."

No one had ever called Holm that, the title of a younger son of a FirstFamily. Never. And now he realized his friends in Druida hadn't addressed him by any sort of a title at all after his disinheritance and before he and Lark moved here. Some new pang and assault to his sense of self to cope with every day. Tiresome.

The man walked from the entry chamber into the large room now graced with huge mats in the center and others rolled up against the walls to use as necessary or for, Holm hoped, seating for observers. Pime Allspice stared around as if he'd never seen a physical training area.

Holm let him gaze his fill, as he scanned the man himself. Didn't move well, beginning student, but limber and good enough body, Holm sensed potential.

When GraceLord Allspice met his eyes, he smiled and Holm became aware that the shy smile didn't quite match the studious — and sharp — gaze. "I work with T'Ash. I'm a merchant specializing in gemstones."

Holm's good friend T'Ash had sent the man. Holm could only hope it wasn't part of a sale or bargain between the two.

No. Do not take insult that this might be a pity student. Put that out of his mind, and deal with the man as-is. "My first question is what you hope to get out of a course of training with me?"

A flush colored the man's face and freckles stood out. "As you may have noticed, I'm not a graceful guy. I'd like to, uh, get better balance. Move well." He flung out a hand, barely missed grazing his knuckles on the wall. "Like you."

Holm nodded. "This we can work on, bringing you to be more physically balanced. How are you at meditation, and emotional balance and grounding?"

This time Allspice's smile flashed quick and sincere. "I'm good there, and mentally, too."

"Excellent." Holm himself had finally become grounded himself in the last couple of months. Didn't want to think of his past life. Nothing hurtful to distract him from the needs of his pupil.

Allspice cleared his throat. "Also, my oldest daughter has found her HeartMate and we will be having an elaborate wedding ritual, including paired Earthan dancing. This training will help me with dancing?"

"Absolutely, but perhaps you should simply consider working with a dancing master."

The man stiffened as if Holm had insulted his manhood.

"I've worked with many dancers," Holm said. "They're fine athletes."

"I want to learn to *fight*!" Allspice took a deep breath. "Gael City isn't the great town with big criminal problems that Druida City is, but I've had tough elements come into my store and try and threaten me. I've reported them to the guards, but I am not ... I am not a man who inspires fear in others."

"So you'll also need to have a *presence*," Holm said. He stood straight, thought of himself as he'd been as the arrogant

HollyHeir, *knew* that he could fight and win against any man in this city.

"Zow. Yes, like that! A *presence* so I won't be seen as an easy person to be intimidated. I'm not, but I need the—"

"Attitude," Holm said, releasing into a more casual manner. He made a show of scanning the man's body. "I think we'll have no problem with meeting your goals. I believe you have potential, you just have to be trained into it. You could make a very good hand-to-hand fighter."

"Thanks!" Excitement lit within the man. Holm had done that, and it felt satisfying. In the first minutes he'd met with the man, Holm had inspired his new student.

"How long of a course do you wish to sign up for?" Holm asked.

"As long as it takes." Allspice set his chin.

"I think you'll find as we go along, that you will like the movement of your body, the exercise, the discipline, and want to make it a part of your lifestyle. Not only will I be offering lessons, but I will be opening the studio as an athletic club and offering such things as group melee nights, ah, et cetera. There will be membership levels."

"Sounds really good. Can we start right away? I brought some casual clothes, but I'll need some standard training robes. And belts, I want to win colored belts as I advance." More anticipation from the GraceLord.

"That will happen," Holm assured him. Mostly the guy had energy he needed to smooth out, and physical training would certainly do that.

After Allspice went into the Men's Dressing Room, Holm crossed to the front door and closed it, put a keep-warm spell on the caff and cocoa, and placed the pastries in a special glass no-time, an appliance that would keep the food as fresh and the same temperature as it went in.

It had been a long, long time since he'd been a raw beginner, beyond his own memory, but occasionally he'd seen G'Uncle Tab give a lesson or two to newcomers. And Holm *had* listened when his younger brother, Tinne, who was to have inherited The Green Knight Fencing and Fighting Salon, was being instructed by Tab in how to train ...

Then Allspice came back ... in ragged clothes Holm would never be seen wearing, even within his own home. The GraceLord was sensitive to his physical appearance, and with being thought of as manly, but cared nothing about the statement his clothes made. He also knew his job well, or T'Ash wouldn't work with him, and Allspice had the pride and confidence of a successful man. Now Holm had to learn that kind of self-made confidence, too.

That he had such an interesting man as his first pupil pleased Holm.

He took the GraceLord back to his early childhood grove study physical exercises and basic defense, then worked up to more impressive moves. By the time they finished a septhour and a half lesson, one hundred five minutes, Allspice could work through a simple drill pattern with enough proficiency that Holm told him he could practice it on his own with few mistakes.

After the lesson he and Allspice talked in the atrium. The GraceLord authorized payment to Holm and signed up for twice weekly private evening sessions for three months. A good start, but Holm had thought he'd have a whole class by now ...

Then loud and raucous young male voices projected into the building from outside the front door Holm had opened.

"Food!" One shouted.

A slap. "Not before we test the mighty Holm *Apple*!" sneered another.

TENSION BUILT BETWEEN HOLM'S SHOULDERS. HE ROLLED it out.

When the owners of the voices swaggered into the entryway, Holm saw a group of six expensively dressed and groomed teenagers — perhaps new adults at seventeen. Surviving SecondPassage and becoming an adult tended to put an arrogant step in a young man's stride.

Holm relaxed. Just. Easy.

He smiled with casual good humor. "Greetyou," he bowed, "boys."

Snarling and scowls. The largest, but not the oldest, strode forward, chin jutting and chest out. "We're here to see your studio and if you can teach us anything."

Holm could teach him manners, for sure. Instead he raised a brow and said, "Do you have names, or do you prefer to be anonymous?"

With superior attitudes, all of the youngsters stated their names and titles. All Heirs to a noble House, as Holm once had been. At a couple of the introductions, Allspice's face went immobile and he faded back against the wall. The merchant had recently gained his noble title, a GraceLord, and Holm recognized higher ranked boys than Allspice and those from longer established Families. Both of which counted in Celtan society.

"Greetyou." Holm inclined his head. "I'm honored you grace my studio." Only Allspice seemed to hear the slight sarcasm. That one smiled.

"And how much training do you have?" Holm asked the teens ranged in front of him.

"Enough to beat you, handily," said the highest ranked one, a GrandHouse Heir of the oldest Family, one whose main Residence was located in Druida City with a secondary estate here in Gael City. Holm knew of the young man's father, the consort of the GrandLady holding the title, but that GrandLord didn't patronize The Green Knight in the capital city. Holm couldn't figure where the youngster got his training.

And they would beat him? Handily? Holm suppressed a laugh. He waved to the dressing rooms. "Do you care to change into fighting robes?" If they did, he'd be able to gauge each's skill by his belt. He already knew none of them had a natural Flair — psi power — for fighting, like all of the Hollys.

He noticed GraceLord Allspice staying and watching, lines in his forehead as if worried. Holm winked at him and the man calmed and leaned against the wall.

"Nah," said the largest young noble. "We won't be sweating or harming our clothes."

The most elegant took the time to brush a tiny lint speck from his cloth trous.

So be it.

"All right," Holm said. "Sounds like you prefer a melee, with the rules as stated in The Green Knight Fencing and Fighting Salon?" He paused, "And followed by other studios, training halls and salles of note."

The teens shrugged up and down their line. "Yeah, sure," said the largest. With a Word his shoes fell from his feet and he walked into the center of the training room in his non-slip liners, stretching as he went. All the others followed. Holm noted two didn't activate spells on their liners to keep traction. The new mats weren't as slick as the polished wooden floor, but a guy could certainly misstep and slip.

Holm had coated his bare feet with general fighting and anti-injury spells developed by the Holly Family.

First he'd take the two youngsters foolish enough *not* to coat their liners properly. Three of them stood around, not warming up. He anticipated all of the teens would make beginner mistakes. Or what would be considered beginner mistakes by his G'Uncle Tab and the rest of the Hollys.

Strolling out on the floor and shaking out his limbs, Holm stood before the semi-circle of young men. He didn't need to warm up since he'd been active the last septhour. With a glance at Allspice, he said, "GraceLord Allspice, would you do us the honor of timing us for a ten-minute free-for-all-melee-match and giving us the start notification?"

"Certainly," Allspice said, touching his wrist timer. He looked at Holm, who winked.

"Go!" Allspice said.

Two rushed Holm, he pivoted, blocked their hand blows, grabbed one and spun him into the other, pushed them both at the next two charging toward him. All went down, one tumbled right off the far edge of the mat — out of the fight.

Five.

Holm waited and watched the upright two dance forward with poor footwork. He hopped forward, swept out a leg and caught them both. *They* went down, one with a harsh, "*Ooof*," the other with a long riiipp of costly fabric. "My trous!" yelled the most fashionably dressed. Yes, he'd split the crotch seam in the back, showing an ass covered in a pale blue breech-clout. Holm grinned.

The young man flushed, hurried away to the side of the room, off the mat, clapped his hands to his butt and began muttering a mending spell.

Four.

Who all sped at Holm at once. He moved toward them, fighting left to right, blocking kicks or blows, sending them off the mat and out of the fight, then stood solitary in the middle of the room, not even breathing hard.

"Two minutes gone," GraceLord Allspice said with a satisfied lilt.

One stayed on the floor groaning, but the rest, with the

energy of youth, hopped to their feet and stood on the far side of the room, looking angry and dazed and confused.

Holm clapped his hands sharply, pointed to the space in front of him. "You new adults, come here and make your formal bows to me."

Slowly, more from their spinning wits than any reluctance, Holm thought, the young men walked to the center of the room and lined up before them. They bowed in a ragged line, but made proper bows to him as Master.

Holm studied them. "If any of you have problems with training with me, leave now. I don't need to teach those who don't respect me, particularly since I've demonstrated my skills to you."

The biggest, most truculent said, "I'm staying."

"Master," Holm corrected.

"I'm staying, Master."

Holm scanned the line, thought more than peer pressure kept them together and here. Curiosity, an ambition to win against him someday. That might happen, years from now. Meanwhile he'd given them goals, as individuals and as a group.

Then he bowed in return, flicked a hand at the dressing rooms, "Clean up. Dismissed."

The teens galloped into the men's dressing room to shower — and compare bruises, and brag. Holm went over to where Allspice stood.

"That ... that ..." Allspice shook his head. "That was an education. Worth the gilt I already paid, for sure." He held out his arm in greeting-goodbyeing and Holm clasped it after a quick Banish Sweat spell. This time the GraceLord's grip revealed the underlying firm confidence of the man.

"Papa?" called an even younger voice than the new adults, this one female.

"Coming, Dica," Allspice replied and gangled toward the

atrium. Still, to Holm's eye, the GraceLord already moved better. Holm would settle that always-too-cerebral man into his body.

"You said to meet you here and I came and have been waiting and waiting!"

Holm glanced at the man who gave him a lopsided smile. "Our part-time nanny would have dropped Dica off about five minutes ago. I'm very late in taking her to GroveStudy and arriving at my own shop, but some things are worth changing plans for."

Holm smiled and a spurt of satisfaction rushed through him. He'd pleased GraceLord Allspice, who'd tell all his friends about Holm's studio.

Allspice greeted and kissed his daughter who sat on a chair against the wall, a wide-eyed child of about five delicately munching on an almond pastry, then the man went over to pour himself a caff.

Holm crossed to where the girl sat on a gold-painted, tapestry-cushioned chair only a female would choose, and squatted before her and held out his hand. "Greetyou, I'm Holm Apple." And for the first time ever, it was easy saying those words. Because the child would never have heard of him before, probably never heard of the Hollys, and would judge him only on what she saw and heard and how they interacted.

She took one hand away from the large pastry, looked at cinnamon and powdered sweet on her fingers and said a spellword to clean them, then held out her free hand to him.

He kissed her small fingers and she giggled, high and delightfully. After he let her hand go, she immediately went back to eating, and Holm said, "You know, your father is training with me to learn to move better. To dance better," he amended.

Dica swallowed and announced, "Papa's a GraceLord now.

He tested and he passed, like in grove study, and we are all nobles. Me, too!"

Holm nodded. "That's an achievement."

She put the last, too big bite, into her mouth, chewed and swallowed, cleansed her hands with a spell couplet and jumped down from the chair. "I can dance!" She whirled, then marched, then stepped a partial pattern of a formal dance, and finally hopped up and down waving her arms.

"Very nice," Holm said. "I can dance, too." He did the same pattern of the formal dance, suppressing memories of his old life, then smoothly transitioned into a simple fighting kata.

"Oooh!" Dica gasped, put her hands over her mouth, dropped them and said, "Can I learn that?"

Holm noticed Allspice giving him the beady eye of a man getting hustled. Holm rolled a shoulder. "She's not too young to start training."

"Hmmph."

A roaring group of young men exited the dressing room into the large training room behind Holm and Allspice. There came an, "Oof, watch it, clumsy!" and a body hitting the mat, rolling to his feet and stomping after his friends, then "You watch it, stupid!" Shoving.

Holm didn't see the action but could predict it accurately enough, and he'd heard sounds like that all his life.

Allspice scooped his child into his arms. Holm tucked his thumbs into his maroon and sky blue belt — the highest color and level a fighter could wear — it might not be Holly green, but he'd won the right to wear the belt, and would do so. He smiled at the GraceLord.

"Training is good for defending herself, too," Allspice said gruffly.

"Or just avoiding pushy-shovey."

"Handling it easily." Allspice nodded. "I'll consider it."

Holm rocked back on his heels, met Dica's gaze. "You could bring your friends, I could start a Young Beginners group." He'd have to tap his G'Uncle Tab for advice, but by the time Holm set up the class, he'd know what to do.

With narrowed eyes, Allspice said slowly, "Training here would also mark my change in status from Commoner to GraceLord." His gaze flicked to the doorway to the large chamber where Holm sensed the young men standing.

"Duels and feuds aren't common here in Gael City but a man holding a title must be able to defend himself." Holm's voice went flat despite his struggle to pretend to be unaffected by recent events.

"That is so." The GraceLord stood straighter, prouder. "There are expectations of what a GraceLord is and can do."

"I'm a GraceMistrys," Dica enthused. "GraceMistrys Dica Allspice."

"Yes, absolutely," Holm said, and bowed to her.

Allspice set his girl down and took her hand, bowed to Holm with the correct inclination of his torso for Holm's status. "We'll think on it."

"I want to be the only one studying," Dica stated. "Not my sister. She doesn't get to come here and learn to dance and avoid pushy-shovey."

"She must be busy with her HeartMate and arranging her marriage," Holm said. He and his HeartMate hadn't had a formal ritual ... yet. Something to think of, but the very thought of Lark eased emotional aches.

"That's right," GraceLord Allspice said.

The young men hovered around the threshold between the training room and the atrium, several casting glances at the sidebar and drinks and pastries.

Setting his hands on his hips, Holm swung on his heel to snag the gazes of the teens as well as Allspice. "What you all must know is that the final status in this studio depends upon one's fighting ability, not one's outside rank." A couple of the young men were Heirs to a GrandHouse, a higher level of nobility than Allspice's new GraceLord title.

"And because you are the teacher, you know the most!" Dica said.

"That's right," Holm stated. He rolled his shoulders again and knew everyone in the building now understood that he could take them all, and all at once.

"Come along, Dica, we are late for our daily activities," Allspice said.

"Yes, Papa." She glanced over her shoulder. "Merry meet, Holm Apple. That's the proper goodbye, now, 'Merry Meet' and you have to say—"

"Merry part," Holm repeated the ingrained words, bowed to her as her station allowed.

"And merry meet again!" she caroled, then traipsed with her father outside to the sidewalk and to the north.

Holm waved GraceLord Allspice and his daughter off, well-pleased that he'd gotten their business. The GraceLord would tell his merchant friends of Holm. More, when he began moving better, others would recognize good training and come.

The most skilled, but not the largest, young man paced forward. "I was wrong in thinking I could best you at fighting. My apologies," he said.

"Accepted," Holm said. "It takes a strong man to apologize for his mistakes." Holm's father, T'Holly, couldn't manage that, disinherited Holm instead.

The youth relaxed, smiled. "Thank you. I would like to sign up for an intensive course for the full year, and the highest level of membership to the studio athletic club."

"Fine." Now Holm conjured the business calendar sphere he'd prepared the day before, and they worked out the details.

Each one came forward to apologize for their hubris, either in clear words or a grumble, and set up instruction. Holm quoted the young men the price for a yearly course and membership to the salon, and not one of them blinked at the cost. As he would not have two months before. He'd always been able to buy any item, any service, he wanted at the moment he wanted.

After the young men tromped out of the building, still loudly discussing the quick melee, the studio fell quiet.

Holm could not recall when The Green Knight Fencing and Fighting Salon had ever been quiet. For the first few minutes he busied himself with refreshing the drinks, and adding tubes of fruit juice, and revealing hearty sandwiches in the glass no-time.

When the studio remained empty, he made notes about his new students — seven — and the fighting levels the teenagers stated they'd attained. He would test them all, and since they liked being in a group, he'd plan more melees for them.

As for Dica Allspice, Holm sensed that her father would enroll her in a young beginners class. Holm would definitely ask his G'Uncle Tab for a class syllabus.

His G'Uncle Tab and Holm's brother Tinne and his wife supported him. Of his immediate Family and good friends, only Holm's parents shunned him. Bad enough.

He couldn't even put on standard music that played through the day, commissioned by The Green Knight. Because his Mama had written the tunes and just hearing them hurt.

The outer door swung open and a middle-aged noble lady and her grown son entered, and Holm picked up one more student, the son. Men would come first, he understood, since Celtan males remained larger and stronger than women, more aggressive.

The rest of the day people dribbled in and out, mostly looking around or consulting with him, four signing up for a few months of classes.

Holm stayed two septhours after WorkEnd Bell to enable those with regular hours—middle class and merchant class—to drop by. He hadn't planned a fancy reception for folk to stop in and look around, and maybe that had been a mistake, but he felt better projecting a business-like image than a social club that offered training. His studio placed the social club factor strongly in a secondary position.

G'Uncle Tab's The Green Knight Fencing and Fighting Salon, a salle operating for over two centuries, was seen as that, a place where people of a certain social class congregated as well as a teaching center. Holm didn't think he could aspire to that, yet. In fact, he continued to fumble with his social standing and interactions. He'd managed fine today, in his studio, with business and fighting, but a reception that needed fine conversational slipping between social and business was beyond him at the moment.

The evening brought him three more pupils, some referencing Allspice and the young men ... and eight full scry inquiries and appointments for the next day by the young men's relatives, all of whom pre-paid for individual consultations and a lesson.

So by the time Holm's HeartMate, Lark, and the two cats sauntered into his place of business at MidEvening Bell, he'd booked a full day.

"The rule for Fams are the same here as in The Green Knight." Holm frowned down at the young cats.

They stared around as if they hadn't been in the rooms before, sniffing the smells of the people who'd come and gone and left their scents, particularly sweat-odors.

"You will repeat the rule back to me, please," Holm insisted.

His own FamCat, Meserve, looked up at him with wide eyes and lifted the top of his muzzle in a sharp kitten-smile, but said nothing. He snapped a paw at his thinner brother. *You say the rule, first!* Meserve insisted. *This is My place and My FamMan, and You are the guest!* Holm got the idea that Phyll had treated his brother as a "guest" in Gael City HealingHall, a secondary position Meserve hadn't liked.

Phyll grumbled until Lark picked him up, and held him in front of Holm, saying, "You must repeat the Fam rule in this studio for my HeartMate."

Fams have to stay off the main floor of the fighting room, off the mats and behind the lines, Phyll muttered mentally.

"Yes," Holm and his beloved said in unison. "And you, Meserve?" Holm prompted.

Fams must stay off of the main floor of the fighting room, off the mats and behind the lines, Meserve mimicked his brother. Then sent at glance at Phyll. *And if a Fam breaks the rule, he must leave and can NEVER come back. And *I* can go into and out of and into the office whenever I want, and YOU can't. YOU must ask permission.*

Lark choked on a laugh, then as the young cats tumbled away and played hide-and-seek among the rolled mats, she asked, "How did it go?"

"Fairly well. Not quite good enough to keep the business going for more than six months, even at the low end of my budget, but ... I have clients."

She laughed, stepped up and hugged him again. "Of course you do. And six months breathing room, right now."

"I suppose."

"We will celebrate, I have reservations at the Brigantia on the river." She tilted her head as if listening to the shrieks of their Fams. "They have an outdoor area for Fams."

"I'm impressed."

"So you should be, it's the best restaurant in Gael City. Good, healthy food."

Holm grunted. Lark leaned in and kissed him, drew back a bit and swept her tongue over her lips. "Mmm, taste of HeartMate."

Just her throaty voice had him considering other uses of a nearby mat, but she stepped back and waved a hand. "You go take a waterfall and I will close down the place."

"All right."

"More than all right, we are fabulous. Both apart and together."

That wouldn't stop her from lancing his wounds.

As he strode to the Men's Dressing Room, his mind focused on business again. "I have a full day tomorrow, Playday, the first day of the weekend. I hadn't thought of it before, but the three weekend days might be my busiest days. I should stay open."

Before he ducked into the room, Lark hurried up and placed a hand on his biceps. "I won't let you overwork yourself!"

He grinned. "That's what you think. You overwork *yourself*." But he gave a decisive nod. "For the first few months I think I'll have to put a lot of time into this place." Even to himself, he sounded cheerful.

Looking forward to a *good* future of sharing his skills, contributing to his Family, if not supporting them.

THE YOUNG FAMCATS TELEPORTED HOME BEFORE LARK AND Holm finished dessert. Though the walk from the river took some time, the balmy summer night and the interesting new environs of a slower-paced town and nearly wild green space gave them both surcease for a busy day.

She kept an eye on Holm and their HeartBond wide open for any smudges.

Animated and enthusiastic, Holm told her of his students, and as she glanced at his profile in the sunset she realized at a visceral level that he'd changed, wasn't the man he'd been before the Hawthorn-Holly feud.

He'd never be that man again.

Even now she didn't think he'd ever have become so unforgiving as the current T'Holly. For one thing, Holm's composer Mama raised him with music and creativity and beauty. For another, he'd experienced the nearly inconceivable ordeal of being shot into space in a starship escape pod, landing far north of Druida City, and managing to trek with his brother all the way back.

He hadn't spoken of that experience to her, and she thought it might only dribble out of him during the rest of their lives. Since she believed he'd worked through any emotional issues the tribulation had caused, she wouldn't prod him about them. But she would continue to reveal and help him cleanse his current distress and welcome the future with little thought of the past.

Stopping on the top of a high arch of a bridge over a river, she tugged at him to pause, too. He glanced down at her with a quizzical expression.

"You will never be as intransigent as your father," she said.

He blinked, his eyes shuttered. When she sent her continuing stream of love to him, he pulled her close, then turned with her and they watched the river burble by, leaves and twigs carried along in a rush.

"That is probably true," he said.

"You've had a harder life, as well as a more difficult time in claiming your HeartMate."

He squeezed her waist. "Got her, though."

"I have you, too."

"That is true."

"You are now, and will be, a far different man than if you hadn't been excised from the Holly Family."

She noted the new unsteadiness in his breathing, but continued to spur him to work through his heartaches.

"That's also right. I've changed in two months, drastically." He sounded bitter. She ignored that. He paused. "And though you've been very supportive in my time of trial," his mouth twisted, but he went on, "you won't hesitate to inform me when you think I'm going wrong."

She leaned her head on his arm. "I love you, unconditionally, but I want a whole and happier you." But she knew he'd referenced his mother. "And, yes, I will let you know if you falter in any treatment of our children."

He flinched. "We'll have children."

"I have no reproductive problems, nor do you. Your parents engendered two children, and so did mine. We should be able to count on two, also."

"Not ready," he mumbled.

"The environment of our beloved planet has limited human expansion through sterility and sickness. I'm sure by the time the Lady and Lord gifts us with a child, you'll be ready." She felt ready at any time, but didn't believe she'd quicken soon.

Before she could stop herself, as she had so many times before, she said, "Your mother was wrong to stand by and let your father disinherit you."

"My Mama—"

"Is wrong." She sucked in a breath, let it out, but he already disentangled himself and moved away. Not quite loping down the steep bridge. She envied him his sure-footedness. When she caught up with him, she grabbed his hand. He didn't pull away, but he didn't look at her, either.

And she *felt* his anger at his parents. "I know you've worked on ridding yourself of anger at your parents—"

"Yes. And it's returned. Perhaps because *you're* angry at my parents, too."

"Yes, something to work through, together." She let a smile twitch on and off her lips. "But I have an upside that I don't dislike my father nearly as much as I did." Her turn to pause. "And I grieve that my brother died when we were estranged and I was angry at him."

Holm grunted and she felt the quick pain that shafted through him at the thought of such an event. "All right, you've got a point."

They walked fast, both of them expending the energy of their anger. One way of handling it, she understood. Activity first for Holm, then meditation and contemplation, and finally the tremors of emotions wracking him. She rarely saw that particular stage, unless she prompted it like a few evenings before.

She couldn't help thinking about the mother he loved, and how she'd chosen to stand with her husband and allow the disinheritance of her son.

Lark would never let that happen, and she'd have to work on her own anger at his parents at hurting her HeartMate. Maybe she'd try Holm's process.

She managed to keep pace with him and not lose her breath ... noted when the anger burned away, and the tarnish on his self-confidence had diminished. Still, the smear lingered.

And she assured herself that the gift she'd ordered for him would shrink his self-doubt further.

THE NEXT MORNING, HOLM ATE LIGHTLY AND KISSED HIS beloved Lark before he left, holding her, sinking into the kiss for support and comfort more than lust. He muttered, "This second day of my business being open is as daunting as the first. Even though I have a full schedule and think more people will come since it's the weekend. I might be able to put together a few on-the-spot melees. Fun for all."

"If you say so."

"When do you think this, ah, apprehension at going into my work might stop?"

"When do you?" She'd sent the question right back at him. Firstly, when he could support himself and her and their kittens and Clam, their household. Which he didn't say aloud.

Then he seriously considered the question. "Maybe, if I ever get enough students to hold the business together for a full year ..." He knew his budget down to the last item now, and the golden figure that would mean success ...

"You'll do it," she murmured, hugged him tighter. They stayed together, embracing and rocking, until Meserve whined, *It's time to teleport to MY studio!*

Lark laughed and released him, stepped back, but trailed her fingers down his cheek. "I'm working today until standard WorkEnd Bell at the HealingHall to study how it runs over the weekend, but I'll come over to your place this evening and bring supper."

"I still have some sandwiches in the no-time." He paused, considered whether mature men might want to snack on those during the morning and decided they would. He'd have to check the inventory of the no-time and restock it.

And though he'd mostly signed up boys and men as students, he should consider including pretty and delicate pastries that might tempt women. Maybe he should buy a larger glass-fronted no-time, especially if Dica Allspice and other children came to train. Lark would be glad to tell him what to keep for young and growing bodies.

She pecked a quick kiss on his cheek. "Should I bring dinner?"

"Yes, I'll take you up on your offer, my Lark, thank you."

"And I'll have a surprise gift."

His heart gave a bump. He treasured the gifts he received from her, always wonderful. "Great."

A press of his love's soft lips on his mouth, then she patted his face. "Later."

"Later."

We go now! Meserve projected as he hopped to Holm's padded shoulder. *I will see all the new clients and observe how inferior they are to My FamMan.*

Holm snorted and Lark laughed.

Phyll lifted a leg and began grooming. *I am HealerCat, I will go back to HealingHall today and check on all Our patients.*

Smiling at the sibling rivalry, Holm counted down and teleported into his tiny office in his studio. He'd already memorized the light of the windowless office, as well as the scent, but it would take time for him to know the training room in all its sun and shadows and seasons.

And today he found his rhythm, managed to be a lot like his previous self. He did *not* pretend he interacted with clients in The Green Knight ... that could only lead to heartache and disaster.

His manner must have been congenial enough, because he signed up every one of the pupils who came to him. In the afternoon, the lords related to the teenagers who'd come in the day before also paid for a full-year's membership and the highest level of the social athletic club. Holm only had to deflect a few comments regarding the Hollys and the Apples and his circumstances — through a smile with gritted teeth.

Meserve, of course, enjoyed all the admiration and questions aimed at him, and confirmed this was *his* studio, but he would allow other Fams to visit.

The place was busy enough that he called in a trio of good people from the merchant guard guild to help him with students in the afternoon and evening, and he oversaw everything, moving from group to group ... when groups came and lingered.

His new clients ate all the food he'd stocked, so when Lark arrived with a basket of hot pasta and green sauce, herbed warm bread and fruit for dessert, Holm's stomach rumbled. He stowed the meal in the no-time as he led her into the training room where three groups of students worked

Along the far wall drilled and tumbled an advanced group of men who'd trained together since grove-study and usually met in parks during good weather. They seemed interested in an actual formal training center, but put the notion in Holm's head that he should make an outdoor area in the overgrown grassyard behind the building to keep them coming. More gilt to spend.

A few beginners practiced settling into their balance off to one side. And the young nobles he'd met the day before who came with their fathers had stayed to hang around. Now they occupied half of the mat as they squared off in twos as sparring partners.

Stopping with Lark in the center of the room, Holm studied her. The Healer robes she wore gave her good range of movement, but not as much as fighting robes. "Time for your first lesson," Holm said.

"What are you talking about?"

"All of our women learn to fight," he stated.

"All of your women."

"The women who wed into our Family. And if guys marry my female cuzes, they have to hone their skills, too." He knew his grin held an edge. "The FirstFamily GreatHouse Holly has run to male Heads of the Households for generations."

"Maybe that's part of the problem."

That rocked him back on his heels. "You think?" Actually made him pause. But he could still feel the press of emotions behind his eyes. A lack of control here and now was not possible even with his beloved HeartMate.

"Perhaps you're right," he said roughly.

She stared into his eyes, said, "That's the first time you referred to the Hollys as your Family and your traditions. I'm proud of you."

"They're my former Family."

Her head tilted. "Perhaps you don't have the name anymore, but no one can deny that you have the blood, or the Flair that comes down through the blood."

He grunted, stretched tense muscles. "You stretch, too."

She nodded. "All right."

And she did, very well, and he thought of something else. "How long has it been since the Head of your House, the House of Hawthorn was a female?"

Chuckling, she shook her head, "Too long, I think, also, but we are not them. We're younger, more flexible mentally and emotionally." Her chest rose and fell and she said, "Being able to speak of the Hollys in a near conversational tone, is a big step in our Healing."

"Ah." He slanted her a glance, took her hand and sauntered back to the middle of one pad. "Show me your best defensive moves."

She blinked. He smacked a wet kiss on her lips, murmured to her, "See, you'll grow, too. You won't be the same woman as you were before the feud between our Families."

Her eyes widened. "You're right. Though since I've received my HeartMate and experienced and Healed during the feud, those events changed me, too. As will being the Head of the Gael City HealingHall and living here, living with Clam, two Fams and you." She brushed a kiss over his jaw. "But, yes, through this activity alone, I'll change. I'll change directly because of you. Because I never would have trained for fighting before."

He offered the smile he saved for her, along with a little heat in his eyes and through their bond. "You'll learn better balance and defense ..."

"And personally experience how a body moves and feels in a fight," she responded ruefully.

He angled his head in agreement. "That's right."

She stroked his cheek. "Worth it." Then narrowing her eyes, she said, "I still know more anatomy than you."

"Perhaps."

Holm glanced around the area, and people who'd been watching them, most faces showing approval. He took a couple of paces back. "All right, let's see it."

Appearing flustered, she adjusted her Healing robes, then did an acceptable basic self-defense drill.

Before she turned her flushed face to him, Holm let out a quiet sigh, glad to his marrow that the feud ended.

Then he went up and worked with her quietly for a half-septhour, focusing on her, but aware of most watching his teaching methods. Luckily, he felt as if his G'Uncle Tab looked over his shoulder ... and patience came easily for his lover.

She smelled of all the best herbs when they walked back toward the atrium, her Healing robes having released scent when she sweated. When he sniffed, he figured she might just have more herbs bespelled in her clothes than he. And a couple he didn't recognize as anything except Lark ... or Healer.

With one clap of her hands, she gathered their Fams,

who'd been jumping and rolling with the beginners and their trainer, and said, "I'm using your office scrybowl."

"Right."

He watched her hips move under her long tunic and trous as she entered his office and closed the door.

Then people thronged around him.

The full club of men came up to him and each bought a year's membership in the social club. A few asked about training classes for their wives, who would feel welcome here, in Holm's Training Studio, where they hadn't in the more informal club.

When he'd filtered through them, the remaining three lords attached to yesterday's youngsters quizzed him about Family memberships. Holm calculated quickly and gave them a figure, changed their memberships and said he'd notify the Family when he anticipated scheduling women's classes.

He'd have to hire at least part-time trainers, and definitely the female merchant guard he'd spoken with earlier in the week.

Talk spilled around the room about having sisters and daughters as part of the social club. Like Druida City society various social clubs existed at different levels, but status in this training studio would be based on skill.

Groups split and mixed. Holm announced the studio would close in a septhour and checked on the all groups and trainers that would continue to drill. Then he and Lark went out to the small, cracked concrete square that held a rickety wooden table and benches.

She opened the containers and the scent of the food hit him like it hadn't for weeks, and he blessed the Lord and Lady for a full day of good work and ate his full portion of noodles with green sauce.

So did she.

Guiltily, Holm grabbed another minute or two to enjoy

the day before he stood. Lark followed and with a sweep of her arm, she translocated the dishes, probably back to their house. She kissed him and he felt their HeartBond, love washing from her to him, spreading through his body, relaxing the last of the tension in his muscles lingering from self-doubt. Tomorrow should be better.

THEY WENT BACK INTO THE TRAINING ROOM AND HOLM announced a last melee, figuring it would take less than a quarter septhour, and that his clientele would like knowing he'd stay open past his usual hours.

Lark watched the melee and offered to do quick Healing spells afterward, since she'd spent more time as an administrative head that day. Another boon the clients liked, though Holm made sure everyone knew that particular service would not be standard or often.

He counted those who'd headed into the Men's Dressing Room, and knew who remained.

Then one of the noble heirs who'd left popped back into the room, appearing excited. "FirstLevel Fighter Apple, and FirstLevel Healer Apple, I believe you're wanted out front." He vanished back outside.

"Excellent!" Lark said. “Everything regarding my gift is on time."

Holm allowed Lark to tug him out to the front, leaving training room and entry doors open.

Their FamCats, who'd been gurgling and growling and playing hide-and-seek in the bushes, ran to them.

Is that it? Is he bringing the present? Meserve shouted.

Yes, yes, yes! Phyll answered. *See, it floats beside him.*

Holm turned and stared along the sidewalk. A sturdy man in overalls and a cap marched toward them, carrying a toolbox. The framework of a scaffold on an anti-grav spell accompanied him, and a large wrapped package, also bespelled, floating along.

With narrowed eyes, Holm examined the piece's length, breadth, width, glanced up at the empty spot above the door where he'd planned on having "Holm's Training Studio" painted.

Lark turned to look at the man too, and they stood side by side, their bodies touching. She beamed at the sight of the workman.

He stopped in front of them and inclined his head, "First-Level Healer Lark Apple?" he asked.

"Yes," she said.

The man grunted. "Got a sign here." He translocated a piece of papyrus sticking out of one of his chest pockets to Lark's hands. Holm leaned close to see the writing, but she blocked him.

"Yes, this is right." She handed the order back to him and shimmied in excitement.

With careful efficiency the man set up the scaffolding, mounted it, placed his tool box down and opened it. When all appeared right, he glanced down at the package, flicked his fingers and the wrapping completely vanished.

Holm and Lark gasped and the FamCats squealed as the green slab shone with the polished hues of rich malachite.

Other people stopped on the sidewalk, gathering to watch the workman attach the stone sign above the door. All Holm's remaining clients and his trainers flowed from the building to observe.

At that moment, the workman yelled, and Meserve screeched, hopping back as a little piece of stone from the lower left corner fell away, broken off the main slab of malachite. It hit with a puff of crumbling green dust.

"Lady and Lord!" Lark exclaimed.

"Sorry, missus," the workman said. Lark stared at him, probably due to being addressed in a way she'd never contemplated.

The man teleportation-hopped from the ladder to scoop up the bit, and touch of green dust around it. Staring at them, he said, "We will be glad to re-do the whole piece, and get the sign up tomorrow morning before WorkBell ... or ..."

"Or?" Holm asked.

"We'll just charge you for the engraving, for the work, you get the material free."

Holm had never haggled for anything in his life. He jerked a nod. "You do that. I want this up now."

"Yessir." With a little suction spell he sucked up all the malachite dust on the ground into the hollow of his palm, spit on them and the edge of the stone. He teleported back up to the short scaffold and fit the piece back onto the corner. Then he glued the fractured fragment back onto the larger sign with a tube of stuff he pulled from his overall pockets. Saying a short spell, he buffed the corner. Frowning, he rubbed the cloth over it again, then glanced down at Holm and Lark. "Looks fine to me. Good enough for you?"

The fault in the malachite vanished in a dark grain of green. No one could see it unless closely scrutinizing.

The small FamCats materialized on the workman's shoulders and he jerked, then hunkered into his balance. Holm thought the guy suppressed a swear.

Meserve leaned over to press his nose against the corner of the piece, and sneezed. The workman flinched. *There is a teeny, tiny crack no thicker than my whisker,* he announced. From the way the guy hunched, he heard the FamCat and felt disappointed.

It is fine! Phyll sniffed loudly on the man's far shoulder. *I can't see the crack with My amazing vision at all!*

"All right, then," Holm said. He met the man's gaze and opened his arms, "Come on down, Fams."

They teleported to his shoulders, and the worker heaved a sigh.

"Thank you for your work," Holm said.

"Thank you," Lark said, somewhat stiffly. Holm felt her aura of disappointment that her gift hadn't been perfect.

With another spit on the softleaf and rub on the corner, the man got to the ground, packed up his gear, gave a courteous tug at his hat to them and left.

Holm's friend T'Ash could have mended the stone to the molecular level with a spellword, but he held a FirstFamily title and great Flair. This man made do, as Holm did.

Lark slipped her arm around his waist, and Holm let his breath sift out with pleasure. He had Lark, his HeartMate, his own small family, and this very business.

"Don't focus on the crack," Lark urged. "Did you *read* the sign?"

He hadn't. Craning his neck, he saw the golden flow of lettering, "'The Green Man.' Thank you," he ended gruffly.

Placing her hands on his shoulders, she met his gaze. "You *are* the Green Man, a fighter of renown who people will come to train with." She gestured to the boys and his trainers and a couple of others who'd lingered. "You have a fine reputation."

"Thank you." He glanced around the street. People still watched, students yet remained, the FamCats radiated pride, and words tumbled from him. "My new life."

"Yes!" Lark grinned.

And the sun hit the sign, made it glow, revealing deeper tones and shiny streaks that had been hidden.

He wasn't useless.

He wasn't Holm HollyHeir of Druida City, but Holm Apple of Gael City, but he could still practice his craft, his *Flair*. Be a good man of good character, support himself and be supportive of his family, his Lark and Phyll and Meserve ... and even Clam.

And he — they — wouldn't just survive, but *thrive*.

At that moment, his Calendarsphere buzzed in a brand-new pattern. It had totaled up the gilt he'd made that day, and he'd reached his goal.

Just at the beginning of this week he'd stood in this place and wondered how long it would take him to make a career for himself in Gael City. With his own rep, his skills, and a little help from his friends it had taken ... Two. Days.

His future, here with his Family and these students and trainers who gathered around him, stretched before him like a wondrous road of adventure.

He turned his back on the past, gestured to the sign above and raised his voice. "Welcome, all, to The Green Man Salon!"

He held his HeartMate as his Fam licked his ear, a couple of his new students thumped him on the back and people cheered.

HIDDEN STONE

This story is a prequel to ***Heart Search***, that book featuring Laev T'Hawthorn as the hero and Camellia Darjeeling as the heroine. So if you want to see more of Laev and his hunt for his Family heirlooms and his struggle with his relations, not to mention the black tom and the little calico, please read ***Heart Search***.

And if you prefer to know of Garrett's difficult backstory as the sole survivor of the Iasc sickness and how that makes him vital to the whole planet of Celta, and perhaps see him take the big fall into love, then you should read ***Heart Secret***. Naturally, his band of animal informants are featured, as well as a precocious kitten.I hope to continue with a few more stories of Garrett Primross, Private Eye, as they come to me.

Please know that my primary genre is romance and both ***Heart Search*** and ***Heart Secret*** are sexy books and may not be appropriate for minors.

HIDDEN STONE

Druida City, Celta, 421 Years After Colonization, Spring

Garrett Primross stepped out of the welcome warm spring sunlight and into the shabby building that housed his private investigation firm. He rolled his shoulders to release the tension between them. He'd totaled up his current revenues and knew he could only afford to rent this hanging-on-by-fingernails-to-middle-class location for two more months without a better income.

But he'd find some solid clients, work hard at that.

The smell came first, farm-animal-pungent overlaid with simple cleanser.

Then he saw the big black cat, long hair tangled and scruffy, lying in front of his office door. One of Garrett's animal informants that he called Black Cat Two. A trail of blood droplets led from the back end of the hallway to the cat, along with a couple of bloody pawprints. Black Cat Two's upper haunch showed hair matted with blood, and a crust over a semi-circular cut.

With a sigh, Garrett muttered the unlock spell on his door, pushed it open with his foot. He murmured a coating spell on his tunic, then bent down and scooped up the cat. He was a big man and though the cat was large, too, the body beneath the fur felt skinny.

Thwapping his tail back and forth against Garrett's arm, the cat sniffed and said mentally, *I have a case for you.*

Well-spoken cat, obviously smart enough to become a Familiar Animal Companion bonded with a human.

"I've made it a policy not to work for animals," Garrett replied, setting the cat down on one of his worn client chairs. Seeing scratched hands in his future -- even if he had fast enough fingers to do sleight-of-hand tricks -- Garrett simply grabbed a jar of Healing ointment from his bookcase, opened it and set it by the cat.

Who sneezed. Then lifted his upper muzzle to show his fangs, dipped a paw daintily into the gel-like mixture, hissed at the feel and flexed his claws. As he covered his paw and worked on his injury, his narrowed gaze met Garrett's again. *I have worked for you many and many days! You should do this for Me!*

Garrett had learned early to be hard-hearted with cats. They'd turn everything into an advantage if they could. "You've worked not quite an eightday for me," he corrected, then pointed out, "You got fed. And shelter from the weather with the rest of my band of Irregulars who nose around for me."

Associating with low life cats! Some don't even think in words-for-humans! And, he shuddered, *even must be in the presence of dogs and foxes!*

"Terrible for you," Garrett murmured. He wiped the inside of the jar with a softleaf and put it back.

"Yesss," the cat hissed audibly.

Angling his head, Garrett said, "And I think that I've even given you a pinch of catnip for a good investigative tip on my last case."

Only what I deserved. A pause. *I could use a pinch now, too.*

"For nothing."

For bringing you a new very wealthy client.

"I've had private detective cases for intelligent animals and actual Fams before, and gotten 'paid' with some not-so-valuable stuff."

Another hiss. *Valuable to Us.*

"That's right. Valuable to you, not to me." He gestured to an old and pitted piece of metal on another shelf. Then he squatted down just outside claw range and passed a hand over the cat, muttering a spell to augment the Healing balm. The cat's fur lifted, dried blood and tufts of fur fell away and odor rose.

Garrett waved a hand to initiate an embedded office housekeeping spell. It sifted sluggishly through the room, touching him and the cat. Still, Garrett noted the feline's wound scabbing over, so at least his own Healing spell worked fine.

The cat gave a surprised grunt, his eyes widened and he grinned, but he didn't, of course, thank Garrett.

He retreated behind his desk and sat, staring at the intelligent cat.

After a couple of final licks of his wounded haunch, Black Cat Two sat up in the chair.

Garrett decided to wait for the tom to speak again, a technique that often worked for him. To amuse himself and keep in practice, he rolled a small gilt coin across the knuckles of his hands, watching the cat.

You are not interested in My case! Black Cat Two sounded surprised.

"Nope, and are you telling me that you thought six days of work was sufficient to hire me?"

"Yesss."

"Wrong."

Lifting his muzzle in an elegant motion he must have copied from someone else because Garrett sensed that the cat himself had never been a companion or lived in a house, the feline said slyly, *What if I told you it is a FirstFamily FamCat who would hire Us?*

Yeah, that had Garrett slipping the coin into his palm and focusing on Black Cat Two. "A FirstFamily FamCat," he repeated slowly. The twenty-five FirstFamilies had funded the starships's voyage to Celta and remained the most powerful in wealth, status, and psi power--Flair.

"I don't particularly like nobles. Not much interested in

working for them." The words rang with more truth than Garrett felt comfortable revealing. And, yeah, having rich clients from the highest level of Celtan society might be lucrative, but came with disadvantages.

They'd expect everything done their way, wouldn't they? And for him to follow detailed orders? Not to mention the fact that he'd had to move his private investigation business from Gael City to Druida City because he'd done work for a GrandLord and when Garrett had solved the case and fulfilled the terms of the contract, the noble had stiffed him and smeared his rep, too.

Absolutely had to be more cautious working for any noble than a regular commoner middle-class person who paid their bills on time.

An HONORABLE FirstFamily! the cat assured, as if he'd heard an echo of Garrett's thoughts.

"Like I said, don't trust animal clients, and don't trust nobles."

You need the gilt, the feline pointed out. *Your nip is inferior to what I can get on T'... on the estate.*

"But you don't get it as often from them as me, huh? A feral cat? Particularly since a FamCat lives with this FirstFamily?"

Fams remained rare, and despite himself, Garrett ran down the twenty-five FirstFamilies and what intelligent animal companions they might have. Birch -- none he'd heard, Rowan, Alder, Willow ... the Willows had FamCats for sure ...

We – You -- would make much, much gilt, Black Cat Two tried more persuasion.

A consideration, since he'd moved this business to Druida City less than a year ago and ... scraped by ... If the cat told the truth and Garrett played this right . . . He matched his brown-eyed gaze with the green-gold of the cat's. He'd learned to stare them down.

Ostentatiously lifting a paw and separating his pads to clean them more, Black Cat Two looked away as if to concentrate on his task.

"And you want a cut of this case."

I could negotiate for you.

"No."

The cat huffed.

"But you could introduce me to this *FirstFamily FamCat.*" Garrett curled his lip in disbelief.

Black Cat Two hopped to his feet and glared. *You doubt Me! It is Black Pierre of T'Hawthorn Residence!*

One of the most powerful Families of them all. Very wealthy, the defunct GreatLord had once held the most important position on Celta, Captain of AllCouncils.

Garrett checked any incoming scries. Nothing, no new clients. He'd closed all his cases and been paid. He glanced at Black Cat Two. "Black Pierre, eh?"

Yesss.

Flipping and playing with the coin again, Garrett leaned back in his creaky chair and considered ... and recalled rumors that FirstFamily lords and ladies bought collars ... jeweled collars for their animal companions. Maybe other gems, too. Hadn't he noticed a FamCat with ear studs?

"Does this Black Pierre have gems ... jewels that he might pay for my services?"

Maybe. But the feline in Garrett's client chair looked aside.

With a grunt, Garrett said, "Just how does some FamCat who lives in a FirstFamily intelligent house, a Residence, have any troubles at all?"

Now Black Cat Two met Garrett's eyes. *The housekeeper accused Black Pierre of stealing!*

Yeah, that might diminish a Fam's influence in the Family.

Maybe lose him some prerogatives. Cats were all about status and prerogatives and a comfortable life.

"Your injuries have anything to do with helping Black Pierre?" Garrett asked.

Yesss! Black Cat Two showed gleaming fangs. *It was the pigs.*

❦

AFTER THAT ANNOUNCEMENT, BLACK CAT TWO SHUT UP except to repeat that the T'Hawthorn FamCat would pay well and was expecting them. So Garrett slung the cat around his neck and headed out to the public carrier for the trip into the portion of Druida City called NobleCountry. The trip took less than a seventy-minute Celtan septhour.

To Garrett's surprise, the small greeniron gate in the tall wall running along the lengthy side of T'Hawthorn estate opened for Black Cat Two, who'd told him to call him, simply, Black. Unable to enter through the shieldspells, Garrett lingered outside the grounds. They had to wait for a Hawthorn guard to come and clear him.

While they stood by, a small, plump calico cat bounded over and addressed them.

Hello, Black! Hello, Man With Black. She glanced up at Garrett with such trust in her yellow eyes that he realized she -- and probably the cat with him -- were under a year old. Something he should have noted before.

Black, after you got hurt, I looked all around the pig place and even under the pigs like Black Pierre said, but didn't find anything, she announced.

"Searching pigsties," Garrett muttered. "Sure sounds like a good and a well-paying job to me."

The cats sniffed in unison. Black lifted his nose. *I will go get gilt coins for You from Black Pierre, he has some.*

"That I'll believe when I see it." And Garrett would prefer gems.

I will wait here, the little calico with baby fat said. *Black Pierre doesn't like you much, Black, but He asked You to help.* A slyness entered her gaze and she looked aside. Hiding something, as all cats did all of the time. *Black Pierre doesn't like Me at all. I will stay and this Man will pet Me.* She gave Garrett a winsome look.

He shrugged and hunkered down, but in the back of his mind, the amount of time he'd already spent on this "job," kept ticking by, adding up.

As Black ran from the gate in the direction of the gray and vertical Earthan-like castle in the distance, the pudgy calico traipsed through the shieldspells and thin bars of the gate to rub against Garrett. *You smell like many Cats and dogs and foxes! You smell good!*

"Thank you," he said, and stroked her, scratched her muzzle and around her ears.

She wriggled and purred. *I like being Outside the gate more than Inside. For now.*

"I hear you."

She added, *Black Pierre does not like Me, but Black does.*

"I could see that."

With a side-glance smirk she said, *But pigs do not mind Me. *I* did not get hurt by pigs!*

Garrett snorted a laugh, picked the little cat up and stood and scanned the area. The high stone wall surrounding T'Hawthorn grounds appeared nearly new, the rich Family kept it so well. The greeniron gate also looked new, and the path clear and well-defined with no roots to trip up a foot.

The fragrance of Hawthorn blossoms hit his nose and he knew massive hedgerows of the tree must be planted all over the grounds. Naturally. And this FirstFamily estate covered a significant amount of land, and that would take an equally large amount of gilt to maintain.

Nobles. His lip curled. What could they know about real problems? You had money and status and power, you could take care of anything.

Finally, a young woman dressed in a guard uniform of Hawthorn colors jogged toward them, her face scrunched in a dissatisfied expression. The wind brought her grumble to Garrett, "All this way for a damn feral cat," she muttered. "Nothing but problems from cats, lately."

I want down now. I am the lowest Cat in status, and the guards don't like to see me. The female cat wriggled from his arms, leapt away and slunk into space between bushes that seemed too small for her.

The guard's expression smoothed as she saw Garrett, and she slowed to a walk as she examined him, taking him in head to foot. With her dark hair and purplish eyes, Garrett thought she might be a distant Hawthorn relative who worked for the GreatLord as security.

Just beyond the gate she stopped and nodded to him in acknowledgment.

He bowed with slightly more respect than her rank demanded.

"Your name and business and why you didn't come to the main gate?" she questioned.

"Garrett Primross, Private Investigator." He plucked one of his new holographic cards from a tunic pocket and tried to sound not-too-stupid as he said the next words. "Requested to come here by the FirstFamily T'Hawthorn FamCat, Black Pierre. I was led here by another FamCat, a young long-haired black one."

At least she didn't fall on the ground and roll with laughter as he would have. No doubt she respected her Family and Fam companions more than he.

She reached through the gate and took his card, stepped back to glance at it. Then she tapped his card against her palm, but didn't trigger the embedded images. "I've heard of you," she said, to his surprise. "You're the P.I. who uses animals as informants." She smiled, and it didn't look derogatory.

"That's right. I have a Flair for animal communication."

"Makes sense." Now she rolled her eyes. "Black Pierre, such a demanding FamCat." One last scrutiny of Garrett, and she moved up to the gate. Placing her hand against the shield-spell, she sent energy and murmured spellWords to drop it for him and unlocked the gate, then stood aside for him to walk through.

Against the long wall grew equally long and thick hawthorn hedges. Of course.

Once beyond the greenery, he bowed again, "Thanks."

"You're welcome." She closed and locked the gate behind him, snorting as the calico cat zipped in. "Cats are nothing but nuisances." Then the guardswoman raised the section of shieldspells again. "We'll be notified if you leave the estate by this or other lesser-known entrances, or swim away from the beach into the ocean. And if you enter the Residence, the House will monitor you."

"Got that."

"Please check out at the front gate main entrance when you're finished with your business here." With a wave, she left, loping back to her station.

Follow Me, said the calico who sauntered from the bushes. She led the way up the clear path. *We will go to the kitchen door. Old, fat Black Pierre stays mostly in the warm kitchen now. He was the old lord's FamCat, the one who died, but Black Pierre did not die, too, like some old Fams do. Now Black Pierre prefers to be the chef's Cat.* Her tail waved in punctuation that Garrett didn't quite understand, except that she didn't respect Black Pierre and seemed to think everyone old. He figured most were, compared to her.

They'd rounded a bend in the path, and the ocean that T'Hawthorn land bordered on throbbed into better hearing, when Black Cat Two -- Black -- shot up and dropped a small leather pouch he carried in his mouth down before Garrett. The bag clinked as it hit the ground, and when Garrett opened it, he found eleven medium-sized golden gilt pieces.

"Interesting," he said.

There will be more gilt, Black Pierre says, if you take the case.

"Explain this case to me," Garrett said, weighing the gilt in his hand.

Like I said before, the housekeeper accused Black Pierre of stealing!

"Food?" asked Garrett. Cats stole food all the time. "Treats? Catnip?"

No such thing as stealing those. Food and treats and nip are Ours.

"Uh-huh."

Said Black Pierre stole a Family thing! An important Family treasure!

"Did he?"

Black Pierre gets all He wants all the time. Why would He take some Man thing? If He wanted Man thing, the lord or the chef would have given Black Pierre the Man thing.

"What sort of man thing?" Garrett asked, as they walked through an arch stating "Kitchen Gardens" with a signpost showing multiple arrows: Vegetable, Herbs, Spices, Edible Flowers ...

I don't know. A thing Man uses, not Cats. Stup to say Cat stole, even if one part was shiny and another part could be a bed. Black paused, his tail flicked. *Not a good bed, not like a fat pillow.*

Like any of that made sense. Garrett would be interviewing Black Pierre. Great.

When they got close to the Residence, Black stopped. *I*

have been good. I started to look in the pig place for Man stuff. Then I got You and brought You here and told Black Pierre. I got the gilt pouch and gave to You. Now I get to go rest and tend My hurts!

The calico licked him on the nose. *You told Black Pierre about nothing in the pigs?*

Yes, Black affirmed, and, treading lightly, he passed Garrett. Calico followed him.

Guess neither of them would be introducing Garrett to the former GreatLord T'Hawthorn's FamCat. In his mind the clicking counter of on-the-job minutes continued. He already figured Black Pierre wouldn't want to pay him any more gilt than that in the pouch he'd put in a trous pocket.

A FEW STRIDES LATER, HE REACHED A LARGE FLAGSTONED terrace outside an equally large door that must lead to the kitchens. Though big windows were set in the fortress-like castle wall, metal shutters framed the glass, and Garrett had no doubt they functioned. The shutters would have been necessary when the castle was new, but now the Residence, as an intelligent home, could defend itself.

Lying in the spring sun on the flagstones curled a fat, long-haired but perfectly groomed and shining-furred black cat. Garrett figured that spells also kept the terrace warm.

He picked up a polished dark redwood outdoor chair and placed it close to the cat, and waited. It wouldn't like being looked down on.

Black Pierre stretched and flexed long-clawed paws before opening his yellow eyes and staring at Garrett. Who noted the more-than-usual intelligence in the FamCat's gaze. But then, that cat had been the animal companion of a First-Family GreatLord strong in Flair psi power for ... over a decade.

Garrett thought of the younger black cat's words. "You have a problem you think I can fix?"

"Grrrrrr." Black Pierre sat and his fur ruffled. The upper skin of his muzzle rose, showing good fangs. *I was accused of taking a Family treasure! ME!* His tail thrashed.

"What kind of Family treasure?"

Instead of answering in mental words, the cat formed images and sent them to Garrett's brain. A long oblong item tapered at each end, chased with silver along the sides. A flat rectangular piece of deep purple tinted fine leather with additional pieces of leather on each side. And Garrett still couldn't figure that one out.

I told the new, young Hawthorn lord that I did not take, but no one except Me assured him. No one said they'd taken it. And it remains missing! "Grrrr."

Then, as if rage prodded him, he leapt to a wide windowsill and perched on it in the sunlight. *Then the young lord realized other objects had gone missing. A big mess.* He grumbled in his throat and stared off toward the sea.

"And you didn't take any of the Family treasures."

No! What would I want with them? His muzzle lifted. *I have anything I want.* A sniff. *Including the best food from the best chef on Celta.*

The cat did show a significant bulge around the middle.

"So you didn't take them, yet you remain accused."

"Yessss," Black Pierre vocalized with a long hiss. *Huathe was an honorable man, and I am an honorable Cat. We are an honorable Family!*

"Uh-huh. But no one's speaking up to defend you."

Stup humans. A lift of the muzzle. *They think that blaming a Cat makes everything easy and right. No one must do anything to find the items, the young lord will be satisfied with the explanation.*

"I understand."

Flicking of the tip of cat tail. *He will not. Huathe instilled in Laev great honor.*

Maybe. FirstFamilies were touchy about their honor. And unlike other powerful men, Garrett had never heard that the Hawthorns contracted with people, got work out of them, and refused to pay. Too proud for that, and, yes, too honorable to break their word or contracts.

There might be a FirstFamily noble who'd be dishonorable, Garrett didn't know and hadn't cared to find out, never thinking to associate with them, but not a Hawthorn.

"So there continue to be missing items, including the one you were accused of taking."

Yes.

"And it bothers you that you're accused of stealing. But you still live here with every comfort," Garrett pointed out.

My status is threatened. They would not dare to turn Me out, but they might not let My new FamMan, the Chef, give Me treats ... or buy Earthan catnip grown on the starship for Me. I would have to put up with an inferior nip.

"Terrible," Garrett said.

Yesss. He stood on the windowsill, wide enough to accommodate his bulk, paced back and forth..

I have been a Good FamCat. Always. My honor is besmirched.

Those words pinched at Garrett. "Not good to have a smeared reputation."

No. I will not allow humans to speak ill of ME. He turned his gaze on Garrett. *You will fix.*

"We'll talk," Garrett said, then asked, "What's with the pigs?"

The kittens found a couple of Family items while frolicking in the pigsty. Black Pierre snorted. *Kittens.*

"What kind of valuable items?"

A bit of pretty jewelry shaped like a dragonfly. And at that, Garrett focused on the gleam around Black Pierre's neck. A collar made of lambenthysts, worth a small fortune. Even one of the jewels would pay Garrett well. Squinting, he saw a hole in each ear, too, though the cat didn't wear studs.

"Doesn't sound very important."

Pretty enough it caught the calico kitten's attention. Housekeeper said it is a lovely piece of excellent craftsmanship. At least a half century old.

"All right, I get it, treasured heirloom."

One would think so.

"Which one?" Garrett pounced on the phrase.

The young lord, Laev, Black Pierre sent to Garrett's mind.

"But not the old lord ... Huathe?" Garrett persisted.

The cat radiated insult. *I have been accused of stealing objects!*

All right, dead end there. Garrett winced inwardly, a literal dead end as the lord had passed on. Garrett vaguely recalled he'd died in his mistress's bed. Not a terrible way to go.

Yank his thoughts back to this "case" taking his time, and maybe costing him gilt. "What other items were found in the pigsty?"

A little stuffed goat, much the worse for wear.

"Laev's childhood toy?" Garrett pressed.

Black Pierre licked a paw. *I do not think so, older than him, retrieved from a toy box in the nursery. I do NOT go to the nursery,* the FamCat ended haughtily. *Nothing there of interest to Me.*

"Of course not."

The cat leapt down from the window, began sauntering toward the door. *Time for my treat.*

"Obviously that takes precedence over speaking with me."

Yes. I have told you what needs fixed. Fix it.

"Uh-huh. But before you disappear into the kitchen, what does the Residence have to say about these missing items?" Garrett wasn't sure what all an intelligent house sensed, and what kind of memory it might have, but may as well ask.

Black Pierre glanced over his back at Garrett. *The Residence is quiet on this. It has not spoken to Me, though I have requested information. It does not inform the young lord that I did NOT take the object. I do not know why it is so recalcitrant.* The feline sniffed in contempt. Which is probably why the Residence didn't speak with the FamCat.

They could be trying.

FAMMAN! Black Pierre demanded at the door, then issued a yowl. *Time for My treats!*

The door whisked open, showing a young teen-aged girl with a harried expression. Garrett figured she must be the lowest kitchen maid. Black Pierre strolled inside.

"Greetyou," said a male voice behind Garrett. He stood and turned.

A TALL YOUNG MAN WITH NOBLE-STYLE LONGISH BLACK hair stared at Garrett. As he strode closer, Garrett met his steady violet gaze, the color denoting the Hawthorn Family. Though he dressed in the richest of clothes, he moved with a walk not as arrogant as Garrett expected, not truly the walk of other FirstFamily members he'd seen around and about in the city. Surprising. His face also showed a few lines deeper than a man of approximately thirty should hold.

"Greetyou, Garrett Primross, Private Investigator." T'Hawthorn, the man must be the GreatLord himself, stopped outside longsword point and inclined his torso.

The guardswoman must have told her boss of Garrett's admission to the estate.

Though Garrett had rarely used the formal salutations that nobles preferred, he, like everyone, knew the courtesies. He just hoped they sounded smooth. "Greetyou, GreatLord T'Hawthorn." He bowed, but didn't think it was the proper degree. Fligger. All right, he shouldn't care, but something in the man's gaze and manner engendered reluctant respect. As if the guy *had* weathered significant storm-problems in his life.

Who'd have thought that?

Wait, hadn't there been a duel between the Hawthorns and the Hollys? And anyone going against the warrior Hollys would be bound to lose. And this man *wasn't* the late T'Hawthorn's son. Probably his Son'sSon. So something happened to this new lord's father.

Garrett really should have done some basic research before he'd left his office ... with a cat. But he'd treated the "case" as minor. Somehow it didn't seem as negligible now as he thought.

The man picked up a redwood chair and placed it next to Garrett's, dropped down into it, and Garrett sat, too. With his arms braced on the flat ones of the chair, T'Hawthorn tapped his fingertips together. When he noticed Garrett's gaze focused on his hands, he gave a tired smile and stopped the movement. "My FatherSire's habit."

Going straight to his own largest concern, Garrett said, "Black Pierre feels insulted at being accused of stealing a Hawthorn Family treasure."

A twitch of the lips up from the GreatLord. "Of course he is."

"He informed you that he didn't steal the item?"

"Yes."

"Do you believe him?"

The nobleman sat up straight in the back-slanted chair. "There's no reason for him to lie."

Garrett paused but went with honesty. "I've had significant dealings with cats, and have learned that their reasons for lying don't match humans, that they can lie casually, and take the truth casually."

After huffing a breath, the GreatLord said, "I believe Black Pierre."

"The Fam also stated other Family pieces are missing."

T'Hawthorn's face hardened. "Yes. I'm just beginning to figure out what they are." His violet gaze met Garrett's. "And, yes, I'm fine with hiring you to find the lost heirlooms."

Garrett almost jerked upright himself, but though tension ... and anticipation of a lucrative job ... jerked through him, he kept up a nonchalant attitude. "I can do that."

The only reason to work for a noble was a huge amount of gilt. He drew in a breath. "I'd like a retainer for this particular job."

"Of course." The man frowned. "You anticipate finding the Family treasures and returning them to me?"

"Of course."

"Then you'll need enough gilt to buy items back. Your bank and account?" T'Hawthorn asked.

"Cascara Bank, Garrett Primross, P.I."

"Right." He gestured. "Let's start with fifty-thousand."

Garrett thought he absorbed the shock of that pretty well, though he did straighten and have to clear his throat before he asked, "How many objects -- Family heirlooms -- do you think have gone ... astray?"

The lord's mouth flattened. "I have no idea." Anger lived in his tone.

Garrett cleared his throat. "Have you asked the Residence?"

The younger man stood and Garrett got to his feet, too. T'Hawthorn turned away, his body stiff. His jaw flexed. "The Residence and I are currently undergoing a power struggle."

Raising his brows, Garrett stared at the nobleman. He'd never heard of such a thing. "I can't imagine a GreatLord not controlling a house." He didn't, quite, sneer. And he shouldn't have asked, noble matters that didn't affect his work meant nothing to him.

T'Hawthorn flicked his fingers and began strolling along the shady side of the house, where the lawn yet showed frost. Garrett kept up pace with the lord.

"I could wipe the Residence's current personality, of course, but I am reluctant to do that, since I grew up with it and it's been the same since before my birth."

"Ah," Garrett said, with a greedy urge to ask more and more. None. Of. His. Business.

"But, no, I have not asked the Residence if it knows what has happened to the items." Anger burned in his eyes. "I have no doubt it knows and is not telling me. Perhaps even other members of the Family know what happened to the objects. My FatherSire certainly knew."

Since that guy had been elected to the most powerful position on the planet, Garrett figured so.

Laev's jaw clenched, released. "But none of them are speaking to me."

"The FamCat Black Pierre did."

That had Laev's shoulders relaxing as he snorted. "Because one of the staff accused him of taking something. A break in the silence, or, rather, notice that something was wrong that I didn't know about."

"So the cat might have kept the secret, like the rest of the Family, indefinitely. And you believe he didn't steal the objects."

"That's right. He wouldn't have said anything if his pride hadn't been pricked. And if he thought the item would add to his comfort or his status in any way -- say a priceless tapestry pillow embroidered by one of my ancestors, yes. But I think a writestick and blotter with the Hawthorn coat of arms stamped on the furrabeast leather -- no."

Finally that made sense. "Where was the desk set kept?"

"I'm not sure. I don't think in here, but perhaps." The nobleman shrugged. "I didn't work in this room, but in my own office," he gestured toward a different part of the House. "So I didn't know the leather set," his mouth twisted, "which I liked particularly, was missing. My FatherSire preferred a desk set presented to him by *his* father when he became an adult. Green and gold. I packed the pieces up myself and had them placed in storage in one of the attics."

"All right. And you think most of the Family knows what's going on."

T'Hawthorn hesitated. "Some, yes, I do."

"But they've made no effort to retrieve the treasures."

"Not that I know of." The man shrugged. "They aren't *great* heirlooms. I'd have missed the most valuable and most cherished pieces."

"All right. My first order of business is to conduct some interviews here. Do I have your permission?"

Waving a hand, T'Hawthorn smiled tightly. "Speak to whom you wish. Perhaps someone will tell *you* what they won't reveal to me."

Now this sounded like an easier case than Garrett had anticipated when first speaking with T'Hawthorn. Merely winkling out a secret. From a FirstFamily full of pride and discretion. And members who'd probably look down on Garrett as a commoner more than this GreatLord who'd hired him. Not to mention a sentient Residence who seemed snotty enough not to talk to the new head of the Family.

Garrett would earn his gilt, after all.

THEY STOPPED BY A SIDE DOOR OF THE RESIDENCE AND T'Hawthorn entered. Garrett trailed after him into the flag-stoned hallway. A couple of meters later they turned into a richly carpeted wider corridor, then stopped at a polished and carved door of golden hawthorn planks. *This* must be a real Family antique and heirloom, for sure.

T'Hawthorn pushed open that door with fingertips, trod across stacked Chinju rugs that had Garret's feet sinking into them. The lord hesitated only a moment before moving behind the equally imposing carved desk that must have been used for generations, then settling into a new comfortchair that would conform to his body. He gestured to the two antique chairs facing the desk. Garrett took the one with embroidered jumping goats instead of the more feminine dragonflies. Dragonflies and goats again.

Drawing in a breath, T'Hawthorn projected his voice mentally, as well as speaking loudly. Garrett got the idea his words reverberated throughout the castle. "Garrett Primross, a private investigator, has been hired by me to find the missing Family items. I am authorizing him to speak to whomever he needs to in order that he can discover what happened to those items *and return them*." A pause. "Please do not test me on this, or the individual will find herself or himself on a tour of Hawthorn properties, starting with the small lodge in the north, as of immediately." The echo of his voice died.

The GreatLord shrugged. "That might work." He frowned at Garrett. "I hope you're good."

"I'm very good."

T'Hawthorn tapped the latest model of a scry panel. "T'Reed Bank, transfer fifty thousand gilt from my personal account to Cascara Bank, Garrett Primross Private Investigations's account."

"Yes, T'Hawthorn," stated a deep voice. "Done."

"Thank you," the lord said. "End scry."

Garrett blinked.

"T'Hawthorn Residence, I expect you to answer GentleSir Primross's questions also," the nobleman said.

And that got only silence.

T'Hawthorn met Garrett's eyes and this time his smile was more of a wintry grimace. "Right."

His calendarsphere flicked into existence. "Scry discussion with the saffron farmers in ten minutes." This voice sounded chirpy and cheerful.

The lord inclined his head to Garrett. "If you'll excuse me?"

Garrett stood. "Of course. Who do you think I should speak with first?"

"Our housekeeper, Alma Hawthorn." A line creased between his brows. "She should be in the main sitting room now," and he gave precise directions. Obviously he knew his staff's -- his relatives' -- schedules, but Garrett got the idea that this was something a regular lord might ask of his intelligent house.

When Garrett entered the sitting room, an older, tall and comfortably plump woman rose from a chair. Her lips pursed. "Garrett Primross."

He bowed. "Yes, GreatMistrys Hawthorn," he gave her the honorific she'd expect.

With a short nod, she sat again, but didn't indicate he should. So he crossed over to a floor-to-ceiling window and leaned against the frame. Smiled and said nothing. She sat, spine straight, disapproving expression, hands quiet in her lap and stared at him.

He let the silence stretch until it reached the edge of discomfort, then pretended to be conciliatory, "GreatMistrys Hawthorn, as you just heard, T'Hawthorn --"

"Laev," she corrected with the smallest sniff.

"Laev T'Hawthorn," the most he'd concede to her, "has become aware of some missing Family heirlooms, and requested that I investigate the matter on his behalf to locate the items and return them."

"You are a Primrose?" she interrogated Garrett, ignoring his own question. "I thought that line died out a generation ago."

"A distant branch," he muttered. "My people moved to the south. I'm the last of us."

She narrowed her gaze. "Hmmm. Where in the south?"

"Near the Smallage estate." He gave her his coolest stare. "Where the Iasc plague started."

With a sharp breath, GreatMistrys Hawthorn flinched back in her chair. Yeah, there wouldn't be any more questions about *him* now.

"The late Nivea Sunflower Hawthorn perished of the plague seventeen months ago," she murmured, looking away, out the sitting room window at the beautiful spring day. The cloudless deep blue sky acted as a lovely backdrop for the heavy white blossoms of the hawthorn hedges that delineated every section of the estate. Spring flowers bloomed too, and all the lingering morning frost coating the grass had vanished, leaving the yard lush.

Almost absently, the housekeeper stated, "And the Healers believe a trace of the sickness damaged the late Huathe T'Hawthorn."

Garrett didn't think the Iasc plague came in "traces," but he kept his mouth shut. The absolute last thing he talked about was his experience -- as the sole survivor -- of the Iasc sickness. He'd only brought it up because he thought the mention would distract the woman. As it had.

"She -- Nivea Sunflower Hawthorn -- was a very sad person. Spoilt and angry and sad." The words sat in the quiet of the luxurious house.

Garrett didn't know how all those might mix together.

"May she be blessed during her time on the Wheel of

Stars and may her next life be more fulfilling." The housekeeper sounded doubtful.

So was Garrett, since being a FirstFamily GreatLady -- but Nivea Hawthorn hadn't lived that long, had she?

"Wasn't she the lady of the house, acted as hostess when she was here?" Garrett asked.

A hesitation. "GreatLord T'Hawthorn lived in this Residence all of his life, as most of us who are Hawthorns and staff do. Much of the time, his mother acted as hostess, until she passed away." The housekeeper lifted her chin, her mouth tightened. "Then T'Hawthorn kept the control of this household firmly in his hands." Her gaze challenged Garrett.

"If T'Hawthorn could run the AllCouncils, I'm sure he had no problem here, with a Family staff," Garrett murmured. Unlike the new GreatLord ... who most of the staff would have seen grow from a child.

The housekeeper stood, brushed at her elegant tunic. "And that's all I'm going to say." She marched to the door.

"One moment," Garrett edged his tone with steel. "I understood you accused the FamCat, Black Pierre, of stealing a writestick ... a shiny piece to play with, maybe. And a leather desk blotter to sleep on."

She stood with straight spine. "*I* didn't. A member of the kitchen staff did. A cook-in-training, a girl perhaps envious of Black Pierre's new relationship with the chef." Another smoothing of her tunic, as if she usually wore an apron during her work. One that would remain white and crisp all day, Garrett thought.

"Black Pierre's relationship with the chef," Garrett repeated.

"That FamCat joined our household during the feud between the Hawthorns and the Hollys and bonded with FirstFamily GreatLord Huathe T'Hawthorn," she emphasized the Family's status as if Garrett wasn't all too aware of it. He stretched a little. She noticed the gesture, but didn't comment on him, continued to speak about the situation, "When T'Hawthorn passed on to the Wheel of Stars two months ago, Black Pierre did not transfer his affections to Laev, but to the chef."

"I see." Must be tough on Laev, another slight by his Family.

The housekeeper inclined her head. "At the time the cook-in-training spent her nights in the chef's bed, then Black Pierre came, and he did not like the young woman and ..."

Yeah, Garrett could see the dynamic. "Where's the cook-in-training now?"

"I thought it best that she be reassigned to another of the estates." The Hawthorn housekeeper waved a dismissive hand. "The one nearest our new cinnamon growing concern, many kilometers from here. I believe she is creating new recipes using the spice, a better use of her Flair than as a cook-in-training."

Garrett grunted, then put his understanding into words, "I see." And he did, the jealous girl had let her anger get the better of her and brought a hidden secret to the notice of the new GreatLord and had to be moved before she spilled more beans.

With a final inclination of her head, the housekeeper whisked from the room.

Garrett sat and thought for a while. Definitely a conspiracy. Or at least a Family secret no one planned on telling him ... or Laev T'Hawthorn.

Garrett would put the idea to a final test. He raised his voice, "Residence?" he called on the intelligent house, wondering if it would be as condescending as the housekeeper.

No response. "Residence?" Garrett projected his voice. Nothing. He moved to the window and began tapping on the glass, varying the pattern at random, then hit a beat of a song he liked. One written by GreatLady D'Holly herself, wed to the greatest enemy of the Hawthorns. Interesting to see if the Residence would recognize the tune.

After one song by the lady, others flooded Garrett's brain and he began humming as he drummed his fingers on the window.

So, how patient were sentient castles? Surely, such-long lived beings must learn patience. Garrett could tap and hum and contemplate what to do next, or occupy his mind with the cheerful fact that he'd get paid well for this particular job. Idly, he said, "You know, I charge by the septhour."

A whoosh and the huge fireplace across the room shot flames up the chimney, heat radiated out. "Garrett Primross, private investigator," a hollow-sounding voice issued from ... maybe the chimney, maybe just the air around him though he'd noted no audio speakers.

"Yes, that's me."

"I have requested references on you from the other Residences. No one knows of you. No FirstFamily lord or lady has hired you. We have only heard that you botched a case for GrandLord Cowitch at his estate in Gael City."

Garrett's jaw clenched, but he said evenly, "I wish *I'd* had references of GrandLord Cowitch before *I* worked for *him.* If you have any concerns about my honor or reputation, I suggest you speak with GreatLord T'Hawthorn about me." That might get the two personages talking again, though currently it was to Garrett's benefit that they didn't. Still, he'd liked the look of Laev T'Hawthorn.

A long pause, then a quiet voice just audible over the crackling fire. "*We* have never conducted business with the

Cowitches in the four generations since they became a Family."

"I guess that's telling, since I'm sure the Cowitches would like to associate with the Hawthorns, and have sent in a proposal or twelve," Garrett paused, then curiosity pricked. "And have any of the FirstFamilies signed contracts with the Cowitches?" He thought they might have. The Cowitches rose too high in status too quickly for the Family not to have a boost from a FirstFamily or two.

"Only to their detriment, but that has nothing to do with this business."

Garrett didn't find out who, too bad. "You brought up my reputation. Like Black Pierre, I don't like having my honor tainted. I'm sure before I leave today, T'Hawthorn will have a contract -- a *fair* contract -- drawn up for me to sign. I will abide by the terms, as I have always done. In fact, I continue to honor my confidentiality agreement with Campsis Cowitch despite the fact he's never paid me past a minimal retainer and has spewed insults about me."

"You are discreet," the Residence stated.

"I'm a private investigator, I'm interested in solving problems and I deal in secrets."

Heat pumped from the fire along with a few muted pops

Garrett offered, "Every family has secrets, commoner to noble. You can trust me to keep yours."

"Huathe T'Hawthorn stated that I am not allowed --" it stopped. A creak, maybe like it recalled that Huathe Hawthorn passed two months ago. Since the house itself could span centuries of life, months passing might not mean a lot. Sometimes. "I am not allowed to speak of this matter."

Definitely a Family secret.

"No?" Garrett ladened his voice with disbelief.

"I prefer not to speak of this matter to you, Investigator Primross."

At least the being gave him some respect.

"All right, what *can* you tell me that might help?"

A long pause. "I believe the last piece to go missing is an inexpensive signet ring with a tiny diamond made for a younger Hawthorn daughter a century ago."

"Ah. Do you have a precise description, size of the ring, metal? The quality of the stone, the diamond?" Garrett figured that Laev T'Hawthorn would be able to tap Great-Lord T'Ash, a blacksmith and jeweler, for knowledge about the ring. Its value, whether it had come into T'Ash's hands, what *he* might know of it, rumors or whatnot. Heady notions, that Garrett could actually be working with the FirstFamilies. *Honorable* Families.

"Our inventory described the ring in detail. I have told GreatMistrys Alma Hawthorn to give you a papyrus copy of the account of that piece."

"Thank you. And, my final question, what is your opinion of Laev T'Hawthorn?"

The fire sucked out and the temperature in the room dropped to downright cold.

"I thought so." Garrett stretched. "But, to me, T'Hawthorn seems like an intelligent man." A few years younger than himself. "And an astute businessman and entrepreneur," he paused. "As his FatherSire taught him to be. Tell me, T'Hawthorn Residence, did the late Huathe T'Hawthorn respect and admire his heir?"

A snapping twang that Garrett couldn't identify.

"So why do *you* not respect the current T'Hawthorn?" Garrett asked. Could it have anything to do with the thefts?

The silence lasted so long that Garrett gave up and began walking to the door. He'd put his hand on the latch before the being answered.

"Laev married an unacceptable woman against the Great-Lord's wishes. Laev would *not* listen to any of *Us*."

Garrett felt at a disadvantage because he didn't know enough of the Hawthorn history as he should have. No use but to reveal his ignorance, and let the Residence look down its nonexistent and supercilious nose at him. "When was this?"

"In the year four hundred and seven, when the boy suffered his SecondPassage at seventeen."

"Seventeen," Garrett repeated. Lord and Lady knew most boys -- new adults -- made mistakes at that age.

"The boy didn't listen to us. None of us."

"But they -- Laev and his wife -- lived here, right?"

"The GreatLord relented, against others' advice, and allowed them to move back from Gael City years ago. But the dreadful mistake continued."

"In what way?" Garrett pressed.

Shutters over the fireplace clanged shut. "Laev has your contract ready." The door opened. Garrett shrugged and sauntered out of the chamber.

WHEN GARRETT STEPPED FROM THE SITTING ROOM, THE young maid he'd seen before shoved a piece of papyrus into his hand and hurried away. Oh, yeah, sure, the Residence and the Family would Reveal All to him. He snorted, glanced at the inventory sheet, then folded it and put it in a tunic pocket.

He took his time walking back to T'Hawthorn's home office, what they'd call here the ResidenceDen. Fancy cloth lined the walls, and if not cloth, murals, and if not murals, then richly tinted walls with wainscoting. Carpets and rugs that looked old, but kept in perfect condition.

Because of the great psi power the Family had, the spells

they coated the Residence with, imbued into house and grounds ... and had for centuries.

Couldn't forget that, the sheer Flair these people commanded, especially Laev T'Hawthorn. And though the old, late GreatLord had impressive wealth and power, every generation demonstrated more Flair, so the younger lord would be innately stronger than his predecessor.

Garrett allowed himself the nigglings of envy at the wealth and beauty of the house and furnishings ... but as he walked through the halls -- the too cool halls -- he reminded himself that the GreatLord's Family hid secrets from him. That many of his relatives held little respect for him. That his Residence didn't speak to him and even the FamCat preferred the chef to the new head of the Family.

The case had flipped on Garrett. It was no longer about Black Pierre, but about Laev T'Hawthorn. The man superseded the cat, not because of his humanity, or because he now paid Garrett, but because his need was more.

As expected, when he entered the ResidenceDen, T'Hawthorn sat behind the desk and gestured to a printed papyrus contract. "My funds are transferred to your account, but have a hold on them until I scry to release the gilt after we sign the contract."

Garrett nodded. "Good enough." He sat in the leaping-goats embroidered cloth wing chair and gathered the two page contract to read.

"It's a general contract for services, billed on a septhourly rate, to include a fair retainer and enough funds to purchase missing items. Open to renegotiation by either of us when the original terms have been met. That would be finding the thief as well as my Family treasures, and the recovery of those treasures as much as possible."

"Yes," Garrett said, and wished he'd brought one of his

own contracts. But he'd thought he'd be working for a cat, and how would the feline sign, with a paw print? Not that cats believed contracts to be important. Mutual self-interest deals with equal to win or lose on both sides worked best with them.

He scratched out a couple of phrases and reworded the contract, signed it and handed it back to the GreatLord. "I'm sure your housekeeper reported on my conversations with her and the Residence, particularly with regard to my to-them-less-than-stellar-qualifications."

T'Hawthorn stiffened. "I will make my own determinations. While you conducted the interviews, of which I only received a short summary, I contacted the Gael City Guildhall with regard to your business and they informed me that your company remains in good standing there. They have removed all disparaging remarks from GrandLord Cowitch since a number of businesses have filed suits against him for breaking contracts, non-payment, slander and libel." T'Hawthorn gazed at Garrett, tapped his fingers together. "You haven't filed suit against the man."

"No."

An inclination of the head. "I think you should."

Garrett shrugged. "Not worth it, his insults made me move up here to the capital where I anticipate getting more and better paid work."

"The FirstFamily GreatLord T'Birch has also filed suit against Cowitch."

"There you have it, then," Garrett said. "The GreatLord probably lost a whole lot more gilt than I did and will get paid first from any suit."

"I understand." T'Hawthorn's eyes deepened to purplish and Garrett sensed anger scratched at the man -- at dishonorable practices? "I also spoke with the Captain of the Gael City Guards for information regarding you and your services. She stated her respect for you and that she'd never known you to break a contract, or a confidence. She also said she believed you to be one of the most courageous men she'd ever known."

"Oh." That would be because the Captain knew the circumstances of Garrett surviving the plague. He cleared his throat. "Good to hear."

The GreatLord stared at him and Garrett stayed stoic. Then the man took a writestick and initialed the changes to the contract, signed and sealed it with spellwords that tugged at Garrett, making him aware of the promises he'd given. Placing his hand on the pages, T'Hawthorn made a copy for Garrett, and a third he sent to the GuildHall cache to be filed.

Then he stood and walked around the desk. "That's all well and good, but this is what matters." He offered his forearm for Garrett to clasp.

Garrett stood and they matched in grip and a sympathetic energy ran through Garrett and probably through the lord, too. If they'd ever had to do a spell together, merge their Flair, they'd work well together.

Interesting, but not all together surprising.

"So the Residence did not speak to you of me," Garrett said.

"No."

Garrett allowed himself a brief smile. "The house is concerned enough about you that when it lagged in answering my interview questions and I pointed out that I charged by the septhour, the Residence spoke up."

T'Hawthorn grunted. "More concerned with Family funds than with me, though we have all we need for generations, and I'll be making more during my lifetime. The Family is secure forever."

Garrett believed him. "You are correct in that T'Hawthorn Residence is angry with you."

The man slanted him a look that showed Garrett had stated the obvious.

"Because of your wife."

A rush of color flooded the man's face and his expression went stiff and impassive. The GreatLord had been so open, Garrett hadn't thought he could become so completely unrevealing. He went back to sit in his comfortchair, but this time his hands stayed still. But his jaw flexed, and he said coolly, "It's well known throughout the noble circles," he slanted Garrett a look, "and I'd thought throughout the whole strata of Celtan society, that I wed a woman whom I believed to be my HeartMate."

And what the fligger did that mean? Of course any First-Family child would wed a HeartMate, that was one of the reasons those Families stayed on top. They wed for Flair, and Flair psi power came more often to the children of Heart-Mated couples than not. Most people who had HeartMates wed with them.

But the man evidently meant something different than what Garrett heard, so he parsed the words and listened to the echo of *whom I believed.* "Not your HeartMate, then," Garrett said, taking his seat.

"No. And I thought all of Druida City, if not Celta itself, knew that, too." T'Hawthorn's face continued devoid of expression, his voice flattened due to bitterness. Then T'Hawthorn ended, "Everyone gossips about the First-Families."

True.

Not getting anywhere here, change to what Garrett really wanted to know. "Did you love your FatherSire?" he snapped.

"Yes!" T'Hawthorn replied. Then he sank his face in his hands and scrubbed it, speared his fingers through his hair. "Yes. I loved him. We'd -- and me and my father -- had ... distant relationships until the Hawthorn-Holly feud. But when my father died in a duel, and we lost the feud and the whole horrible situation came to a messy end," T'Hawthorn flapped a hand, "my FatherSire mellowed."

The new GreatLord raised his head, his face pale, his eyes reddened. "I disappointed him immensely, but he stood by me, and loved me."

"That's good to know and remember," Garrett said.

"You think such questions apply to this case?" T'Hawthorn asked.

"Maybe. It's additional background for me."

T'Hawthorn rose stiffly so Garrett did, too. The GreatLord gave him a short nod. "If you'll excuse me, I need to leave for a business appointment."

The first time the man had lied to Garrett. "Fine. I have a few more interviews here--"

"Be at home," T'Hawthorn said not quite automatically and met Garrett's gaze for a few seconds, then said, "I think we understand each other and will work well together. Please call me Laev." He offered his arm once more and Garrett grasped it in beginning ... acquaintanceship.

"I'm Garrett," he said, then felt foolish. Of course a noble would call a commoner who worked for him by the first name. Well, Cowitch hadn't since he hadn't recalled Garrett's name on the few occasions they met.

T'Hawthorn, Laev, smiled as he dropped his hand, then continued on to a corner set with a square rug that Garrett belatedly realized served as a teleportation pad.

The door opened and the housekeeper bustled in, "Wait, Laev, where are you going?"

Obviously the Residence had been listening in and reporting on their conversation.

Laev T'Hawthorn stepped onto the rug and sent her a bland look. "Out for business."

"You don't have any appointments on your calendarsphere!"

"Later," he said aloud, but sent Garrett a private telepathic stream. *Do what you can to follow this case through.*

Garrett also replied mentally, *I will be searching for some of your lost items this afternoon.*

Lave looked surprised. The housekeeper sidled toward him. "Now, Laev, dear ...."

But T'Hawthorn vanished.

The housekeeper whirled and hissed out a breath. Garrett wondered if she'd been hanging around too many cats. He had, but he made sure he didn't mimic their behavior.

"THAT MAN!" HER HANDS FISTED, AND WHEN SHE CAUGHT Garrett watching her, she smoothed both face and fingers.

"He *is* a man, and a FirstFamilies GreatLord, and I've gotten the impression that the loss of these treasures came as a shock to him."

She sniffed. "Some treasures."

"Nothing you'd care to claim?" Garrett asked mildly.

"Nothing to cause so much fuss." She swept a glance around the room, as if noting changes the new lord might have made, focused on the comfortchair, the up-to-date scry panel, then frowned at the corner where Laev T'Hawthorn vanished. "But he won't give up on this situation and he won't listen to us."

"Just as he didn't when seventeen?"

"None of your busi--" she stopped.

"The Residence told me, and I think the past very much affects this case." He raised his voice. "Residence?"

"I hear," the Residence said with a tight creak.

"How long has that ring, the last item to go missing, been gone? he asked.

The housekeeper gasped, clutched her arms, curled into herself. Oh, yeah, Garrett nosed down the right trail.

"Sixteen months." A whisper on the air came to Garrett.

He tensed and repeated, "Sixteen months."

Mouth screwed narrow and shut, the housekeeper marched from the room.

"That is correct." The Residence fell silent.

Over a year -- three months over a year -- and no one said anything to Laev Hawthorn until a ... kitchen worker became newly jealous of a cat and a chef.

Garrett had to push this. "Sixteen months. The late GreatLord Huathe Hawthorn knew of the thefts, then."

After a few seconds, the Residence said, "Yes."

"But he didn't report them to the city guards." As soon as the words fell from his mouth Garrett knew them to be stupid. Of course the lord wouldn't report personal Family thefts to the guards. And no one else of the Family *who kept this secret for all these months* would go against the GreatLord's wishes.

And the old GreatLord hadn't bothered to contact a private investigator like Garrett either. So he knew the thief.

The case cracked wide open.

"But why did he ... allow the thefts?" Garrett asked.

Another pause. "We did not discover the thefts for some time since the items were ... are ... very minor heirlooms. Not worth finding."

"In the former GreatLord's eyes."

"Yes."

"But not in the current GreatLord's mind."

"Apparently not."

And disappearing sixteen months before. Well, there could only be one thief, then, right? Laev T'Hawthorn's estranged wife, Nivea Sunflower Hawthorn. The woman no one liked, the wife the Residence still seethed over.

But GreatLord Huathe Hawthorn loved his Son'sSon and would not have told him a grief like that, that Laev had married a woman who would steal heirlooms from the Family. Huge blow to the pride and honor of the man, not to mention the honor and integrity of the House.

"The late GreatLord discovered the thefts after his daughter-in-law died," Garrett said matter-of-factly.

"Ye-es," the Residence slowly confirmed.

"And GreatLord Laev T'Hawthorn only recently discovered antique items had gone missing. After his FatherSire's death."

"Yes." A long creaking groan of a wood sigh from the Residence as if reluctant.

Since he hadn't gotten an answer before, Garrett said, "I ask again, T'Hawthorn Residence, did the late GreatLord T'Hawthorn respect and admire his heir?"

Again the house didn't answer. So Garrett changed the question. "Did the late Huathe Hawthorn love Laev?"

"Of course."

Garrett said, "I would have thought that such a long-lived and intelligent being such as yourself would be more accepting of mistakes." But apparently such a generational, immobile, smart ... person ... would hold a grudge longer. Certainly wouldn't recall its own youth or any errors it had made in that dim time.

"So you, Residence -- and many of the Hawthorns -- know that Nivea Hawthorn stole from her husband's Family, from you, but kept it quiet from Laev."

And Garrett got the feeling that the Residence would have squealed and scolded if the old lord hadn't forbidden it.

But they'd gone beyond the point of denial of the thief.

"Do you have any idea what she might have done with the

items? Other than translocating them to the pigsty for kittens to find?" As far as Garrett knew, those two items were the only found treasures.

"Rumors have come to my ears that Laev's late wife might have made gifts of our items to her own minor noble family."

Though another noble house should have "Family" capitalized, it sure didn't sound so when T'Hawthorn Residence used that tone.

"The Sunflowers," Garrett confirmed.

"Yes."

"Surely not items marked with Hawthorn symbols."

"I do not know."

But the Residence still knew more than it was telling. "What else did she do with the pieces?"

A low grumbling and the fire lit in this chamber, popped and hissed. "She might have given gifts to her lover or lovers that she met in Druida City."

Boom! The air concussed around Garrett, stopping his hearing, a not-so-subtle way of ending the conversation.

He rubbed his ears. "Right." He bowed toward a camera he'd noticed in the corner bookshelves. "Thank you for your confidences, T'Hawthorn Residence."

No response.

"I'll see if I can find and restore the treasures."

This time when he left the room, a long *Ha, ha, ha, ha* echoed on his heels all the way to a back door.

First he'd check out the pigsty. After that he'd make rounds of antique shops. A tingle at the base of his neck told him that the woman might have actually sold other heirlooms, and he should follow that track.

Buying back the ones she'd given to the Sunflower Family, who must not like the Hawthorns either, would be easier, so Garrett felt he could wait on that a bit.

Finding the woman's lover or lovers would take longest.

He got directions to the home farm and walked through the sunlit day. Winter had truly passed, not to come again until after the turning of the new year at autumn's Samhain. The air tingled along his skin, the ocean adding humid fizz and scent, the touch of salt on his lips.

A huge amount of land, T'Hawthorn estate in Noble-Country, still a part of Druida City, within the walls, but complete unto themselves, the FirstFamilies.

But tended and groomed. The grassyard seeded more than four centuries ago, smooth and already spearing up lush.

And on the way, he puzzled out the Laev-Nivea background from what folk had concealed and revealed. Laev had been seventeen and undergoing his Passage to free his psi-power, fever dreams, or just past that time, when he'd married the girl

Probably a quick meet and marry.

And he'd believed her to be his HeartMate.

Since the woman had shown herself to be selfish and greedy, Garrett didn't think it too much of a stretch to deduce the girl had manipulated Laev into thinking she was his HeartMate, even if she knew she wasn't.

Garrett didn't think the girl had been much older than the boy, another new adult, and what seventeen-year-old girl would pass up the opportunity to become a member of one of the FirstFamilies, the highest in status and greatest in wealth and power on the planet? If she'd been alive now, she'd be a GreatLady herself, able to sit on the FirstFamilies Council and vote.

She didn't -- maybe couldn't -- suppress her ambition to rise to the highest stratum of society.

And the boy didn't -- couldn't -- listen to older and wiser heads who maybe knew the girl wasn't his HeartMate.

Perhaps she rationalized that she'd make Laev a good wife, an excellent wife, though she wasn't a HeartMate.

Garrett had to stop and swallow as reverberations of his own life crashed over him like the sound of the ocean surf in the distance. He'd been giddy in love with a girl, a girl who wasn't his HeartMate -- and he'd known he had a HeartMate -- and only wanted to be with Dinni. He'd thought they'd have a wonderful life. He still thought so.

But, because he'd had a HeartMate, Dinni wouldn't marry him. She wanted him to find and marry his HeartMate.

Obviously minor noble Nivea Sunflower had not had the loving nature of a commoner woman like Dinni Spurge.

Did that leave Laev T'Hawthorn in a better circumstance than Garrett Primross? Laev's wife pretended to be what she was not, married him for her selfish reasons, even if she planned to be a good wife. And would have stayed married to him forever. Naturally Laev would never subject his Family to the great scandal of a divorce and tarnish the Family name and reputation.

Garrett's lover had stayed true to herself, had given him up for selfless reasons, didn't believe she'd be a good wife if Garrett had an unknown HeartMate. And Garrett had never gotten to marry his Dinni, knew she wed with someone else.

Grinding pain for himself and Laev T'Hawthorn, either way, he supposed.

He turned away from the ocean and toward the farm that would make the Family self-sufficient, if necessary.

STRIDING THROUGH HAWTHORN HEDGEROWS SEPARATING areas of the estate, he continued to the pigsty, easily discovered from an odorous whiff.

The pigsty. How damn fliggering petty for a woman to throw her husband's Family's treasures away like that.

Garrett understood she must have been an unhappy

woman, but he'd been unhappy in his own love himself, and hadn't acted so poorly ... shut that down.

Wrinkling his nose more at the contempt he felt for Laev's wife than the smells of the porcines as they now jostled to a trough and ate, he figured Nivea Sunflower Hawthorn had felt such contempt for her husband and his Family, too.

Though the Residence and the Family was wrong to continue to blame Laev. And the woman herself was dead. Garrett shouldn't continue to judge her.

Hello! The little calico pranced around his boots.

"Greetyou," he found himself saying, the word seeming appropriate for being on this estate. "You here to check out the place for more items?"

No. There is nothing from the big house here. I would have sensed if anything had been there. Even if covered up in deepest mud. Even if tromped on by many, many hooves. I knows what Hawthorn stuff feels like now.

Garrett looked down at her and saw a resource.

"Is that true?"

Yes, very true.

"How would you like to earn the best catnip on the market?" T'Hawthorn could afford it.

A gasp, whisker quivering, whole small, plump body trembling. *Nip, all for MYSELF!*

"Yes."

Not to SHARE? Not with ANY ONE?

"Nope."

She sat on her butt, yet still wiggled with impatience. *What do I have to do?*

"I'm taking you into Druida City proper, to the shops for you to sense any Hawthorn objects." Antique stores and pawnshops that might still have a piece or two of the Hawthorns. After sixteen months. Right. But best to try.

Go out into the streets of main Druida?

"Yes. I'll be right there with you."

Her little muzzle lifted. *We can do this!*

"Yes."

For prime catnip grown and sold by the starship Nuada's Sword!

Uh-oh. And he wondered how she knew of that. Might cost as much as any antique object Garrett might find. Still, his line item expense report to T'Hawthorn would look interesting. Maybe it would make Laev smile. Garrett already figured the man carried around too much intensity.

Not helped by his Family or Residence.

I will sniff with My excellent nose and listen with My excellent ears and FEEL with my sensitive pads and all the hairs in My fur!

"All right."

To his amazement, Laev T'Hawthorn had ordered a Family glider to be pulled into the drive for Garrett's convenience. He waved away the Hawthorn driver, who'd been leaning against the long front of the vehicle. Garrett would rather not advertise where he was going and be reported on.

He didn't quite sneak calico cat into the big vehicle, but he masked her entrance. And on the seat he found three pouches of golden gilt coins, separated the amount of five hundred, then stashed the rest in the vehicle safe, passcoding it shut.

Calico ignored the coins, pressing her paws and nose to the side window. Thrilled, she burbled all the way into the busiest part of town.

Resting against the plush seat as the glider navigated the streets, Garrett considered which shops the late Nivea Hawthorn might have sold her husband's treasures at.

Would she have pawned them? She'd have had to be careful with anything that held any Hawthorn coats-of-arms or symbols ... like the purple leather desk set and writestick. Garrett would be lucky to ever find those, the objects that started this whole thing.

Too bad because he knew Laev T'Hawthorn cherished the things.

Pawnshops, perhaps, but not as likely as other stores. Less busy places and those not frequented by the FirstFamilies, or maybe nobles at all. Lesser nobility ... like she'd been before she'd determinedly married up. Tricked Laev into marrying her. Yep, still judging a dead woman, even when he'd admonished himself not to. Had to work on that.

But it seemed she continued to make trouble even after her death.

If she actually sold items ... and would she? Garrett thought so. An angry woman would do that. Dump minor items in the pigsty, sell better pieces, give away others to her relatives and, if the Residence was to be believed, her lovers.

They entered a square a few blocks away from CityCenter and he parked the glider in one of the usually-open spaces for such a vehicle. Only the rich could afford a glider.

Garrett liked the public carrier system, but no doubt the glider got him here faster, and before minor shops closed.

Respectable. Wouldn't Nivea Hawthorn want that? A respectable shop that would pay her good gilt. Perhaps a store she'd usually sneer at?

Oh, yes, the more Garrett tried to get in her head, the less he liked her.

So he left and shielded the glider, and smiled as Calico hopped around, squealing with delight at being somewhere new.

The third store he and Calico entered, she stilled in his arms, and he felt the prickle of her interest.

Something is HERE! Some Hawthorn thing! She leapt from

his arms, went over to the wide shelf of the left front window, stretched tall and pawed at a small item.

No one objected since no one stood behind the counter. Bells attached to the door had rung when they'd entered, but he and the cat still had the shop to themselves.

The object clinked to the floor, and, sure enough, when Garrett moved over to pick the piece up, he found a ring. Since he couldn't examine it well in the dim light, he flicked a small burst of temporary light into existence, studied the ring and the papyrus that described the heirloom. There did appear to be some sort of etched symbol, perhaps the listed dragonfly, engraved on the inside back of the ring.

Glancing down at the cat, he said, "You're sure this a Hawthorn piece?"

It smells-hears-feels like Hawthorn! I will show You! Her mind brushed against his and widened, and his own Flair spiraled out to meet hers, and he felt as she did. *Sensed* as she did, the smell-sound-vibration-feel of the ring that spoke to her of ... reverberations of *rich time-centuries* of T'Hawthorn Residence.

Her focus sharpened until she projected the mental-emotional resonances of the Hawthorns themselves.

See, smell, feel, listen? she ended, full of satisfaction.

Yeah, he responded to her mentally, but when his blurred vision cleared, he found he'd braced himself with a hand on the wall to stay upright.

This particular Familiar Companion Flair felt a little too alien for him to use, but he honed in on the *feeling* of the Hawthorn item. Cool, not radiating huge emotions. The original faint sense of pleasure when the young girl had received it.

Garrett pondered the basic feeling-sense he'd gotten from Calico that she designated as *Hawthorn.*

Clean and cold and edgy.

Risk.

That brought him up short. Risk. Not ambition or greed or anything else, but *risk*, the basic characteristic of the Hawthorn Family. If they hadn't been one of the highest, wealthiest, most powerful Families on Celta, they'd be adventurers.

But that's what got them to Celta, wasn't it? The Earthan ancestors of the Hawthorns had risked everything to come to a new planet ... had plunked down a lot of gilt to finance the starships, and be encased in a cryonics tube for the voyage. Sure sounded risky to Garrett.

Risk might be a hallmark of the Hawthorns, but not for Garrett. He'd be risk-adverse, despite his profession. But he'd rarely been in danger ... on the job.

Surviving the Iasc plague was a different story. One he never wanted to revisit. So shove it out of his mind and focus on the now ... Of Calico giving a tiny mew so he'd let her out of the door.

It's Black! she caroled in Garrett's mind. *He's here to play with Me!* Then a very, small private whisper along with a detailed image. *This is where You should translocate the Very Good Nip. Under my pillow under the bush next to the back wall of the stridebeast stable.* Then a loud, *Later!*

She bounced out of the store as he cracked open the door for her, careful not to jingle the bells. Just waiting to see how long it would take for the proprietor to show up.

GARRETT TUCKED THE HAWTHORN INVENTORY BACK INTO his pocket and studied the ring. It appeared to be the cheapest of trinkets, dull with grime. Puzzlement filtered through him that the store owner wouldn't bother with a slight *polish* spell. He felt an etching when he slipped his pinky along the inside, but it seemed as if no one else had bothered to scrutinize the piece.

A minute later someone finally responded to the sound of the bells that had rung when he and Calico had walked in.

"Yeah?" Ah, this girl, too, looked slatternly and completely bored.

Garrett glanced at the sign high on the wall behind her. "Huper Clubmoss's Fine Collectibles? Huper?"

She snorted "'A course not. I'm his Daughter'sDaughter."

Her eyes narrowed in calculation as she noticed the ring in his fingers. "Very valuable," she said.

His brows lifted. "I don't think so."

"But you want it, I can see that."

Yeah, he'd probably expressed a little too much interest, and hadn't put it down when she'd walked in. So he smiled charmingly at her and flipped the ring, caught it on the tip of his little finger, rolled it down to his palm, flipped it again to the back of his hand and sent it back and forth over his knuckles. "Very good for sleight of hand," he admitted.

"Oh, you're one of those fake magicians," she said sourly. She stared at him, let her gaze sweep him up and down, and he understood that though she didn't care for his blunt-featured face, she liked his strong body just fine.

She sidled up to the counter, thrust out her chest to show how her lush breasts strained against the sheen of her cheap silkeen tunic. "I can let you have the ring for forty gilt," she purred. "And perhaps some other considerations ... like a drink with me at a caff house."

That's not what she really wanted.

A boy of about twelve strode in. Saw the ring in Garrett's hand and scowled. "That's too low a price, Erzia. That's a genuine item, that is, gold and diamond."

The girl cuffed at his ear, but he ducked. "You think lots in here's genuine items when what our MotherSire sold was trash." Her lip lifted as she surveyed the dusty shop, filled with jumbled items.

"Not true," the boy said stoutly. "A good man with good character, MotherSire was." He scowled and crossed his arms. "You and mother should let *me* run this shop. Then it would make a profit."

"You belong in GroveStudy." She dismissed him, continuing to concentrate on Garrett.

Garrett gave a half bow to the boy. "I'll pay sixty gilt for the ring."

"Still not enough!" the youngster said. Eyes sliding to his sister, he came around the counter and held out his hand to Garret for the ring.

"Josey, you're not supposed to touch things in the shop!" the young woman scolded.

Dropping the ring into the boy's hand to see what would happen -- after all, Garrett wouldn't be paying for the thing, Laev T'Hawthorn would -- Garrett watched as Josey picked it up, rubbed it on his sleeve and muttered some spell Words. Dirt and dust and grit vanished to reveal gleaming gold, and sparkling gem.

"Lady and Lord!" the girl gasped, goggling at her brother.

"I think there's engraving inside," the boy said, then, "Lightspells!" he ordered and three small sunlike globes circled the ceiling, removing all gloom and casting the shadows of sharp-relief, and revealing the deterioration of the shop.

He stared up at Garrett, his face impassive. "Two hundred sixty gilt," he said.

The inventory listed the ring's worth as three hundred ten golden gilt. So the boy knew more than he thought, but not quite as much as he should.

"Done," Garrett said, using his sleight-of-hand and a

touch of Flair to pull gold coins from an inner pocket and reveal them stacked on his palm.

Sister and brother gasped.

Garrett tumbled the gilt into the boy's hand, and said, "I'll want it wrapped well and a receipt."

"Of ... Of course," the young woman said.

"You really *must* let me take over this business," the preteen said.

His sister said nothing as she created a pretty box and set the ring inside, then began wrapping it elegantly in beautiful red paper flocked with gold, obviously something she preferred doing instead of selling. She'd cleansed and polished the counter before she translocated heavy papyrusboard for the box and fancy paper.

Since taking his gilt, they both became more cheerful, and Garrett leaned on the counter and asked his questions. "Do you have any idea who brought the ring in to sell?"

She paused in her creasing of intricate box folds. "No."

"I'm sure your MotherSire would have kept an inventory. I'd be ... grateful ... if I could see it."

"Why are you so interested?" The woman's eyes narrowed. "Did you know that ring was here? How did you find it?"

He could have explained, but would rather not. She didn't impress him as a trustworthy person and she already had a lot to gossip about. He didn't want to give her more. Not his name, not his profession, and certainly nothing regarding Black Pierre, the Hawthorns or Laev.

The boy, who'd sidled to the edge of the deep window display and begun picking up objects and cleaning them with Flair, said, "I was in the shop with MotherSire when he purchased the ring. I remember who brought it in."

That didn't surprise Garrett, and from the small smirk on the boy's face, Garrett guessed they'd just made a very good profit, despite the lad not knowing the true value of the piece.

"Oh, Josey!" the girl huffed, but said nothing more, continued to work on her intricate wrapping. No doubt considering the amount of gilt he'd paid for the ring demanded her best. A change of attitude he liked. She seemed to be going easier on the boy, too.

"So?" Garrett asked casually, "A man, younger than me?" Would the boy describe a male who might be Nivea's lover? If so, that would be a lead.

"No, a lady. Very snoot-- very fashionably dressed. Didn't treat MotherSire well, so I remember her." Josey scowled. "Pretty enough, golden hair, light brown eyes, tan skin."

A golden woman, hair, skin, eyes ... Garrett had noted a painting of Nivea in the corridor outside the ResidenceDen.

"MotherSire laughed when she left, said he didn't mind being insulted since he bought a very valuable ring for a very low price." Josey's face screwed up as if fighting tears. "That was sixteen months ago. He dropped dead the very next week. So I remember."

"Do either of you recall a desk set? Dark purple blotter, black and silver writestick. Perhaps with a coat of arms engraved--"

Both siblings stiffened.

"We wouldn't take anything like that!" the boy said. "We are honorable dealers. We do not buy or sell anything from nobles unless they prove they own it." He crossed his arms and jutted his chin. "And that's our reputation, too. Everyone knows that!"

Garrett slid his gaze to the young woman who finished making a bow of long red curls. Her mouth had puckered in distaste, and she said, "It's always more trouble than it's worth to purchase an item that might be stolen. Josey's right, we wouldn't buy something with a coat-of-arms unless we knew the noble. Our MotherSire particularly would not have done so."

One more tweak of the bow and the girl announced, "Package is done!" She set it at the edge of the counter, smiled brilliantly. "Sure you don't want a nice cup of caff?" Another view of her breasts.

Garrett did a slight inclination of the torso. "Thank you, no, GentleLady." He gave the boy the same bow. "GentleSir."

"Come in anytime!" she called as he left with a ringing of bells above the door, and he heard Josey's determined statement. "I'll be taking over the shop. I'll convince Mom."

And as he left with the ring, Garrett reflected on the parallels of this particular case. This time Laev and Josey. He'd met two young males, of widely different backgrounds, with their skills and intelligence dismissed by their relatives. He thought young Josey had finally proven himself to his sister, and maybe to the rest of his family, whoever they might be, at twelve.

Laev T'Hawthorn, FirstFamily GreatLord, a man of thirty-some years, still had to prove himself and gain – regain -- the respect of his relations.

As for Garrett, at about Josey's age, he'd been doing a man's job in the stables of the Smallage estate.

OUTSIDE THE SHOP, GARRETT GLANCED AROUND, BUT SAW no sign of the FamCats. Using the scry in the glider, he ordered the smallest amount of Earthan catnip on sale for the young calico cat and had a member of the starship crew send it to T'Hawthorn Residence cache with a note for Laev.

He weighed the fancy box and bow in his hand. Now the conundrum facing him was to decide whether to go along with the Family and refuse to reveal the greed or fury, or worse, pettiness, of Laev's dead wife to the man himself. Or leave the guy with a better image of his late wife.

Not something Garrett would usually worry about. But he didn't delude himself that this new scandal wouldn't get out and smear Laev's and the Hawthorn's name and pride even more.

If he continued the quest Laev had sent him on, his inquiries would prompt talk and speculation. Gossip.

Like any other social circle, Garrett figured the FirstFamilies would gossip about this. And about Laev, a man who'd just succeeded to a title.

A man who'd made a terrible mistake that the highest lords and ladies might still talk about, one that showed his judgment, at the very least, to be poor ... at seventeen.

But the man and the Family would take a definite hit. Lose honor, lose some of the prestige the former lord with the towering reputation had built.

Garrett had been wrong.

Nobles *did* have problems. And some that gilt and power couldn't fix. Even if Garrett discovered every single item the woman had purloined ... had sold or given to her Family, or, even worse, tracked down gifts to her lovers .... Even if Garrett returned all the heirlooms to GreatLord T'Hawthorn -- something Garrett didn't think was possible -- the fact that his wife had betrayed him in such a shabby manner would hurt the man.

And Garrett liked Laev.

But he'd been hired to do a job. He'd signed a contract, sealed the deal with an arm grasp. So, really no choice.

He had no doubt that after Laev T'Hawthorn moved through his anger and grief, he'd see the implications of what could happen to his Family's position and influence if Garrett continued to try and recover the missing treasures.

Laev could make that decision.

Garrett had determined the thief and found and returned one stolen heirloom, they could both consider the contract fulfilled.

With a low level dread at having to reveal to his client that his lady had betrayed him, Garrett exited the glider when it pulled up before the impressive front entrance of the castle. He strode up the steps and the elaborately carved wooden double doors over steel swung open. The Residence in action, since not one member of the household stood in the small atrium, nor beyond in the larger hall.

Good with directions, Garrett took the corridor to his left toward the ResidenceDen. "Is T'Hawthorn back?" he asked. If not, he'd leave the box on the man's desk and make an appointment to meet with him tomorrow. He wanted to get this delivery of bad news over with.

"As you surmise, Laev is in the GreatLord's ResidenceDen," the house said and fell silent.

"Uh-huh." Garrett sped up, taking another turn or two down empty hallways. Human instinct not to be around the boss when misfortune hit.

This time when he entered the ResidenceDen, Garrett became aware of an elegant purple rug showing the Hawthorn tree and shabby at the edges. Mostly he noticed it because Laev stood frowning down at it.

"Nice rug," Garrett said into the heavy silence.

Laev raised violet eyes to meet his, gestured elegantly. "You want it? It's yours."

"Rather be paid in gilt," Garrett said.

A not-happy smile hovered on Laev's lips. "This would be in addition to our contractual arrangements. You can take the rug away with you today."

Cleaning out. "Fine." Garrett went over and stooped to touch the carpet. With great effort he translocated the rug to his apartment. Then he wiped his sweaty forehead with a softleaf.

"I got the catnip." Humor showed in Laev's eyes as strolled to his desk and held up a tiny bag. "For one of the animal informants you use?"

"Nope, for one of the feral FamCats on your estate."

Closing his eyes, Garrett formed the *location* image that Calico had transferred to his own mind, sent that mentally to Laev. An instant later the catnip vanished and Garrett heard a telepathic cat squeal of glee. Yes, he and Laev T'Hawthorn worked together well.

Garrett placed the exquisitely boxed package on Laev's desk, along with the papyrus inventory.

T'Hawthorn glanced at the sheet. "A girl's ring, a gift to a daughter of the house found and returned. Excellent."

"Glad you think so."

For himself, he'd like an emotional blow, bad news, shot quick and clean. "You should sit and brace yourself."

The lord's smile faded, his body tensed. He glanced at Garrett then sat behind his desk.

Garrett took a position behind a chair. He might need to make a fast getaway.

"All right," Laev -- T'Hawthorn with the grim expression -- said.

"Your wife Nivea Hawthorn purloined the items."

Devastation flashed across the man's face and he flinched. At some point in time he must have loved his wife, cherished her, and been totally betrayed.

A man who was held to be -- and held himself -- to the highest, most honorable code, had been manipulated and betrayed by a deceitful woman. He'd brought that woman into the heart of a Family too proud to stoop to dishonor.

He sat still, eyes darkening to purple, saying nothing, only absorbing the blow and the various ramifications, and unspeaking for several moments.

Garrett didn't press him.

"Thank you," T'Hawthorn gritted.

And Garrett felt the rawness of his pain. "I'll be going now, and send you an itemized bill for today's work. You can let me know if you want me to continue--"

"Yes. I do." The man's voice sounded downright rough.

"I have other leads and think I can reclaim some -- perhaps most -- of the missing pieces."

"Good."

Garrett met the GreatLord's bleak gaze. He bowed deeply as a mark of respect man-to-man. "Merry meet," he said, then winced.

A crack of laughter erupted from T'Hawthorn, then he breathed a couple of times as he held Garrett's glance. "Merry meet, friend Garrett."

"And I'm thinking you're definitely glad for me to 'merry part,'" Garrett said, considered the man whom he'd shocked with such an emotional blow. Laev had taken it, and committed to taking more, doing the right thing for his Family, even though scandal would whirl around him. "Merry part, friend Laev. And we will meet again."

As friends. Garrett never would have thought it, not of a noble, not of a noble of the highest status.

He used the last of his energy to teleport away to his warm and homey apartment.

Today's case had shone a light on his own life, his own past, his nature. Had revealed his own prejudice against nobles, when some were more courageous and honorable than he'd ever expected.

He valued his own station, situation, *life* more.

And he'd gained a friend.

HEARTSTONES

I was asked by a writer friend to contribute to an anthology: *Debris & Detritus, The Lesser Greek Gods Running Amok* (edited by Patrica Burroughs, published by Story Spring Publishing L.L.C. of Pekin, IL, in 2017). Since then I've revised it slightly and added a ***new ending.*** Both Zane and the House, Debris and Detritus, will be featured in another books.

HeartStones

424 Years After Colonization, Druida City, Winter

SOMETHING -- SOME SOUND, SOME *PAIN* KICKED HIM INTO consciousness. Splintering agony ripped through him. Yes, someone *broke* his front door. The pang sharpened as it hit the metal hinges of the door, then dulled a bit as the hurt traveled through his walls and floors, then eventually dissipated through his whole three-storied house self.

Pain more than he'd felt ... long, long, long time.

Ssshhh, whispered through him, as a wisp of alive-ness inside him but apart from himself surged. The being trailed energy that soaked into each of his fibers. Riveted, he watched himself mend and grow stronger.

He's aware!

Then we must withdraw. He can Heal himself.

A while later he turned his attention back from his beams and stones to ponder what happened. A *kick* brought him to full awareness and kept him there. The kick on his slammed door. *His* door, part of him. His main portal to the world *outside.* And odd that he sensed a *world* outside.

A different type and temperature of air against his rough outer walls than the smooth inner ones.

He began to sense many things, put them in order. Think.

Live.

Primarily, hurt. The smashing of the door hurt. He whimpered and *strained* and the small pieces of the front door rose and set back in place. Still aching, he sent ... energy ... into it, soothing himself.

Better.

But still the door didn't quite fit and a gaping crack let the cold winter air in.

Now silence lived within him instead of the noises. No mumbled words that he'd been aware of for a while and that had stirred him, reminding him of other times and sounds and voices of beings that moved around inside him, vibrating on his floors.

Yes, he *remembered* other voices, a snatch of back and forth between two beings long ago ... *conversation.*

His oldest memory -- words echoing through him, bouncing off his interior walls instead of soaking into them, then. *"If I am debris, then you must be detritus."*

He turned over the syllables, again and again, began to get meaning from them.

Debris and Detritus. He liked those words. Said often

within his walls, the words fit him, because they'd shaped him.

Now as he *thought* them, he tried to form them in sounds. Odd creaks, not like the smooth facility he'd sensed from those who'd originally made the words. But those sounds, the first words said by his own self, echoed through his walls, sank into his stone, seemed to anchor his being.

He was *Debris and Detritus.*

The concept of self floated through his mind, new and sparkly thoughts.

A vibration outside his walls, *outside*, heavy, stopped near his broken door -- oh! from a *mobile being!* Additional ideas tumbled through Debris and Detritus's mind-self. He was *not* a mobile entity.

That odd being forced the door in, scraping and hurting. Debris and Detritus let wind whistle through his rooms, giving noise to the pain.

"Huh," the mobile *person* grunted, bootsteps stomping on the floor, through the tiled hall of the entryway, into the round mainspace of marble. "Yep, definite squatters stayed here. Kicked in the door. Left a lotta trash. I'll call in a report that I'm doin' a sweep of the house. That'll keep me here and out of the police guardhouse until end of shift. Good."

The new being mumbled a word, one with weight that fizzed the air around it. And Debris and Detritus experienced another recently-remembered sensation, the inside of the mainspace chamber held less dark, became brighter with *light*.

He liked that.

"What's this? A hundred silver coin?" The new person made a series of deep sounds and radiated ... *amusement.* Another concept came to Debris and Detritus' new thoughts. Laughing.

"Those fliggering squatters left something besides trash

here. They'll sure miss that. And I've got it! Only fliggering thing of value in this cruddy building."

More laughing. "Huh. This'll come in handy. I'll stay to end of my shift, follow my regular pattern so they don't look at me for stealing that brooch. Only twenty more minutes. But then gotta get out of the city with the jewel. Immediately. Live good for the rest of my life." The bright white bathing his walls vanished from the mainspace.

The air in his rooms changed as the mobile entity traversed every chamber, light coming and going. As the being thumped up his staircase, Debris and Detritus *listened* to the words coming from the entity.

"No one here in this stupid, trashy, place."

That made an odd and different pain inside him.

The person kicked more *stuff* from the center of chambers to along baseboards. "If it weren't for finding that silver piece, and for giving me a good excuse to hide out alone until end of shift, I'd be long gone from this abandoned and rotting house."

Debris and Detritus creaked in surprise at more insulting words. He checked, fast. No rot lived within him.

Vibrations back from his third floor down the stairs and into the mainspace, then a ping sounded, a non-being-made noise. Then came a wheezing huff. "That's it. Shift over. Report in, then teleport straight outta Druida--"

Mumbling, then a whoosh of once-occupied-air and the being vanished from Debris and Detritus' space. But as he left a clink sounded as something fell onto the marble floor.

Fascinating object, full of pulsing energy, giving a heavier *feeling* than the true mass of the worked minerals. Debris and Detritus drew it toward his essence, his *thinking stones* and surrounded it with energy, kept it safe. He liked the feel of it.

Then no more sounds or vibrations, either inside or close to his outside walls. Silence and not-light, *dimness and dark,* gathered within him and he had much *time* to recollect the other noises and beings and conversations past, from long ago.

He considered time: minutes, septhours, days, weeks, months, a year.

Terrible *event* happened perhaps four years ago. Something he disliked--*hurt*--recalling. The end of the sounds and warmth and light of mobile beings, the beginning of emptiness.

Thoughts feathered at the edge of his brain, that portion of him he understood consisted of his *stones.*

There had been two mobile beings, persons, people. An old couple who had ... talked to each other? Communicated?

He knew that word now, conversation and *communication* -- ideas sent to other intelligent beings.

He scoured his memory and it flickered like ... like the fire in his fireplace in the mainspace he had once felt, close to his stones. And he felt, then *considered*, things he'd heard and what the people had read aloud and those words that had echoed in his walls

Debris and Detritus recalled the last deliberate touch of those two, near his stones, and their words. "Shouldn't be long now, other Houses are Awakening," the higher voice had said, smoothing a hand over the fireplace surround.

The other part of the couple replied in a deeper voice, "He will reach critical mass soon, of Flair that has sunk into him from this ground and atmosphere of Celta, of all the Flair his inhabitants have given him over the centuries."

"Like us. We've shared our psi-power magic Flair", said the first.

"Like us. We wanted to stimulate a house to become a Residence, and leave a legacy, and we have done so. He will Awake soon."

A loud breath from the higher voice. "We won't be here."

"Maybe, maybe not."

That conversation went around and around in his mind. He had much time to be, and remember and contemplate.

To come to decisions.

He needed ... people.

He needed *Family*.

Somehow he'd get them. He would *keep* the next ones who came.

ONE NIGHT LATER.

Zane Aster had heard a whisper of treasure ... a treasure lost in Druida City.

While on duty, a venal city police guardsman had pinched a jeweled brooch from a GreatLord --a stupid deed. From that Lord's sentient Residence -- an even more unintelligent action, since the Residence eventually figured out who'd stolen the item. And, the worst and final idiocy, the guardsman-thief had misplaced the brooch.

Reward money had been offered.

As he stared into his thick, expensive brew mug, Zane wondered if he'd been supposed to hear that rumor. If it had come to his ears because his Family worried about him.

He sat in a luxurious noble social club frequented by all but the highest of society, his ass cradled by a thick cushion that conformed to his butt, the furrabeast leather chair tilted slightly to accommodate his wretched back.

If he'd been whole, he'd be down in a low-class tavern frequented by sailors and other treasure hunters like himself, but his pride wouldn't let him go back there in his crippled state.

Glugging down the last of the ale, he acknowledged his Family *should* worry about him. With his sight fading along with his *finding* psi-power, his Flair, he wouldn't give himself good odds of making it to spring.

He might not actually commit suicide, but he wouldn't take care of himself, and there were plenty of ways to perish if you just didn't give a damn whether you ate or how much alcohol you drank or what streets you wandered down drunk and wearing expensive clothes.

What he had to look forward to tomorrow was another Healing session. Maybe the Healers would break his spine again, or plump up the pads in his spinal column or something equally nasty he didn't want to contemplate. The Healers could fix his back ... eventually.

They had no clue how to stop his blindness.

Or the diminishment of his Flair.

And he couldn't just stay sitting on his ass and contemplating a very bad future.

So he called for a hot toddy to go -- and exited the warm social club by the main door into the snowy night instead of calling for a glider to take him home.

The wind cut into him, despite cloak over jacket and tunic. He didn't have enough Flair, psi magic, to bend a weathershield over himself. He barely had enough power to activate the warmth spells on his clothing.

As he walked through the streets no more than a half kilometer from his own home neighborhood, he acknowledged that he'd made a mistake in not summoning a vehicle. Even his clothes and the false warmth of the alcohol in his blood didn't keep him from shivering.

Unless that was just another symptom of the damage he'd gotten in the underwater accident.

Still, when he reached the crossroads where he should turn left, instead he angled right, tripped over the curb of the sidewalk, then slid his foot to test the height and stepped onto it. Because he heard the faint wispy notes of a melody that called to the heart of him, to what had once been his primary Flair. A whiff of an odd but compelling tang curled into his nostrils ... the scent of treasure.

He plodded on through the blue-gray evening, ignoring the warm yellow or white blurry rectangles of lit windows as he passed still open businesses and apartments above them. He should go home, to GraceLady Aster's Residence, his MotherDam, mother's mother.

Where he'd be fussed over and nagged, and he'd hate every minute.

But he could not ignore this final opportunity to hunt for this last treasure before his talent failed.

Time to accept that the large and drifting flakes of snow in the evening light weren't what dimmed his sight. That deteriorated all on its own. And the sensation of his Flair for finding a prize should have been a lot stronger, sizzling through his nerves, buzzing along his skin, especially since FirstFamily GreatLord Ivy's recently stolen bauble was more than a brooch, some sort of magical Family artifact.

Zane simply continued to put one foot in front of the other, following the whiff of energy and magic of that power-imbued treasure, calling himself foolish with every step. And he traveled from an upper noble class part of town to an area of deserted streets devoid of inhabited houses.

The colonists from Earth had built Druida City, sure their descendants would populate it and the world beyond the walls.

But Celta was a tough planet for the humans. Though individuals lived longer, the sterility rate was high and the birth rate was low. The colonists' grasp on life still slippery.

So the city had never been full, and this part echoed with emptiness.

Finally, he stopped in front of a tall, narrow house in a row of tall, narrow houses. His vision cleared for a few instants and he saw protruding rounded bowed windows on both the first and second floors, a balcony on the third, and the whole façade embellished with elongated designs.

A very elegant and beautiful building. And if his eyes and back and feet didn't throb with aching, he might have been able to call up from memory the Earthan architectural style this row of homes had been modeled after.

But his sight did flicker from the dim evening of reality to gray fuzz to a blank darkness, and he couldn't quite make out the exterior sculpture.

He *could* see that the tall and narrow door with a half-round top showed a large, and recent, gaping split. Zane sniffed, flexed his fingers, stomped his feet to move his sluggish blood a little faster and stimulate his Flair, used his talent. Yes, the treasure awaited inside.

The icy wet of the iron door latch nearly seared his hand, and with a grunt and a shove of his whole body, he forced the thickly paneled door open. It scraped across the floor -- a not-wood floor, unusual.

A spurt of anger zipped through him that someone had damaged the door, and he used his tiny amount of energy left to mend the wood fibers, by feel, not by sight. Made the door whole, straightened it on its hinges.

His balance failed and he windmilled and managed to set his shoulder, not his bad back, against the wall as he panted. Probably shouldn't have fixed the door, though he'd locked out the wind and weather.

He blessed the Lady and Lord for being out of the spitting sleet, if not out of the cold. He breathed and felt the warmth of his breath against his face as he moved forward through the entry hall, extending his senses. He passed doors on his right and left, he thought, then tripped on a low threshold from one room to another and stopped. A touch of sweat filmed his armpits.

His breath came ragged and harsh, sounding too loud. Did the material of the walls cause sound to echo? Or did he strain more to *hear* since his sight faded?

The drips from his clothing plopped around his feet and since standing in a puddle didn't appeal, he scuffed his toe around and found even and solid ground.

Dark filled the interior of the abandoned house and he hesitated. On one hand he could pretend his sight didn't decline in a night-black room. But he cherished even the slightest haze of pale gray that he could see. Which might vanish during the night.

Find the treasure and go.

So he stood tall, and probed the room with his senses and pushed at his psi power to *work*.

Oddly enough, the room felt circular, with a bank of colder, tall glass windows curving some meters ahead, looking out on the back. Not that he could see.

He tilted his head, noticing that the reverberations of the small noises he made sounded unusual. Slowly stretching out an arm, he touched a smooth pillar. Ah, more small columns must grace the room. Probably marble. He sniffed. Smelled like marble.

And, yes, something not of the house, new to this environment, throbbed in slow and heavy pulses. A great magical artifact indeed. After inhaling through his open mouth, he tried to taste the essential magic of the artifact, thought he got a tang of bitter ivy. More overwhelming was the flavor of the house -- sweet like golden honey, another peculiarity.

Blinking, he peered into the darkness, saw nothing, no glow from the brooch which should blaze to his Flair-sight. He swallowed the despair coating his throat, shuffled a couple of steps in and past the pillar. Turned in the direction of the ivy taste, the whiff of Flair, the tiny hum of a magical artifact out of place. The jewel that needed to be returned to the Ivy Family where it belonged and would be cherished.

"Just get the brooch and go," he muttered.

So he ignored his blindness and strode to the right into the room. A chill breeze whisked through the place, his foot came down on a piece of thin papyrus and he slipped, toppling backward. His head hit the column, definitely stone. His mind spun dizzily as he fell, then his wits got swallowed up by a more gentle darkness than that of blindness.

THE MOBILE BEING WITH MALE GENITALIA--A *MAN*--LAY TOO still on Debris and Detritus' floor. An unfamiliar feeling, a rising sting, pulsed through his walls. He did not know the name of the emotion and did not like it. His windows on the third floor shivered as his air pressure increased due to the emotion.

No, he did not know this feeling and needed this man, his new Family, to explain it. Explain a lot.

The empty time before the man had come had stretched into an infinity of quiet moments and Debris and Detritus began to realize how much he did not know. Did not understand concepts he should be able to grasp but made no sense.

Debris and Detritus *did* know of time intervals. The small brick area with a sundial behind his not-street-facing walls measured time. The previous mobile beings had told him of time and the sundial when it had been built. That instruction, and the bit of Flair they'd sent him at the time, had made a strong enough impression that he could access it.

But when the man had come and moved so quickly, Debris and Detritus had not been prepared. Especially since the man wanted to take away the powerful sparkling thing the last person had left. Debris and Detritus had swept a piece of flat stuff under his foot to slow him down.

Now the house had two sparks on the floor and it appeared the one from the worked minerals -- the brooch! -- was stronger. That did not seem right.

He did not know what to do and he let out distressful creaks until the man made a terrible sound.

Lady and Lord, his back ached! Worse than his head. Bad enough that Zane couldn't deny that he'd awakened from the chill of pain tears on his cheeks. Taking stock, he thought he'd be able to move, he hadn't torn any muscles or broken any bones. Just wrenched the damn thing.

Concentrating on keeping his breathing even and gentle, he let input lap at him, and sensed the Flair of the Ivy brooch. The last treasure he could ever hunt and find.

It lay on the floor to his right about two arm-lengths away.

When the pain faded a bit, he rolled and that didn't seem to tweak his back as badly as he'd anticipated. He came up against a slight ledge. The odor of old smoke and soot filled his nostrils. Extending his fingers, he touched cold metal. He traced it, discovered a fancy pattern, realized he touched a fire grate.

His fingertips tingled this close to a great artifact. He refused to recall other times when his hands had nearly burned at the proximity of power.

Stretching over the grate and into the fireplace he tried to reach the brooch, failed, and felt the sweat of pain coat him. That would chill him fast in this cold house, better to keep his exertions normal.

Rest again and wait. Don't hurry and use energy he didn't have.

Greet. You, said a mature male voice.

Zane jerked in surprise, let himself subside. "Who's there?" But his own words echoed through the chamber, so he felt foolish. "Anyone?" The harsh grating of that word emphasized that the salutation had been telepathic, mind-to-mind.

A Fam! His heart thumped hard. An intelligent animal companion. Lord and Lady, what a blessing, a being to help him get home.

"Fam?" he croaked. "FamCat? FamFox?" He called out the most common Fam species.

What is Fam? came the question, along with a long creak as punctuation, and his hopes plummeted. The building. This place had become intelligent, as happened to some after a couple of centuries.

Lady and Lord. He couldn't send the House to get help. And it sure wasn't hooked into the network of intelligent dwellings, Houses and Residences, or it would know of Fams.

Hope left him and the chill pain of his body returned. He closed his blind eyes, let dampness ease the aching dry.

Greet you. Hello. Debris and detritus. Please respond, mobile being ... man.

The odd phrase rang through his head, debris and detritus, usually leftover stuff after he'd finished a treasure hunt. Usually swept out to sea ... or claimed by small ocean beings as dwellings. Odd bits that floated away.

Couldn't stay helpless on his back, he scooted to a pillar a few centimeters beyond the fireplace, propped himself against the column. Not an ungodly amount of pain, though his back did crackle during movement.

The sound of rustling surrounded him.

Finally, he croaked aloud, "Debris and Detritus?"

YES! That is me!

Definitely a telepathic voice, maybe not a hallucination, since he would never have imagined that phrase. Eh, he could talk until the last of the pain subsided, take the brooch and leave.

"Debris and detritus is you?" His voice sounded harsh and with an edge.

Yes! Another creak punctuated the word.

"Why Debris and Detritus?" Everyone else on the planet had botanical names, following the lead of the FirstFamily colonists who'd paid for the starships and the trip. Those colonists had formed the culture after what they knew of the Celts -- and the twenty-five sacred trees.

But the House replied, *My former person ... people ... one, two, three, four ... no, only three, I think. One, then two. They were scholars and studied ... studied legends. Ancient legends of the fore-land. The place not here.*

"Ancient Earth?"

Yes! That place, and a place of that planet, Greece.

Zane grunted. He knew a multitude of legends, but barely recalled those.

This notion of planets is odd.

His throat tickled as Zane began to answer and he coughed. His chest hurt, felt a little soggy. Not good. "The humans, ah, mobile sentient beings like myself, originated on the planet Earth and came through space from there to here, this planet we named Celta."

The atmosphere around him thickened with heavy silence.

What am I?

"You are a House. Capital 'h' because you are becoming intelligent--that is, self-aware and able to communicate in a rational manner with other sentient beings."

Oh. A House. Long pause. *What IS a House? Or a house?*

"A house is a building made by we mobile creatures to protect us. A dwelling."

I have a purpose! To protect a Family.

"That's right. From what I know of houses becoming Residences," he cleared his throat where the damp fog had congealed, "HeartStones are placed when people -- ah -- mobile beings, want their homes to become sentient. The stones are blessed and, ah, given energy during rituals and such," he pulled a hand out of a warm pocket to wave vaguely, though he didn't know whether the House could sense the gesture, unless by a ruffling of his atmosphere. "And after a time a critical mass of energy or knowledge or spirit or something, sparks, and you, ah, become conscious and intelligent." Sounded good to him.

So I was WANTED.

"So I believe."

And as Debris and Detritus contemplated that in silence, Zane understood, he, too, had been blessed. His chill lips curved in a self-mocking smile. He'd been more than blessed. He'd been arrogant. Had considered all the blessings of his life -- his Flair, his career, his *sight* as his due as a member of a Family who'd become noble within the first three decades of landing on Celta.

What is a Fam?

"A Fam is an intelligent animal companion who bonds with a person. Cats. Foxes. Dogs. Raccoons, I think, a couple of birds."

Animals.

"Yes."

I know of this. A pause. *Not humans and usually smaller and not bipedal.*

"Usually smaller. Think a horse or two has become a Fam." Gradually, he began to stretch his muscles, test them, especially his back as he sat up straight, shoulders over hips. Easy does it.

I am Debris and Detritus, the House said with a note of confidence not formerly in its tones.

"Greet you." If he licked his lips, the cold would crack them, but his mouth was dry. He rubbed a hand across it. "I am Zane Aster, of the GraceLady Aster Family." Though the lowest of the noble ranks, 'Grace,' the early founding of his Family gave them better status. "And Debris and Detritus is a mouthful of a name, I'll call you D and D."

That sounds ... acceptable. A pause, *Greet you, Zane of the Aster Family.* Now the House sounded wistful. Another pause. *We have exchanged names. What comes next?*

Suppressing a grunt, Zane began moving in increments. He pushed himself to a squat, crab walked back to the empty space he sensed of fireplace instead of wall.

Extending a hand trembling with cold -- had to be cold causing the shivering, not more futile despair -- and his fingers touched a stone, rounded, no doubt a fabulous gemstone, for some reason the facets under his fingers, and the way it ... resonated ... made him believe the gem was a great round ruby. It pulsed like heart's blood.

Yes, now that he relaxed a little, analyzed the input from his senses -- undistracted by Flair -- he *felt* glimmerings of the treasure that had brought him here.

Zane Aster? What comes next?

"Next I take this nice little bauble and hand it back to T'Ivy and collect the reward."

No!

The whole house shuddered with a force that knocked Zane back on his ass, jarring his damn spine again so he sucked breaths through his teeth.

You can't go. You MUST stay! the House insisted.

"Why?" he asked.

I need a person. A Family. We belong TOGETHER.

Zane paused. "You're lonely." He had a big, nosy, and noisy Family, all ready to mend him though he couldn't be fixed.

I will think on that word and concept.

Creaking to his squat again, Zane reached for the brooch.

NO! Static electricity snapped through the room. Zane's fingers curled reflexively, protectively.

"Give me the brooch." Gritting his teeth, he stretched, nabbed it. No electric jolt of pain that his Aster Family Residence would have shocked him with. Guess the House didn't know it could do that.

Or know that it could drop a brick or a ceiling on Zane.

Good.

Bit by bit, Zane straightened to stand--hunched but upright. Soon he'd uncurl from that posture.

Eyes open, he saw nothing but black, but recalled the door opening. He glided one step toward it, then the next.

You can't go!

Impatient with being told, once more this month what he could and couldn't do, he barked, "You can't make me stay." Naturally, he didn't have the strength to teleport. "I can kick in that door I mended." He didn't want to, and his physical strength felt subpar, his back ached.

If you go you will-- Debris and Detritus broke off.

But Zane listened hard, knew the immobile being had nearly said something it might regret.

I can tell you a secret.

"Yes?"

A long pause.

The secret may make you stay.

More quiet, until Zane broke it. "All right, I'm a treasure hunter, so I'm a curious man, tell me."

When the answer came, it was a feathery whisper in his

mind. *All who leave me, leave something behind. It is the nature of ... me. My being. My ... Flair.*

That had Zane straightening to his full height, barely aware of his aching back. His mind played with such a scenario a dozen ways, then he insisted, "That's not all of your secret, is it?"

No. If the person treated me ill, he loses what is most important to him. Loses more than if I like him.

"I don't understand that," Zane replied curtly, but that sure explained finding the brooch here. "You just became aware," he added.

It just happens. I don't do it on purpose. A pause. *I don't think, but if I'm upset -- Maybe.*

"This always happens?" Zane's voice cracked. He couldn't lose the last of his sight, of his Flair, of both, and survive. Could not. Not today. Yes, the House had trapped him.

He turned and pounded a fist on the wall, hurting his fingers. Didn't care.

Why did you do that? D and D asked.

Zane refused to answer.

I feel ... heat from you.

"It's the heat of anger. You know of anger, ire, fury, don't you?" Zane snarled. "Why don't you think on *that* concept."

But he couldn't stay still. If the House had been aware longer, Zane would have thought it bluffed. Couldn't count on that.

As he shuffled to the doorway, turned at the threshold and walked down the entry hall to the main door, he strained to see. And to feel the object in his fingers as more than a brooch, a true treasure.

Gray-shading-into-black sight. Nothing but shaped metal inset with faceted gems.

Face it. He'd already lost his sight and Flair.

Today. *Fligger.*

The tiles under his feet squeaked, then the House said, *You will lose the brooch and the reward if you leave.*

Minor compared to what he'd already lost. Almost he let his fingers release the thing. His lips curled before he replied, "It is not an honorable act, to constrain someone against his or her wishes. To imprison them."

It is not an honorable act to abandon someone! the House shot back.

"I'll come back," Zane grated out.

I do not believe you. This time D and D's voice whispered so tiny Zane couldn't catch any emotion from him.

"Keep the brooch then." Zane let it fall. A wind whisked the artifact away. Setting his hand on the latch, he braced and shoved the door open, and followed it into a blizzard.

His caught breath sucked icy air into his lungs, wind whirled around him, pelting him with snow. He saw white, and thought even if he'd had his vision, it would have been the same.

MotherDam? he called with his mind.

Nothing.

No sense of how to go. He'd turned right into the house, but how many blocks had he walked since the last turn? How many times had he jogged left or right? He couldn't recall because he hadn't paid attention. First rule of treasure hunting, know where you were and how you got there, and he'd ignored that, sunk in despair. Big mistake.

And if he stood out here more than a few minutes, he would die.

If he tried to find his way home, he would perish.

Turning in place, he sensed the quietness of the open door of Debris and Detritus, and returned, shutting it behind him.

The lock clicked shut. He didn't care. Didn't even care when he heard inner bars slide across the door.

You DID come back, the House said tentatively.

"The weather is too bad. I can't make it home in a blizzard. I have to wait it out." He returned to the pillar and slid down it.

Emotion radiated from the man in wild pulses beating against Debris and Detritus' walls, small heat from that emotion sank into the House's floor where Zane sat.

The man did not speak to him further.

What could the House do to interest him again? To make him think about the non-mobile being Zane shared space with?

He had said he was a curious man.

Debris and Detritus stretched his mind, considered all of his contents -- the things transient people had left, and those items the people who had made him had stored near his HeartStones, his brain.

Papyrus instructions, ancient books, audios that D and D had not the skill to access. Memory spheres, but they were too odd and strange for D and D, experiencing the world as a human did. Vizes -- recordings of his man and his woman.

He could run a viz for Zane.

Straining with the effort of a new ability, D and D *projected* the viz from one of the stones in his walls.

There, there, three dimensional holographic images formed.

"If I am Debris, you must be Detritus," the man said.

"What's that?" demanded Zane.

A viz, D and D replied.

An ugly, spiky noise came from Zane, harder emotions flashed from him. "I'm blind, House, I can't see a viz."

Oh, terrible that he'd hurt Zane. *I am sorry,* he whispered in his tiniest voice. *I just wanted you to see my naming.*

The House sounded like a child, and its words stopped Zane's futile and ironic laughter. He wiped his sleeve over the wetness on his face, lingering from the storm, his runny nose. Anything remotely like civilized manners were lost to him.

The future looked -- *was* -- dim. Ha, ha.

So may as well while away the time with the past while the blizzard raged.

"Go ahead," he said gruffly. "Play it, I can hear the dialog, *listen.*"

Very well, Zane, came the high childish voice again. But then, in any terms, Debris and Detritus was a child, even less, a baby with only a full day's awareness. The House's first tones of mature and male were wrong.

"Watch where you're going," boomed a woman's voice. "You've broken the last vase. Left debris all over the floor. Well, I am not going to clean it up this time. It can sit until you do it!"

"No, you're a lump of *in*energy, aren't you? If I'm debris, you're detritus. The detritus that life has left of a woman," said the man whose voice D and D had copied.

A gasp, then a sniff. "Well, Mister Papadakis, I don't think that's very nice of you."

In a lofty tone, the man replied, "We are no longer Papadakis. We are the Family Parietaria, and I missed being a GraceLord by one percent."

Zane snorted. That sounded like an old excuse to him. The whole scene sounded well-worn, though it kept his mind off his aches and his future.

The woman grumbled, "But you spend your days researching and writing about that ancient heritage of yours, and too much time at night, too."

The man gave a sharp gasp and Zane wondered if he'd gotten an elbow in the ribs.

He found himself smiling, more, his back had loosened up and he'd relaxed against the column. His shivering had subsided into occasional shudders, though his exhaled breath still felt warm against his face.

"Fascinating stuff," the man said. "I'm pretty damn sure that primal energies tagged along with us on our starships." Followed by a hiccup that sounded drunk. Then words continued, "Small and large entities. Why not? Our main religion of the Divine Couple is not exclusive."

"An inclusive religion is a very good thing," said the woman. "The easiest way for humans to pick a fight is to base it upon religious intolerance. We brought our religious fervor with us, in many forms--"

"Our beliefs. Energies might stick to those, form into what we believed," said the male, more ponderous.

"Or the major energies of the Divine Couple are real," whispered the woman.

"Who knows?" he grumbled. "And since you complained ..." A wet smooch ... kissing?

Zane straightened from nodding off and cleared his throat. "Very educational." he said. "You can stop that now." He drew in a very cold breath and warning bells alarmed in his mind.

Then he knew. The house was too cold. He would not make it until morning.

Despite the shelter, the cold would invade and he'd freeze to death. With eyes open to dark gray, he contemplated how long it would take for his Family to find him.

Worse came to worse, they'd hire one of the Blackthorns to track him -- the FirstFamily GrandLord with great Flair and an equally great price, or one of that man's distant cuzes with a minor gift. In any event, it would only be to find his corpse -- and the Ivy artifact, of course. If D and D allowed them to leave with the brooch.

Zane's whole body curled as he laughed. Now that his doom had come, he realized he didn't want to die.

Why do you make those noises, Zane? asked the House.

"I'm dying."

What!

"My lifeforce is being extinguished by the cold. Sort of amusing. You came to life yesterday and I die today."

No!

Zane leaned back, kept his eyes open to blackness. "I have no Flair," he croaked. "Not even to call my Family. Not even to light a fire. I'm blind, I can't teleport when blind. I can't leave here and enter a raging blizzard. I would not find my way home."

No, no, NO! said the House. *I will not let you die.*

The House was full of 'noes.'

I cannot have another death within my walls, another decaying human shell. It is terrible. Vermin come. They burrow into me and gnaw on me and bad stuff coats my walls.

That gave Zane pause. "Huh. If you prefer me to die outside your walls, I can stagger some meters down the street." He coughed. It racked his body, lasting longer than he'd anticipated. Well, it wouldn't bother him tomorrow.

No! I want YOU as my Family, the voice in his head sobbed.

Coughing again, Zane said, "There is a fireplace in this room. If you have wood or coal and you can light the fire, I might survive the night." And maybe he should stop talking and just *think* words at the House.

This is why you mobile beings constructed me! I am failing in my duty!

Uh-oh.

Not your fault, Zane projected mentally to Debris and Detritus. *You don't feel the cold, didn't know I needed more warmth than you can give me.*

The ceiling split. Zane heard plaster break, felt chunks rain just behind him. A thump hit a few centimeters near him and he coughed from the dust.

WOOD! cried the House. *A beam, use it for fire!*

Lady and Lord, Zane matched the moan of Debris and Detritus, *Why did you do that! I don't want to hurt you.*

It is done. The pain of the lost beam does not hurt me as much as my ... fear ... for you.

"Sorry," Zane managed aloud, through numb lips. But he scrabbled toward the beam, got slivers as he found the broken edge, ignored his back pain as he hauled the thirty-centimeter beam to the fire.

Then he panted and rested. Even such a short exertion exhausted him. His mind fogged as he wondered how to light the beam. *Too* awful to make the House set fire to one of its bones for him.

Fumbling in his pouch his nearest sister had equipped and fastened on his belt herself, he touched various objects, then found a bespelled firestarter that would work even underwater. No additional Flair needed.

He lit the beam, feeling ghoulish, and rolled to the fire, but began to sink into a sleep he knew he wouldn't awaken from. *Sor-ry, Debris and Detritus ... just too late. I am glad of your companionship, though I am sorry I cannot spare you the distress of my corpse.* He paused and listened to his slow and ragged breaths, the only sound he made. *Debris and Detritus, I think if you REACH OUT mentally, you could contact other intelligent Houses and Residences. You are not alone.*

I AM! You are leaving me alone! The entire House seemed to contract in the wail that trembled through Zane.

Not enough, the House wept in creaks around him. *Not nearly enough. Please do not die, Zane. Please, fight. I do not wish to stay sentient if another one of my beings dies. I cannot bear it.*

A child, no, baby's cry, that Zane could not ignore. He couldn't summon his Flair, but he could gather all the strength he had. *We ... will ... work ... together.*

A pause in the lament.

How?

Zane struggled with sluggish thoughts. Think or die.

You have Flair. As you were constructed and as you stood, the people who lived here gave you strength and energy throughout your lifetime until you became aware.

Yes!

If you can share a little of that with me ...

I can! I WILL!

Right. I don't know how we can share. Maybe if you run some energy down the beam in the fireplace--

*We will work together! *I* know how we can share energy. My HeartStones--*

And I WILL NOT hurt you further, by messing with your HeartStones.

You cannot hurt me through them. I have much untapped energy that I can share!

Maybe he shouldn't put his trust into a newly aware House, a baby, but he had nothing left to lose. Zane found himself clearing his throat, mumbling, "All right then. Tell me what to do."

Stand up and face the fireplace! The order rang in his ears, reverberating oddly as if more than one being addressed him.

Nearly beyond his strength, he forced himself up, staggered, each step jarring his back, making his lungs bellow with breath.

Place your hands on the heads of the sculptures flanking the fireplace. Your reach is wide enough, a high snappish voice instructed, not the House's usual tones.

Zane blinked, saw only blackness, but now that the House mentioned it, he *could* feel the irregularities of sculptures. He moved forward, reached out, and found the tops of the heads of two figures, one male, one female, in the same style as those on the front of the House.

Not just your fingers, curve your hands around the facial features of Debris and Detritus, too! A deeper voice intoned, and now the atmosphere around him seemed to seethe with energy. Heat rose from the fireplace as the beam crackled, burning.

He palmed the faces of the figures.

NOW!

Lightning sizzled, arcing through him and he yelled. He'd tapped into the centuries-accrued energy of the House.

Pain zapped down every nerve, slid over his skin, sank to his marrow, raw power.

He screamed as the force filled him, overflowed, heard the House shriek, too. Definitely felt the whoosh of the beam as it zipped away from the fireplace, lifted to the ceiling, creaked into place.

He connected with the House, they melded together for an instant and his own ribs shivered as the beam became whole, the burned end augmented with Flair and other ... bits of wood left in the rooms. Plaster ladened the air as the ceiling mended to better than new.

He and the House groaned together. As the energies blew through him, he went toppling when his hands lifted from the statues of Debris and Detritus.

He crumpled, stunned.

I love you, said the House. *I will always shelter and protect you,* D and D said in the tone of a solemn oath.

Loving Zane? That was too damn quick, but he didn't say so. Words formed slowly as darkness tugged at the ragged edges of Zane's mind, complete sincerity, *I will always cherish and preserve you. My ... vow ... of ... honor.*

THE MAN, ZANE ASTER, DEBRIS AND DETRITUS' *FAMILY,* lay still. D and D stayed quiet himself so he could sense all Zane's life indicators. He breathed, evenly, steadily. His muscles lay relaxed against the House's mainspace floor, his body *warm.*

They had saved him. Zane would live.

D and D's inner trembling receded. He felt as if he, too, could breathe. Odd that he began to think of himself in mobile entity--human--terms, but so it was.

ZANE AWOKE TO HEAT AND HE *FELT* THAT HE LAY IN A patch of sunlight. Even with his eyes closed he could delineate the ragged swatch of light on his body. He snorted. Eyes closed, right. From what he remembered of the evening before, he wouldn't see anything with his eyes open ... or straining all his Flair.

Both gone forever.

But ... he felt that sunlight. And his normal senses fed information to him, his skin, his brain, with a nearly painful acuity. As if those senses had expanded, no, magnified. Expanded exponentially. He smiled at the alliteration and opened his eyes.

Not darkness, but gray. A wavery gray like smoke. He didn't know what that meant other than he remained blind.

"I survived," he croaked aloud. "*We* survived."

Yes. We survived, the House whispered in his mind. *The sunshine on my outer walls has heated them warmer today than many days lately.*

"The storm has passed and the weather is better."

Yes, Zane.

He could hear all the creaks and soughs of the House, some slight scratching of glass, like branches on windows. But not on this level. Straining his ears, he realized the sounds emanated from one of the back rooms of the third floor.

His breath caught with a gasp that became a cough. But this cough didn't emanate deep from his lungs, racking him.

No, he continued to feel good -- in muscle and bone, skin and tendon. His back felt Healed. No frostburn or windburn on his face.

He simply had no sight and no Flair.

But his senses seemed greatly augmented, a conundrum. Something that had occurred when he'd linked with the House the night before? Or the continuing strange results of the underwater accident that had almost killed him and taken his sight and Flair?

Who knew?

Who cared about the why? He didn't.

With an easy move, he rolled to his feet, stretched, popping joints. Yep, felt good.

"The room is warmer." He turned toward the fireplace, could sense the dimensions of the open interior, the individual pieces of charcoal in the pile, glowing red or white.

His hands recalled the feel of the two carved statues on each side of the fireplace with enough detail that he could form the images, male and female, in his mind's eye.

Slowly he turned in place. His sight yet showed a dark flat gray. But the pressure on his skin, even through his clothes, told him where the columns were, the five tall rectangular windows in the back. He knew how far the ceiling loomed over his head, and the dimensions of the doorway a few strides away.

Turning his palm upward, he commanded, "Lightspell!"

Nothing. Not a bit of Flair for him to draw on, the psi magic he'd felt pulse through his nerves all his life.

Blind and empty of Flair.

Zane? the House sounded nervous.

"I'm here," he said absently, still taking stock. Trusting in this new awareness, he strode across the room, stopped a few centimeters before a column. Raising a hand, he brushed it over the cool stone and frowned, it seemed to him that the pillar was of a light-colored marble ... but not white. Odd.

This whole thing was odd.

The strangest days in his life. He whirled and jogged across the room and through the door, down the short hallway, noting another door on his left that would be the front room with the bow windows he'd seen yesterday evening.

Pretty much his last image was of the house.

ZANE WHAT ARE YOU DOING?

Stopping at the front door, he lay his palm against it and linked with the House.

I FEEL you!

I feel you, too, he replied mentally. *You and I worked together to save me.*

You saved me, too, D and D said simply, *I'm glad you didn't die and rot on my floor. That is scary and nasty and I couldn't go through that again.*

The atmosphere in the room trembled around him as if the air pressure suddenly dropped.

Zane grimaced. "I imagine so." Such a young entity would have hidden his awareness from death and decay within his walls. Perhaps withdrawn so much that he might have perished if Zane had died.

Yes. We saved each other. He stooped and picked up the Ivy brooch-artifact, then added aloud, "I'm going to turn in this piece of jewelry for the reward, file a claim for you and your land so I will be named as owner."

Owner!

"Unless I can file some sort of certificate that you have become self-aware and are your own intelligent person and I am your Family." He paused. "I want everything very legal so no harm will/can come to you."

You will be my Family? A tiny breeze scraped papyrus scraps around the room along with the equally tiny mental whisper.

"Absolutely!" He said it so loud it rang against the walls, more, so it sank into the House so D and D would believe him. "I'm also going to arrange the move from my ... previous ... abode to here, D and D. I'll be back within a septhour, seventy minutes."

You promise?

"My solemn vow of honor, and I have never given that to anyone before." He paused. "Except for you, last night. You should have memories of all the circumstances of a solemn Vow of Honor. I would suffer if I broke it."

I ... care for you. You would hurt me if you betrayed my trust.

"I care for you, too. I'll be back." He paused. "One moment." He strode back into the mainspace, no stumbling or staggering now. He knew his surroundings. Oh, there'd be no deep sea diving and treasure hunting for him anymore, but he had Flair. Maybe not. Not Flair, but he had some sort of talent or gift that mitigated his blindness.

He touched the stylized face of the male, Debris, then the female, Detritus, the sculptures flanking the fireplace. Gave and accepted a blessing.

Then he turned and walked to the front door, said the phrase he'd only given members of his Family before, but, then, this House *was* his Family, now. "I love you, Debris and Detritus. I'll be back shortly."

I love you, Zane Aster of the House of Debris and Detritus. I will wait.

Zane chuckled and slid aside the bars, unlocked the door, and stepped into a cold, clear day. No doubt the sun shone, a white star in the deep blue sky. Pain flickered.

Zane? asked the House.

"I'm all right," he murmured, though no one walked along the street for blocks. He couldn't see the sun or the sky, but he knew that. He took off down the street with a long stride. Someday he might learn how to teleport again, for now he could walk the few kilometers to the GuildHall and turn in T'Ivy's brooch, file a claim for the House.

And he knew he'd left something behind in Debris and Detritus after all.

Despair.

LIKE SMOKE RISING, THE MINOR GODS, DEBRIS AND DETRITUS, removed themselves from the statues of the fireplace. Their attenuated essence twined into the bedrock beneath the House, separating themselves from the newly intelligent being. They had helped the House become sentient, but now they wished to be individuals.

They'd linger, though. Rest and wait and grow stronger for a few decades.

Then they'd leave this sanctuary and run free.

THE HOUSE HUMMED TO HIMSELF, A JAUNTY SONG HIS Family, Zane, had taught him. He tidied himself up as much as possible, found a button from Zane's jacket. He swept it into the pile of other small and interesting items next to the fireplace pillar of Detritus. He cleansed everywhere from the stored Flair he'd learned to tap.

He spent the rest of the time stretching himself.

Debris and Detritus thrilled at the feel of His Person, Zane, before D and D's door. Zane had returned as he said he would! D and D could trust His Person. D and D had sensed that, and gone with his very own judgment and had been validated.

"Debris and Detritus," murmured Zane, and the man

touched D and D's front stone door jamb. The House felt the warmth of his living flesh, and through that flesh the joyful emotions of the man.

Yes? he sent telepathically.

"I am going to affix a plaque next to your door, on the outside of your wall. It announces your name, and that you are an intelligent House, soon to become a Residence."

YES!

"It may hurt a little." Zane sounded apologetic.

D and D creaked a little around the newly fixed hinges of his door. Thought the noise would sound like a human huff. *I am a strong being. The little pain is WORTH having My Plaque.*

All right, Zane sent mentally. *And have you noticed you've started speaking with EmPhaSis?*

I have connected with another new Residence, the Mugwort-Moss Residence. Once known as the Turquoise House. A spurt of pain from his person stopped D and D's explanation. *What is wrong?* he demanded.

I did not SEE you well in the storm and before I lost my sight. I do not know what color you are.

It does not matter, D and D assured him. *I do not know what color I am, either. My Name and Being is not linked to color like the Turquoise House was.*

Ah, replied Zane, then said aloud and the vibrations of his voice hit D and D's front wall stone, "Ready?"

Yes. D and D braced himself.

The tiny pokes and pricks and holes in his outer *skin* hurt, but as soon as Zane set the attaching pieces into his stone, D and D sent his Flair-magic to make the plaque a permanent part of him. And he *felt* the new ... addition to himself, the change of stone to metal, and an additional feeling of ... light.

Zane commented, *The glisten metal of the plaque should be shiny. I feel the warmth of the sun on my body, so the sign will be reflecting light.*

Oooooh! D and D whisked a breeze through himself and sent the song note from that to Zane.

"I'm glad you're pleased," Zane said.

I AM! He sensed that someday he might be able to modify enough to *see* the street. Fascinating!

What does it say? asked D and D.

"It says 'Debris and Detritus House, Aware this Month of Willow, 424 Years After Colonization, Zane Aster Family.'"

Thank you!

At that moment a ... change happened at the edge of D and D's boundary. A massive feeling of *Flair* stood on his sidewalk.

Zane felt surprise with a touch of alarm zip from his new home, his intelligent house, to him. Bracing a hand on the doorjamb, he turned, trying to sense what D and D had.

An ovoid shape seemed to block light and wind, a person. Struggling to master the new sharpness of his physical senses that had nothing to do with mental and personal psi power, Zane said, "Yes?"

And the air took on a heaviness.

"Oh," said the voice of a man that Zane recognized but who he'd avoided. "Zane Aster and, I see by the new plaque, a new intelligent house named Debris and Detritus." A pause. "Odd, and I do believe I've heard equally odd rumors about this House, but that might explain why I was drawn here. A newly acknowledged being and a new bonding of human and House."

Zane felt the ripple of the breeze, the change of the light and figured the great nobleman bowed. "Greetyou, First-Family GreatLord T'Vine," Zane said and bowed, too. He *wanted* to open the door and run and hide inside his new home instead of listen to what the Prophet of Celta had to say.

Zane licked his lips, found the humid air colder than he'd

expected as it dried the wetness from his mouth. "I've lost my Flair as well as my sight ..." and how proud he felt to be able to say that steadily! "So you can't use my Flair to see my or Debris and Detritus's future."

The man's steps came near, stopped slightly outside what would have been Zane's old personal-space boundary. Now he needed more, felt he should have a huge bubble around himself, but he wouldn't reveal that to this guy.

"I don't need your Flair to see your future, Zane. I only need my own. However, there is an old and massive accumulation of Flair on this particular piece of land."

A part of T'Vine's essence, a shadow, seemed to move as if he tilted his head to look beyond Zane and toward D and D. He raised his voice, "Greetyou, Debris and Detritus." Another dipping of air, as he bowed once more. "The people who set and tended your HeartStones did very well, cared for you very much. You are well blessed and imbued with much Flair-power."

"Thank," came the stone creak-crack-tiny-pebble-flake-and-fall audible voice to augment D and D's mental blast.

"You're welcome." Zane heard the GreatLord's voice deepen, grow richer with Flair, as if he used that power to see and reveal the future. "Debris and Detritus, you fear that you will be abandoned again."

Zane flinched and thought D and D's innermost beams shivered.

"That will never happen," a lower, slower, heavier tone carrying Flair. "You will always be well-loved, and remain in -- with -- the Family Zane founds ... weds into. Though Zane himself will be one of the people who stays the shortest time within your walls."

"NO!" both Zane and D and D cried aloud.

"It will be all right, fine ... even ... fabulous for all of you ... Zane Aster and the Family he bonds with." The prophet's voice thrummed with promise bordering on vows. "They will need you more than ... humans usually need an intelligent House and Residence. You will be most prized."

Oh, a tiny word from D and D.

Scary feelings, and the prophecy gave them all too much to consider right now. Zane had to act. He opened the door, it swung easily, fixed forever. "Come in," he offered to the GreatLord, though he and D and D had no food or drink to give the man, or any furniture for him to sit on.

The noble retreated. "I don't think so," he said, a little huskily.

Zane stilled as the notion came that the GreatLord knew more than he told, might *see* even further than he'd revealed.

"As I said, I've heard rumors about this place."

"From whom?" Zane pressed.

He thought T'Vine flicked a hand. "General whispers. And I don't care to leave behind something I can't afford to part with."

"You gave us a service," Zane said reluctantly. "For which we didn't pay, that will count in your favor--"

"Thank you for the hospitality, but no payment required. Merry meet, Zane Aster and Debris and Detritus,"

"And merry part," Zane replied automatically.

"Merry," murmured D and D aloud.

"And merry meet again," ended the GreatLord, then the air shifted and Zane understood the nobleman had teleported away, and more hurriedly than any of them might have anticipated.

Zane stood a few minutes, heard others walking on the sidewalk across the street, but no one coming near. Finally, he said, "You know, D and D, I don't think that you and he *will* meet again. At least, I don't believe he'll come back anytime soon."

D and D answered him mentally. *He is a man with GREAT Flair power.*

"Yes, everyone says so."

And his visions and prophecies are disconcerting.

"Everyone says that, too," Zane agreed. He opened the door and walked in. The whole place smelled better than when he'd left. All trace of smoke and despair vanished under a fragrance of spring blossoms.

He moved through the entryway to the mainspace, turned slowly, extending his senses. "You know, I have a healthy bank account. We need to furnish you, particularly with food no-times, the newest and the best. Then we'll decide what rugs and chairs and beds and whatnot you and I will want and need."

"Thank you, Zane," Debris and Detritus said, but sounded subdued.

Zane crossed to the fireplace, put a hand on the mantle, said softly, "The prophet may be right, who knows? I may be one of your Family who stays with you the shortest amount of time, but know this, Debris and Detritus. No one will ever cherish you or love you more."

STONE IN ZANTH'S PAW

This story was originally written as part of a conference promotion and put on a website under the title of *Zanth Returns To The Beach*. I've since revised it.

This is the only animal point-of-view story in this collection.

Those of you who follow/ed me on Facebook will recognize the story as my second, shorter Staying At Home Story, posted page by page with an image every day.

Chronologically, this story is the last entry in the history of Celta so far.

No, I'm not finished! I have plenty of other story and book ideas for Celta!

STONE IN ZANTH'S PAW

*426 Years After Colonization, Ash Family Beach Estate South of Druida City, Summ*er

ZANTH, TOP FAMILIAR COMPANION CAT OF ALL OF THE PLANET Celta, stomped down the path from his house to his beach. He should not have to do duty on this beautiful, sunny morning.

But Mother Turtle, Swift-In-The-Sea, had mentally contacted him a week ago. She'd told him she wanted to inspect her daughters she'd sent two years ago to be cared for by the animal Healer, Danith D'Ash. Danith was one of Zanth's humans.

After two years, the two littlest of the hatchlings now stood and stretched twice as big as he. Still talked in baby-talk, though. Less than half-baked in Zanth's opinion.

Zanth had informed his Family of Mother Turtle's request. Then the whole Ash Family, T'Ash, and D'Ash and their two sons and two daughters, had come to this southern estate and the large house near the beach where the turtles had cracked out of their shells.

Zanth had saved them then, so now he seemed stuck with them. Mother Turtle had not wanted to meet Danith, like *most* animals in all the planet of Celta should. Otherwise *Danith* would be doing this duty and not Zanth. He grumbled low in his throat.

Even worse, two of Gwydion Ash's mob of gray housefluff bunnies decided to follow Zanth and turtles from the mansion to the beach. Zanth disliked the fluffs.

Anyway, it looked like he led a parade of fools. That detracted from his status.

Still, he kept his tail high and waving.

As he approached the first dune, he could smell the patch of herb he liked to sleep in. Far away from the scary and restless big water. To his nose, the spicy groundcover smelled sweeter than ever. From the buzzing of the insects that liked to sit on the leaves, the herb had spread since last summer into a nice, big mat for him.

But no sleeping this morning. This morning he had to return the two female sea turtles to the damn damp sand and meet with their mother. Both now plodded after him.

They lumbered in his wake, sending falls of sand into the

scruffy brush, and they were s-l-o-w. Even the two housefluff bunnies hopped along faster.

And the turtles were loud, both with their swishing walking behind him — he was silent — and with their mental comments. Every smart being, human and Fam, could hear their mental shouting.

We are going to SEE MAMA! shrilled the first one into his mind and into the air.

Yes, yes, yes we are! the second yelled. *And maybe we will swim with her and sleep with her and BE with her, now.*

Zanth grumbled, *You should be grateful you lived with Us, that MY FamWoman took you in and helped you survive and taught you stuff and how to talk in words more than squeaks.*

Yes, Zanth, TopFam, said the first.

Yes, Zanth, TopFam, agreed the second. *BUT WE ARE SOOOO EXCITED,* she screamed to the world.

Zanth winced and tried to fold down his black ears in reaction, but even weighted with his emerald earring studs, they didn't lower.

You are too loud! screeched one of the housefluff bunnies.

Those Familiar Companion beings hopped behind the turtles, and over them, and around them, getting in Zanth's way.

The Family had spent much, much gilt — money — on the two immature female turtles. For personal protection spells for them. For trips to the local seaside near Druida City and a cottage on that beach. A place FamWoman Danith had gone alone many a time to take care and check on the turtles as they grew. She left her HeartMate, FamMan Rand, who didn't like that at all. She left *Zanth*! For beings who stayed in the big water!

Inconceivable.

All to keep two turtles well and happy.

He snorted. And he smelled — bad odor.

What's that? asked Housefluff One mentally. His nose wriggled wildly.

I don't like that smell! said the housefluff's mate, her own nose moving slightly less.

Zanth stopped himself from wrinkling his own nose. *Dead and rotting thing,* he said. *Always something dead or dying on the beach.* He'd learned that from experience. *The big water is tough on beings.* Zanth thought *all* water was tough on beings. Nasty stuff.

If something not dying on beach today, will tomorrow, he said. He just planned on it never being him.

The female housefluff stopped in her big-footed tracks, one of her large pink-lined ears tilted. *I'm not going up and down dunes to the beach.*

Zanth tossed her a glance. *You housefluffs return home, not that far.*

The female lifted her foot, stared at her pads. *Don't like this grit.*

That's sand, nothing but sand on the beach. And shells, broken shells that become sand, Zanth informed her. Sand and grit got between pads and had to be picked out. Like these beings littered Zanth's life. Turtles soon to be gone, though.

Female bunny twirled and hopped back toward the house, round puffy tail twitching. Zanth stared at it. He'd always wanted to catch a housefluff by the tail.

Forbidden.

He virtuously turned his back on the pair — good riddance! — and continued down the path. A path animals and Fams used, not humans.

Reaching his patch of herb, he had time to inspect it, knead it all over so nice scent coated his pads and paws and under his claws, and got rid of some grit. Then had a short wallow, before turtles caught up with him.

The shelled beings still burbled cheerfully, but this time

only in turtle body language and turtle-mind-speak that sounded like a slow rising and falling hum in his head. Ignorable.

Easier to tune out than the whoosh in and out of the big water, just lurking beyond the last dune. He dreaded seeing that, growled under his breath, and kept pace with the turtles as they went slowly up the incline.

As they topped the last dune, he didn't see Mother Turtle.

Bad smell worse up here, probably horrible on the beach. Zanth trotted down, putting his black and white paws in dents in the sand. A meter before the beach, the land fell abruptly, cut as if a storm had come through. He leapt easily down.

The turtles, of course, squealed as they slid down the sand, tipped onto the beach and fell okay on their bellies.

He turned toward the smell ... something he'd have to take care of since it wafted over his territory ... and stopped.

There, gnawing on a mangled part of a pelican more than a day old, stood a scrawny male wolf. He stared at Zanth with cold yellow eyes and Zanth glared back. He could tell this wolf wasn't smart enough to be a Familiar Companion animal. Almost, but not quite. That made Zanth superior in all ways. He swaggered forward. A strong Fam could always make a regular animal back down.

The wolf growled in a low threatening tone. Zanth noted one of his hind legs looked recently crippled and dribbled blood. Too bad.

Zanth showed his teeth and hissed. In his head he showed the range of his territory, sent warning that the wolf intruded. That Zanth would not tolerate the gaunt thing here, on Zanth's land.

Rumbling came deeper from the wolf's throat.

Zanth sent a clearer picture of boundaries, added words

that would cue the wolf of Zanth's superior status. Not to mess with him. *Take rotten meat and go. Away. Off My land.*

Instead wolf tensed, like he would actually defy Zanth.

And another growl came from a burrow in the steep cut of the land. Another wolf.

Zanth stiffened, alarmed. Fighting two of them could be tough.

When they'd left the big house, Danith had been taking care of a local sick dog who'd eaten something bad and was puking his guts out. Still, she or FamMan T'Ash would hear if Zanth called for help, but he wouldn't.

He couldn't back down. Turtles returning to the sea would know he'd not defended his own land, would tell *everyone* far and wide.

Threat came mentally from the male wolf before him. Dark intimidation and challenge.

Then a breeze stirred the air and Zanth smelled that the wolf in the burrow had whelped not long ago, and a pup was with her. Big wolves would protect pup to the death—Zanth's or their own.

Uh-oh.

Zanth stepped back, bumped into turtles. They were about as long as the wolf and much wider. Wolves' thoughts sounded like they found turtles too hard to kill and eat.

But turtles didn't seem to sense that. They squeaked and moved toward the fast encroaching water.

Come with us, Zanth! We will protect you! the first said.

Yes! the second turtle chimed in. *Water GOOD!*

No! Zanth spit out, looking at them, but keeping a wary side glance on the male wolf. Zanth let his body ease, friendly. Best to get through this problem without a fight that would damage everyone but the turtles.

We talk, he sent in words. Showed image of wolf relaxing, too. Of everyone respecting each other.

The male displayed his fangs. Bigger than Zanth's own.

Making sure he remained *just outside* claw reach, Zanth pressed his paw into the moist sand, leaving a good print. Then with his mind he *colored* the print pink. The symbol for Zanth's FamWoman, the Animal Healer that all smart Celtan animals should know.

The wolf sucked in quick breath, lowered his head a little, gaze fixed on Zanth. He thought of Danith, gave the vision to the wolves, and the large house at the end of the path.

YOU GO. GO TO HOUSE WHERE HEALER IS! he projected to the male wolf, making sure his feeling of helpfulness would echo through the wolf's mate bond, as well as reaching the female directly.

In the lair, the female rumbled in a questioning manner. The he wolf growled, abandoned the piece of dead bird, retreated close to the opening of the den. Did body talk — tail and ears and fur — and probably private picture talk to mate.

Female stuck her head and neck out, appearing as skinny as the male. Stared at Zanth, met his eyes. He sent her his knowledge of Danith D'Ash. How she *loved* animals, all animals, not just Fams. How she would want to help the small Family.

Would coo over the pup. Would *Heal* the male's leg, for sure. Would feed them all good food.

??? A swarm of questions, requests for confirmation of Zanth's info, came from both wolves, loud enough to rouse the dozing pup to yip once.

YES! screamed one of the turtles, as if mentally speaking louder would make the wolves understand better. *DANITH D'ASH IS WONDERFUL!* Her image of Danith seemed odd, using muddy tints instead of pink.

YES, YES, YES, said the second turtle, repeating what her sister said, as usual. But this turtle's images and feelings were clearer than her words. She sent memories of deep comfort from Danith, feeling of love cycling between turtle and woman. Turtle's adoration of Danith.

And how the woman helped the turtles, then let them go free. No cages or pens.

GO UP PATH TO BIG HOUSE WHERE HEALER DANITH IS! confirmed Zanth. *Follow housefluff pawprints and scent.* He thought of the housefluffs, fur sleek over plump bodies.

The male wolf's eyes widened, a small string of drool fell from his open mouth. Zanth felt the female perk up at the image of fat housefluffs.

Oops.

As Zanth checked mentally on the fluffs, found them safe inside the house, the wolves rushed by him. The male jostled Zanth, forcing him away from their den and the path. The female trotted first, carrying the pup in her mouth, but stayed within the sight of the male behind her.

Zanth hopped back, found himself dewclaw deep in water! He opened his mouth to hiss, then one of the turtles bumped him, slid under him and he danced for balance until she lifted him up on her back.

I'll save you, Zanth! Take you safe to sandbar in water where big nasty dog-things won't come! Meet Mama, THERE!

Me, too!

NO! Zanth shouted, but the turtle's head dipped below water ... that slid all around his paws, sometimes covering them!

Already in deep, deep, water. *Take Me back!*

She ignored him.

He stuck his claws in the turtle's leathery skin and she didn't flinch too much. Not as much as Zanth shuddered.

A moment later, the turtle slipped onto a narrow sandbar surrounded by water. Zanth hopped off the turtle's shell onto the spit of land, barely above lapping water. The second turtle arrived, and splashed him even more, droplets on his white fur and his black fur!

He let all the Cat curses he had roll out of him in spitting fury. And the cowardly turtles deserted him!

We be back when you happier, Zanth! We going to send sounds to Mama for her to come. They travel better in water, said the smarter one.

Yes! said the sister.

Zanth wasn't stupid enough to have a hissy fit and thrash around on the sand. But it took some stalking up and down the very slim piece of land before his anger decreased. He eyed the mainland beach, many Zanth-cat-lengths away. Didn't see hide nor tail hair of the wolves. Stretching his senses, he felt Gwydion, also an Animal Healer, open the sick animal door to the wolves. Good enough.

He'd saved *them*, too. Was a hero, as usual.

But stuck on this damn piece of land in the middle of the great water.

What was he going to do?

To call FamMan or FamWoman or some other Fam to rescue him would be to lose great face. The turtles didn't think about status like other Fams, didn't realize the position they'd forced him into.

One of them simply had to take him back. He'd insist. Then he'd say he'd done all this on purpose to show how strong and brave he was. By the time he'd told the story often, he would believe it to be true himself. So he paced until he could send cool, smart words to turtles.

Come on back, now! he called, not putting command in his tone, because turtles responded to coaxing better. Now that he stared out at the bigness of the huge water with no land, he could sense where they swam, nearly see their underwater wakes.

Mama can hear! We will wait for her with Zanth like we told Danith we would! The first turtle started back.

Last week, when old mother Turtle, Swift-in-the-Sea, talked to Zanth in his mind to bring her daughters to the ocean, she'd told him she didn't want to meet any humans. She distrusted them.

Zanth believed her too wary, but maybe she didn't have good judgment as to which humans were good or bad, not being as smart as Zanth.

The sister turtles returned to the sandbar and stared at Zanth.

You happier now? I am happy! Mama comes.

I am happy, too. Excited and waiting for Mama, the second turtle said.

Didn't sound as if either of them would take him back right now. Zanth muttered under his breath and grumbled in his head but didn't say nothing to turtles.

A few minutes later, he sensed a powerful presence approaching. Zanth saw Mother Turtle zoom through the water, reach the damp sand part of the sandbar. Then she came, slow flipper-step by slow flipper-step out of the ocean and onto land, an old and massive being.

Greetyou, FamCat, she said. Zanth wondered if she remembered his name.

She saw her daughters, heard their mental joyful squeals and relief radiated from her. *Good. Good. You two survived.*

Sand spit as the three met on the beach. *Good,* Mother repeated. *We lost two. So I have eight daughters from this most successful clutch.*

Because Me hero, Zanth reminded her. After all, he'd *saved them all!*

She seemed to ignore his words and spoke again to her daughters, *Though we are a family of Healers, neither your sisters nor I could reach in time the two who perished.* A long breath out. *Snapped up by a shark.*

The image of a terrible fish and it eating small turtles smacked Zanth. He jumped back with a hiss. No, not a squeal of terror, a *hiss.* He did it again, just to emphasize that it *was* a hiss.

Mother Turtle sniffed her daughters, told them to stay as she moved ponderously all around them. Went to smack one with a strong flipper and the blow barely connected. She lifted her head and stared at Zanth. *What is this?*

Spell personal armor. Protects young. It had cost a fortune ... or at least a few Fam animal companion placements in the Yew and Blackthorn Families. *Wears off gradually—*

I understand that, Mother Swift-In-The-Sea said.

—so young learn from fatal mistakes instead of being stupid and dead, he finished. Both turtles would have died a dozen times over if they hadn't had such armor.

Mother Turtle huffed. *Well, they were not with their mother, but a human woman who'd never raised turtles. Never wanted to meet her before, dealing with a cat like you is bad enough.*

We loovvee Danith! the littler ones chorused. *She is an excellent Healer of not only turtles but all Fams. And animals, too!*

Hmmm, Mother said. *I sense your Flair, daughters, and that the human woman Healer sparked it. Perhaps you will follow me as Great Healers. This is good.*

One last stare at Zanth, and she said, *I will take my daughters to their brethren and we shall see how well they Heal others. What they might have learned from this Animal Healer Danith D'Ash. If they impress me, I will contact you again to meet with her and perhaps share knowledge.*

Zanth grunted, he himself unimpressed by *her*. Mostly.

Follow me, she instructed her daughters, and began to turn back toward the vastness of the waves.

Wait! Zanth yelled. *Take Me back to the mainland beach!*

Before he could blink, she flicked her flipper and used *Flair*, mind-magic, to move him to her back. He scrabbled and clawed at her neck and she took off straight into the water! Her daughters followed.

He did not like this. No, not at all. In fact, *he HATED* riding through the water, wavelets breaking over his paws. How dare the turtles, *all* the turtles, subject him to such indignities. To *water.* To moving water. To moving *through* water.

At least she lived up to her name. She swam swiftly. No more than ten or so Zanth-lengths from the beach Zanth began to breathe easier.

Until Mother Turtle said, *You fear the sea. You should learn it better and you will fear less.*

Then she *rolled* in the water and Zanth had to release his claws or drown!

She sped away.

He tumbled over and under and salt water in mouth and rubbing fur raw against sharp ground and getting grit stuck between his pads ... He surfaced and saw the beach a meter away and he *swam.* Then his paws hit wonderful, fabulous land. And he rushed against the surf onto the beach, panting. His pads would have sweat with the effort if they hadn't already been wet. Or maybe the salt sweat mixed with the salt water, along with traces of blood from the sharp stones. Leaving part of him in the wide ocean. As a big piece of ocean stone stuck in his paw between pad and toes.

His claws dug in the mud, the wet sand, found more purchase. He scratched at the land, rushed from the water. Stood slick and shaking and far too wet for a small minute.

Ignoring the stone that cut, he ran fast, fast, fast along the path that would only coat his paws with sand and dirt and not the whole rest of him like water did. Coated *all* of him when he'd been thrust into the ocean.

At the top of the dune he stopped, his sides going in and out fast with harsh breaths. Far enough away. The big water never came here except, he heard, during special storms. Now the sun shone and the water glittered and rumbled just like usual.

He'd survived. And he'd learned as Mother Turtle said.

He could swim.

He didn't like it, would never like it, but he could.

And if the water took him again ... at least here on *his* beach, he could survive. He knew the water now, and the land under it, long and shallow enough for him to wrench himself away and reach safety.

If he fought hard.

He always did.

He lifted his foot, stared at the wedged stone, a big piece of sharp shell. Then he sank on his haunches to worry it out with tooth and paw and after long minutes and some more blood, he plucked it out. Like other irritants out of his life, the turtles, the wolves.

All would know he was a hero.

Light flickered over the shell-piece in a pretty way. He could keep it, take it to Danith as a present, or to his FamMan T'Ash to make into a jewel and sell.

His shivering stopped and he squinted at the big water. He'd survived all the ocean had thrown at him.

Looking down at his bedraggled self, he saw he'd lost several whiskers. His nice round head would look lopsided!

Maybe FamMan and FamWoman wouldn't notice.

He touched a white forepaw to his black ears. Both earrings in. Good!

Still, he should indulge in a long grooming session before he returned home. Wanted *no* comments.

He sniffed, the scent of that herb patch he liked to nap in and dream and occasionally munch caught in his nostrils. And he calmed as he nuzzled it, sniffed deeply and appreciated the smell of good dirt and living green things growing out of the ground. Kneading the herbs until they released even more nice smell, he lay down on the thick, soft leaves. He'd snooze a bit, then groom, get the rest of ocean sand out of his claws.

The sun already warmed his fur. He liked sun and land better than ocean. But he respected big water, didn't fear it as much, though he knew it could kill him easily, thoughtlessly. But hadn't today.

Life was good.

Thank you for spending time with me on Celta.

During the years I've been writing the Celta HeartMate series, I've kept track of much, particularly the characters, but also forgot much. For these stories I needed help from readers who follow me on my Facebook page and they were acknowledged before each story when they helped me out. MY READERS ARE AWESOME! MANY THANKS TO ALL OF YOU!

Bright Blessings. Merry meet and merry part and merry meet again.

CELTA HEARTMATE SERIES IN READING ORDER

Please note that these books and stories are primarily romances. They are not appropriate for children.

****means this is a STORY**

FOR BUYING LINKS, PLEASE SEE:

ALSO BY ROBIN D. OWENS

**Passage Through Stone (in *Hearts and Stones)*

**Heart and Sword (in *Hearts and Swords*)

**Peaches Arrives on Celta (in *Celta Cats*)

**Zanth Gets His Boy (in *Celta Cats*)

**Homing Stone (in *Hearts and Stones)*

HEARTMATE

HEART THIEF

HEART DUEL

**Fractured Stone (in *Hearts and Stones)*

HEART CHOICE

**Pinky Becomes a Fam (in *Celta Cats*)

HEART QUEST

HEART DANCE

**Heart Story (in *Hearts and Swords*)

HEART FATE

**Heart and Soul (in *Hearts and*

Swords)
HEART CHANGE
**Zanth Claims Treasure (in *Celta Cats*)
HEART JOURNEY
SCRIPT OF THE HEART
**Noble Heart (in *Hearts and Swords*)
**Hidden Stone (in *Hearts and Stones*)
HEART SEARCH
HEART SECRET
HEART FORTUNE
LOST HEART (Novella)
HEART FIRE
**Baccat Chooses His Person (in *Celta Cats*)
HEART LEGACY
HEART SIGHT
**Zanth Saves the Day (in *Celta Cats*)
**HeartStones (in *Hearts and Stones*)
**Stone in Zanth's Paw (in *Hearts and Stones*)

ALSO BY ROBIN D. OWENS

Please note that these books and stories are primarily romances. They are not appropriate for children.

HeartMate

Heart Thief

Heart Duel

Heart Choice

Heart Quest

Heart Dance

Heart Fate

Heart Change

Heart Journey

Script of the Heart

Heart Search

Heart Secret

Heart Fortune

Lost Heart, a Celta Novella

Heart Fire

Heart Legacy

Heart Sight

Hearts And Swords, a Celta Story Collection

Celta Cats, a Celta Story Collection from Cats' Point of Views

***

The Ghost Series (contemporary paranormal/ghost story romances)

Ghost Seer

Ghost Layer

Ghost Killer

Ghost Talker

Ghost Maker

* * *

Feral Magic, a contemporary paranormal shifter romance e-novella

Feral Magic

* * *

The Mystic Circle Series (contemporary fantasy)

Mystic Circle AUTHOR PREFERRED EDITIONS COMING IN 2020!

Enchanted No More

Enchanted Again

Enchanted Ever After

* * *

The Summoning Series

Average American women are Summoned to another dimension to fight hideous evil, and, yes, with flying horses!

Guardian of Honor

Sorceress of Faith

Protector of the Flight

Keepers of the Flame

Echoes in the Dark

ABOUT THE AUTHOR

RITA® Award-winning author Robin D. Owens has been writing longer than she cares to recall. Her fantasy/futuristic romances found a home at Berkley with the issuance of HeartMate in December 2001. She credits the "telepathic cat with attitude" in selling that book. Currently, she has two domesticated cats (who have appeared in her stories).

She loves writing fantasy with romance or romance with fantasy, and particularly likes adding quirky characters for comic relief and leaving little threads dangling from book to book to see if readers pick up on them (usually, yes! Reader intelligence is awesome!).

Robin spends too much time on Facebook (see link below), loves hearing from readers, tries her best to respond to any questions and has been known to take reader advice for her work. When she receives good reviews or fan mail, she's been known to dance around bored cats...

Contact me here:

www.robindowens.com

robindowens@gmail.com

Made in United States
Troutdale, OR
09/01/2024